WRAPPED
UP IN
CHRISTMAS HOPE

An uplifting small-town romance

JANICE LYNN

Print: 9781952210723

www.hallmarkpublishing.com

To my mom, Brenda Green. Love you.

Chapter One

ANDREW SCOTT WATCHED WITH A grin as his good friend and fellow firefighter, Cole Aaron, raced down the school hallway toward him, both hands clutching at his oversized red velvet shirt. The wide black belt flapped loose on his friend's waist, and his fake jolly ol' belly sagged beneath it.

It was an entertaining sight, but not a particularly surprising one. In Pine Hill, Kentucky, Christmas was a three-hundred-and-sixty-five-days-a-year event. As soon as one December twenty-fifth came and went, the town started preparing for the next time Saint Nick made his appearance.

Which was today at Pine Hill Elementary. That was why his buddy was wearing the red suit, the wig, and all the other Santafication accessories. Cole's girlfriend Sophie had done up his face with leftover Halloween makeup so he appeared to be a rosy-cheeked old man, but it had been up to Cole to get his Santa suit on. A task that had, apparently, been a bit too much for him.

"Sorry," his friend called out. "Wardrobe issues." Cole had stopped by the bathroom for another belly adjustment, but it didn't seem to have worked very well. Andrew and Ben, another firefighter, exchanged an amused glance.

"Best slow it down," Andrew said. "How would it look to the kids if Santa got sent to detention for running in the halls?"

"It wouldn't be the first time I got sent to detention," Cole muttered. "But we'll keep that between us. I wouldn't want the kids knowing Santa ever had to put himself on the naughty list."

"Unlike you two, I was a good kid," Ben said. He wore regular uniform pants and shirt topped by a baseball cap emblazoned with the fire hall's emblem. Andrew had decked himself out in full firefighting gear. It wasn't the most comfortable outfit to hang around in for hours, but kids liked that kind of thing. Firefighters and Santa. They couldn't go wrong.

"Yeah? Look where all that goodness got you," Andrew said. "Same place as us, only we had some fun along the way."

Chuckling, Cole lifted his gloved hand and Andrew high-fived with his pal.

"I had fun," Ben defended, adjusting the bag of fire safety goodies in his arms. "Just because I don't rocket across town on Big Bertha like some motorcycle daredevil doesn't mean I don't have a good time." He puffed out his chest beneath his uniform shirt. "After all, it was this great-looking Kentucky boy who had a fantastic date Saturday night."

Andrew and Cole snorted at his boasting. But Andrew saw no need to mention that he'd spent his Saturday helping his grandparents put up outdoor Christmas lights, and had then stayed for dinner. Not exactly the kind of Saturday night that would win him bragging points with the guys. "For the record, you haven't really lived until you've experienced the thrill of taking Big Bertha for a spin."

"You and that motorcycle," Ben accused, shaking his head. "No wonder you didn't have a date this past weekend."

"Or any other weekend," Cole added, gaining a grin from Ben.

"What can I say? I don't think a woman exists who could ever compete with Big Bertha," Andrew said. So what if it had been a

3

long time since he'd gone on a date? "She's a beauty, dependable, gets me where I need to be. Dating is not a priority in this dude's life."

Fighting fires to save lives and property was. That and taking care of his grandparents. Ever since his grandfather had taken a tumble at the Christmas festival last year, he'd felt the need to keep a closer eye on them. .

Andrew pointed toward the door, decorated with a Christmas tree covered in student-created ornaments. "Well, guys, this is our stop."

He knocked on the classroom door, then entered the room crammed with all three kindergarten classes—about sixty kids and five adults. Andrew recognized one of the teachers as Suzie Winters, who had stopped by the station to talk to Chief about sending some of his crew to speak with the students. He vaguely recognized all the others except one, a petite blond.

She glanced up and their gazes didn't just meet. They collided, held, left him struck with the sensation of deep recognition. He felt as if he should know her...but that was impossible. He wouldn't have forgotten those big, Christmas- tree green eyes.

Those amazing eyes took on a leery expression, as if she didn't trust him. That made no sense. Who was more trustworthy

4

than a firefighter? Especially when that firefighter was delivering Santa Claus to a bunch of excited kids?

"Santa! Firefighters!" A posse of kids launched their little bodies toward them and wrapped their arms around his and his friends' legs like stripes on a candy cane.

But it wasn't the kids clinging to his legs that had his attention. It was the mysterious blonde who filled his belly with the same thrill he got when gearing up to go fight a fire. A feeling of adrenaline, anticipation, and extreme caution for the ever-present danger. But why would she trigger any of that? She stood at no more than five-two or three, and she looked harmless enough. Curious and unable to resist, he winked.

Shock registered on her face. She parted her lips as if to say something but instead she gave a little shake of her head and looked away, leaving Andrew feeling as if someone had just snatched away his favorite present on Christmas morning. Her attention focused on a boy standing near her.

"Okay, kids," Suzie called out to the class. "It's time for Santa and his firefighter friends to tell us about the Christmas coloring contest the fire department is hosting this year. They're also going to talk to us about how to stay safe in case of a fire. My classroom, return to your seats. Miss Stevens and Miss Wilson's classes, find a seat on the reading rug, please, and keep your hands to yourselves."

The kids reluctantly released Andrew's legs. He glanced again at the blonde, now crouching down and talking to the boy. No wedding ring on her left hand, he couldn't help but notice. Andrew made his way up to join Suzie at the front of the room.

Was the blonde a teacher's assistant or a parent volunteer? Andrew didn't date single moms. It wouldn't be fair to let a child get attached, since he planned to leave Pine Hill to follow his dream of becoming a smoke-jumper—a firefighter that parachuted in to combat wildfires. That was way too danger-ous a profession for him to ever consider a serious relationship with any woman, much less one with kids.

"I'm so glad you wore your fire gear," Suzie praised in her kindergarten-teacher voice. "The kids are so excited."

Glancing toward the teacher, Andrew nodded. He needed to get his mind on fire safety and off the blonde.

"Aw look, she has a statue of you on the corner of her desk," Andrew teased Cole as they passed by the Jolly Old St. Nick figurine. The whole room was already fully decked out for Christmas. Cut-out snowflakes, decorated Rudolph faces, tinsel over the dry erase boards. Pretty much the holiday works. "Looks as if you might have gained a little weight since that was made, though."

Physically fit beneath his costume, Cole rolled his pale blue eyes, and then, smiling, waved at the class, and tossed out a few ho ho hos, doing a great imitation of the old guy himself.

"Who's been good this year?" Santa Cole bellowed.

"Me. Me," the kids chanted, their hands in the air as they bounced in their seats. The boy who'd remained in the back of the classroom raised his hand and motioned for the blonde to put up her hand as well, which she immediately did, smiling down at him.

Andrew wasn't surprised she raised her hand. She looked like the kind of "good girl" his Grandma Ruby wanted him to meet and settle down with. He kept telling his grandma that he wasn't ever doing that, but she would just smile as if she knew something he didn't. Grandmas.

While Cole was telling the kids about the contest that would benefit the town's Annual Christmas Toy Drive, Andrew and Ben headed to the back of the room. The blonde and the boy still stood there, and after flashing a smile at the woman, he knelt to speak to the kid.

"Hey, there, bud. How's it going?" he asked, keeping his voice low so as not to interfere with Cole's talk.

The shy little boy's eyes grew big. "Good."

"That's awesome." Andrew held up his hand. "Give me five."

Morgan Morris's pulse was suddenly pounding as if she'd run to the North Pole and back. She gulped back the knot in her throat. Her instant awareness of this handsome firefighter disconcerted her, making her feel as if she needed to shield herself from the rush of unexpected emotions.

It had been almost two years since her husband Trey had died—her soul mate, who she'd met at nineteen. It had been a great love story. She just hadn't expected it to end so soon.

But she tried not to give in to bitterness. A while back she'd made a promise to herself to count her blessings and be grateful for the time she'd had with him. Time that had given her Greyson, the most beautiful little boy to ever exist.

For the most part, she kept that promise, but there were days when the whys took over. Why had Trey been taken so young? Why had her son been left without a father? Why had she been given a taste of what true happiness was only to be left to spend the rest of her life with a heart only half full?

She never got any answers, but those days would pass, and she'd settle back into accepting her new normal. She'd not vowed to remain single but had no interest in becoming involved with another man. What was the point when she'd already given her heart away and had nothing left to give?

Yet, when, with a grin on his handsome face, the firefighter had winked at her, it had been as if someone flipped a switch, lighting up her nervous system with millions of twinkling lights that cast a dazzling glow.

Seeming to be tongue-tied, Greyson smacked his hand against the firefighter's.

"Good job," the man praised him. He straightened and turned toward her. His gaze danced with interest, and no doubt hers shone with fear. Not for herself, but for the way her son was staring up at him with wide little eyes filled with adoration.

The life Greyson dreamed of was standing right there in front of him in full gear, and it was all she could do to not wrap her arms around her little boy and beg him to dream a different dream. One that didn't involve running into burning buildings.

"Ahem." The other firefighter cleared his throat, motioning for the man standing in front of her to join him.

He gave her a crooked little smile, then shrugged. "Duty calls."

She and Greyson watched as the fire-fighters spoke to each other, then opened a bag to pull out plastic helmets and fire safety goodies to give the kids.

"Did you see that?" Greyson asked, looking up at her in awe.

Placing her hand on her son's shoulder she smiled. "I sure did. You got to be the first one to meet one of the firefighters. He must have sensed that you want to be a firefighter, too."

"You think so?" Greyson's eyes were huge.

"It's just a guess, but it would seem so since he came over to talk to you. That makes you special." While she didn't want to encourage firefighting dreams, she did want her son to feel appreciated and seen.

She'd been worried when he'd not rushed over to the firefighters along with the other kids. Was it because he still felt like an outsider to his new classmates and was struggling to fit in? He'd been through so much in his five years. She hadn't wanted to uproot him from his home and bring him here, but when she'd lost her nursing job due to hospital budget cuts, she hadn't had much choice. She'd hoped that a fresh start would be good for both of them—and in truth, she'd been feeling much better since leaving Georgia and their former life behind.

Her son's gaze didn't leave the firefighters, particularly the unsettling one in full firefighting gear, as he nodded.

"It's awesome that our cousin Sophie's firefighter friends are talking to your class today. And I know that her other firefighter friend, Cole, really liked meeting you at Grammy Claudia's after church that Sunday afternoon." She kept her voice chipper. "We'll have to take him up on his offer to give us a tour of the fire hall."

Greyson nodded. "We need to go."

"I'm sorry we didn't get to this past weekend, but my days off didn't match up with when Cole would be there." She didn't have much control over her work schedule at the assisted living center. At her son's disappointed nod, Morgan's heart squeezed. "Maybe one of the firefighters here will know if Cole's working this Saturday. If so, we can go by then."

Although she was anti-anything that might someday put her son in a dangerous situation, currently, she'd encourage most anything that put a sparkle into her son's eyes.

Besides, kids usually changed what they wanted to be when they grew up many times over the years. Hopefully, Greyson would settle on something Mom-approved.

She couldn't deal with living in constant fear due to a loved one's reckless choices. Never again.

"That would be good. If the firemen don't know, we could ask Santa," Greyson suggested, staring up at her with big eyes that held her heart. "Santa knows everything, right?"

"Right, especially who's been naughty or nice." She bet this Santa really did know Cole's schedule. Hopefully, Greyson wouldn't recognize Sophie's boyfriend in the Santa suit. After all, he'd only met Cole once at Grammy Claudia's, just over a week ago. Morgan herself had barely recognized the fit former Marine beneath the padded red suit, white wig, mustache, beard, and makeup. If not for his pale blue eyes, she might not have figured it out. "Plus, you can let Santa know what you'd like for Christmas this year."

"I'd like to meet the firefighters first, though." Greyson looked toward the firefighter in full gear, the one who'd winked and completely discombobulated her. "Then I can ask Santa."

Morgan's chest tightened. Of course, Greyson would want to meet the firefighters first. She took his small hand into hers and gave a reassuring squeeze.

"Absolutely. Come on, let's get you back

at your desk so Mrs. Winters can get you assigned to a group to meet them."

Maybe, if she was lucky, she could avoid meeting them.

Well, at least the winking one.

Because she suspected that firefighter started more fires than he put out, and everything in her warned that if she didn't stay away, she'd get burned.

"I'm going to be a firefighter when I grow up." The towheaded boy eyed Andrew's helmet with longing as he took the inexpensive plastic imitation they were giving to each student. Whereas the other kids had been animated, the boy chewed on his lower lip as he put the red hat on his head, then looked to Andrew as if for approval. Something in the kid's eyes tugged at his chest, making him wonder what the kid's story was.

"That's great." He fist-bumped with the boy. He had no doubt now that the kid was her son. Same big Christmas tree green eyes. Cute kid. But that meant the blonde was definitely a mother. Disappointment hit, though he tried to hide it.

"We need more good men on the crew," he said, loud enough that Ben and Cole both cut their gazes toward him and rolled their eyes. "We'd love to have you join us after you complete your training."

The kid's face lit up. "Really?"

"Absolutely. Fighting fires is important work. Families count on firefighters to keep them and their homes safe. Plus, it may not seem like much, but this," he gestured to the classroom, "is important firefighter work, too."

The boy didn't look convinced. "Talking to kids?"

"You bet. Teaching people of all ages what to do if they encounter a fire is very important. If you know what to do in the case of an emergency, especially fires, you could save your entire family before us guys even show up. That's huge."

The kid's expression turned pensive. "You mean how you stop, drop, and roll if you catch fire, or you crawl to get away from smoke?"

Impressed that the boy had been paying attention when he and Ben had talked to them about fire safety, Andrew nodded. "Exactly. It's vital that everyone, regardless of age, knows what to do in case of a fire. That way, we keep our community safe."

"I'll be the safest firefighter ever," the boy assured Andrew, keeping his voice low. "But my mom won't like it. She'll still think I'll get hurt."

Andrew looked over and saw that the

blonde was snapping a photo of each student sitting in Santa Cole's lap. But she kept sending worried looks in her son's direction. "I understand," Andrew said with a nod. "My family worries about me, too." Not that his family wasn't proud that he was a firefighter. They were, but they still worried, especially his Grandma Ruby. Growing more and more curious about the kid's history, he asked, "How did you decide you want to be a firefighter?"

"I want to save people."

"Good answer, kid." Suspecting the boy would appreciate the gesture, Andrew took off his helmet and handed it over so the kid could hold it for a while. Eyes wide, the kid took it as if Andrew was passing over the holy grail. He liked this kid in ways that had nothing to do with his fascinating mother.

"Since you told me your future career goals, want to know mine?" A goal that he'd only ever told Cole and Ben. Why did he want to tell this five-year-old? No doubt Cole and Ben would say it was because Andrew was as mature as a kindergartner. But as crazy as it was, he felt like the boy was a kindred spirit.

Glancing up from the helmet, the boy nodded.

"When I was your age, I went with my grandma to bring supplies to a family who'd lost everything in a fire, ever since then

15

I wanted to be a firefighter. I love being a firefighter. But a few years ago I volunteered to help fight a wildland fire in East Tennessee, and now I've decided that I want to be a smokejumper. That's a firefighter who fights forest fires that the fire trucks can't reach."

Just the thought of smokejumping and possibly helping to save entire towns had adrenaline rushing through him.

Confused green eyes stared at him. "Then why aren't you a smokejumper already?"

The green gaze so similar to his mother's burned into Andrew with the intensity of the hottest fire, making sweat pop out beneath his uniform. What could he say that this child would understand? No matter how much the desire burned within him, he had reasons why he couldn't just take off and leave Pine Hill. Promises he'd made long ago that he'd always be there for certain people, just as they'd always been there for him.

"Adulthood isn't that simple."

"My mom says that a lot. She doesn't want me to be a firefighter because she thinks it's too dangerous." The kid's face took on a thoughtful expression. "Maybe by the time I'm old enough, she won't worry so much."

"Moms worry." And grandmas, he mentally added. "It's in their job description. Still, it's good that they care so much, so we'll consider ourselves lucky that we have people who love us."

The boy nodded. "My mom loves me a lot. She moved here to give me a big Christmas."

Again, Andrew found himself wondering what the kid's story was. "Nothing wrong with having a big Christmas. Pine Hill is definitely the place for it. The holidays are everyone's favorite time of year."

"Greyson." The blonde gave a nervous-sounding laugh as she stepped up to them. "You're the only student who hasn't had your photo taken with Santa."

The kid gave her a *pretty please don't make me leave* yet look.

"You need to thank the fireman for his time and let someone else take a turn talking to him." She placed her hands on the child's shoulders.

"No worries, Ma'am. Greyson and I were just swapping firefighter stories. I was telling him how our crew could use a good, safety-conscious firefighter like I know he'll be. I've no doubt that he'll work hard and make his dreams come true—in the safest way possible."

Andrew met the boy's gaze and winked conspiratorially. As he'd hoped, Greyson's face lit up and he winked back. Andrew grinned at the exaggerated wink. Yeah, he liked this kid.

The boy handed his helmet back to Andrew. "Thank you and sorry I held up your line."

Andrew reached out and patted the boy's shoulder. "Are you kidding me? I'm the one who held up my line because you're an awesome dude. I enjoyed our man-to-man talk."

"Me, too." The boy eyed him as if he'd just promised him the moon.

It made him feel a little guilty—and maybe a bit undeserving. Andrew was proud of the work he did. But he didn't want the kid idolizing him. He was just doing his job and being friendly to a kid who reminded him of himself as a child.

"Good luck with the contest and on becoming a firefighter. You're going to make a great one."

Digging in his heels as his mother tried to nudge him along, Greyson continued to look up at Andrew. Then, he smiled. Andrew got the impression this happy, full-on smile didn't happen to Greyson nearly often enough. The reaction from the boy's mother seemed to confirm that. Her hand fell to her side and her conflicted gaze went back and forth between him and the kid. Kids deserved to smile—lots. That this kid obviously didn't was a problem. One that made him want to be a problem solver.

"Thank you, sir, and good luck to you,

too," Greyson said, and then to Andrew's surprise, the boy hugged him. His little arms felt warm and tight as they wrapped around Andrew's thighs. "Your secret is safe with me. Pinky promise forever."

The stunned blonde's eyes widened even further at the last comment. Andrew was fairly stunned himself. He and the blond watched the kid skip over to where Santa Cole had finished up with his last kid.

"What kind of secret?" she asked the second Greyson was out of hearing range, looking very much the mother hen who might attack at any moment.

"It was a comment I made about firefighting, nothing more," he said, putting his hands up defensively.

"Okay. I...well, I," she shook her head a little, then gave a forced smile. "Thank you for your kindness. You made Greyson's day. But he shouldn't have occupied so much of your time. Your line is backed up and the other children are waiting to get their firefighter helmets."

"No problem," he assured her. "It was my pleasure. Great kid you have there."

Something flickered in her green gaze, then she nodded and motioned for the next kid in his line to step up. "Jace, thanks for being so patient while waiting for your turn."

Then, without meeting his gaze, she

headed toward Cole's line where Greyson was now talking to Santa.

"Hi," he greeted the kid who'd stepped up to him and handed the boy a plastic helmet while answering the kid's questions. Laughter from across the room caught his attention, and when he looked up, the woman was smiling at Santa Cole.

What would it be like to have that smile aimed at him?

For the remainder of his time in the classroom, Andrew's gaze kept bouncing between Greyson and his mother. Which wasn't difficult as, although she helped with multiple students, she was never far from the future firefighter.

Greyson had gone to his seat, taken out a box of crayons and started coloring one of the pictures in the fire safety booklet. Most of the kids were paired off or in small groups, but Andrew hadn't seen Greyson speak with or interact with any of the other children. No chattering or smiles or laughter. Wearing the plastic helmet Andrew had given him, along with one of the badge stickers Ben had given him, Greyson looked totally absorbed in the coloring book while around him noise and chaos abounded.

His aloneness tugged at Andrew's heart and sucked him in further. It couldn't be easy being the new kid in town.

Cole and Ben joined him, finished with

their groups of kids while he still had a handful left to talk to. Great. He was never last except when it came to leaving a burning structure. Then, he always made sure all his crew was out safely before he himself got out.

"Miss Hilton was wondering if you would have time to talk to her first-grade class, too?" Suzie asked, smiling at them all. "I think the other teachers were a bit envious when they found out I'd made arrangements for you to talk to all of the kindergartners about the Christmas Coloring contest."

"Yeah, sure," Cole agreed in his regular voice, then corrected himself. "Ho. Ho. Ho. Of course, Santa has time to talk to the other good boys and girls."

"So long as no calls come in." Ben patted the two-way radio at his waist. "We've got more coloring books, stickers, and helmets in the truck."

"Thanks so much, that would be wonderful," Suzie told them, clapping her hands together.

"Santa and I will grab the materials from the truck," Ben said. "And if Miss Hilton is ready, we'll talk to her kids while the Pokey Little Firefighter here finishes up."

Andrew rolled his eyes at his buddy, then smiled at the kindergartner who he was handing a red helmet to. "Choose your friends wisely, kid."

"You're lucky you have friends at all," Cole said for Andrew's ears only as he walked by on his way out of the classroom.

Andrew snorted, but refrained from saying anything back. He wouldn't want the kids to think he was insulting Santa. Instead, he turned to the next kid in line. Although his friend had been ragging him, truth was, Andrew knew how lucky he was to have Cole and Ben. He and Ben were lifelong friends, and Cole had just clicked with them as soon as he'd moved to Pine Hill a year or two back. There was no greater friend than one willing to lay his life down for the other. They were those kind of friends. He knew they would literally walk through fire for him, and he'd do the same for them.

Andrew gave the last kid a plastic helmet and thought he was finished when he realized the cute want-to-be-a-firefighter with the pretty mom had gotten back in line.

Andrew grinned at Greyson and said, "Hey, I'm glad you're here. With Firefighter Ben with Santa, I need a helper. Do you know of anyone who would want to help a firefighter out?"

"Me," the boy immediately responded.

"Great. I hoped that's what you'd say." Andrew smiled at the kid. "Let's see if your teacher is okay with you being my assistant when the class goes outside to look at the fire truck. I need someone to sit in the truck cab and keep an eye on things for me."

"Don't think I haven't noticed you looking at Andrew Scott every time one of the kids isn't demanding your attention."

Morgan's cheeks burned Rudolph-nose red. She'd tried to keep her mind on taking photos of the kids with Santa, but Suzie was right. Unfortunately.

Suzie's lips twitched. "Is it because fire-fighting fascinates you?"

Terrified her, was more like it. She couldn't imagine running into a burning building rather than out…and she couldn't bear to think of Greyson doing that some-day. Still, she gave her son's schoolteacher a tight smile.

"Something like that."

"Right." Suzie laughed, glancing toward where Andrew was chuckling at something Greyson was saying. "Looks as if you're not the only one in your family who's cap-tivated. For whatever it's worth, Andrew's a great guy. Born and raised in Pine Hill. His parents had to travel a lot with work so they built next door to his grandparents. He prac-tically lived at their house. He played football with Marty, was the team's star quarterback,

actually," Suzie added as if that should impress Morgan. "He was valedictorian of their
class. And if someone needs helps, he's one
of the first people to show up. Like I said, a
great guy."

Why was Suzie telling her Andrew's life
story? She wasn't interested.

"Oh, and did I mention that he's single?"
Suzie teased.

Morgan didn't want to know his relationship status. Okay, so she had looked at his
left hand and noted that he didn't wear a
wedding band. It didn't mean anything. And
she definitely didn't want the shaken-up-
snow-globe flutters in her belly that knowing
he was single had triggered.

"Not that it matters," Suzie continued,
eyeing where Andrew still talked with Greyson. "He's a self-professed lifelong bachelor."

"He doesn't date?" Why was she asking
that? She didn't date.

"He dates, but never seriously. The moment he thinks a woman is getting attached,
he calls it quits. Mostly, he just casually
dates. My sister, Betsy, went out with him
for a short while. He told her upfront that
he'd never marry or have kids."

"Why?"

Suzie shrugged. "He told her his life
wasn't 'conducive to a serious relationship.'"

Morgan wished that didn't intrigue her.
It couldn't be because of his job. Cole was

a firefighter and seemed happy dating Morgan's cousin, Sophie.

"He's a bit of an adrenaline junkie," Suzie added. "Rides a motorcycle and jumps out of planes. That kind of thing."

Morgan's stomach plummeted. Of course, he was an adrenaline junkie.

There must've been some DNA sequence malfunction that alerted her whenever a thrill seeker was in the vicinity. Maybe that's why she'd kept looking toward him. Because on some level she'd recognized that within him, and it had reminded her of Trey.

"Everyone thinks he'll take over if and when Chief retires." Which meant he'd be a lifelong firefighter. "But it's going to be a lonely life for him if he sticks to that pledge to never settle down."

"Interesting," Morgan mused, still mulling over the possibility of whether her rattled response to him was because he was similar to Trey's love of danger. "I'm sorry if your sister got hurt when he wasn't willing to commit. But at least he was upfront with her. And honestly, good for him for meaning what he said. We have that in common. Although, I don't plan to date at all—seriously or casually." Especially not a firefighter who unnerved her. "Maybe I'll reconsider after Greyson is older, but for now, he's my priority."

Morgan's gaze went to where Andrew

listened intently to whatever Greyson was saying. Were they talking about Greyson's dream to be a firefighter again and swapping stories? She knew that she should direct her son back to his seat, , ,but she didn't have the heart to interrupt. Not when today was the most excited she'd seen him in a long time. They had fun together with just the two of them, and he'd warmed up to Grampy George and Grammy Claudia, but the move hadn't been easy on him.

"Admit it. He's great with Greyson and, as a bonus, is super cute."

Morgan cut her eyes toward her friend and frowned. "His being cute has nothing to do with anything."

Suzie laughed. "Sure, it doesn't. A cute firefighter is talking to your kid and promoting a charity contest that's raising money to buy Christmas toys for needy kids. What's to like about that?"

Knowing that no matter what she said Suzie wouldn't let up, Morgan sighed. "Yes, Greyson seems to like him very much." She didn't bother saying whether or not she agreed. Suzie would draw her own conclusions.

Suzie's hands clapped together softly. "So, you're going to talk to him?"

"What would be the point? You know Greyson and I are still struggling to find our way. We've got enough going on without throwing in a good-looking firefighter." It was good seeing the animated way Greyson chatted with him, though. Which must be why her heart still raced.

An adrenaline junkie firefighter. That alone should turn her off completely. *You'd think I would've learned my lesson.*

"Besides," Morgan continued. "You've already said he's a confirmed bachelor, and I'm not interested in dating, either, so what would be the point?" In all these months since being thrust back into single life, dating hadn't entered her mind until today. She hadn't been prepared for someone waking her insides. "That's why I don't plan to talk to him."

She'd never let another adrenaline junkie get close to her. Not ever.

"If you say so." Suzie didn't sound convinced. "But you may not have a choice."

"What do you mean? Of course, I have a choice. There's no rule that says I have to date again."

Suzie laughed. "I meant about talking to him. Because, don't look now, but your son has a firefighter by the hand and is bringing you a six-foot Christmas present worth writing Santa a thank you note for."

Chapter Two

ORGAN HAD JUST ENOUGH TIME to frown before Greyson and Andrew reached her and Suzie. Greyson really did have the man's hand. His eyes were bright and full of excitement.

"Mrs. Winters, may I have permission to be an assistant firefighter?"

Suzie and Morgan stared at him in confusion.

"What my buddy here is asking is if he can help me while I talk to the kids about the fire engine," Andrew clarified, his eyes sparkling and not leaving Morgan's.

Why was he looking at her that way—as if he knew something she didn't and found it amusing? Had Greyson mentioned something embarrassing about her?

"Can I please, Mrs. Winters?" Greyson looked up at his teacher with such hope.

Suzie sent Morgan a questioning glance. Greyson turned his pleading eyes onto her. "Please, Mom. I'll be good and super careful. I promise."

How could she say no to such an innocent request when it obviously meant so much to her son?

"That's fine, Greyson, so long as Mrs. Winters doesn't mind."

Suzie gave her a look of approval, then smiled at Greyson. "I appreciate you being willing to assist our visitor, Greyson. Thank you for always being such a great helper." She turned to Andrew. "Should we wait for Santa and Firefighter Ben to come back from Miss Hilton's classroom? Or should I line the class up to go outside and look at the truck right now?"

Rocking back on his heels, Andrew nodded. "Since we're finished here, why not go now? It'll give the kids more time to see the truck and ask questions."

"Greyson, please get your coat, then go stand by the door," Suzie said. "I'll get the rest of the class bundled up and lined up behind you."

Greyson nodded, then took off toward his cubby to grab his coat. Suzie walked to the front of the classroom and called her students to attention, leaving Morgan alone with Andrew. He'd been squatted down with the kids earlier. Standing fully upright, he seemed larger than life. Then again, most people seemed tall next to her.

"I'm Andrew, by the way." He grinned at her, again.

Reminding herself that she wasn't interested and could walk away at any time, Morgan nodded.

His eyes danced with merriment. "I missed where you gave me your name."

Breathe in. Breathe out. Stay calm.

"I didn't tell you my name." She swallowed the lump that had formed in her throat. Talking to him shouldn't make her feel this fluttery excitement. Not excitement. Anxiety, she mentally corrected herself. Anxiety that he'd gotten through her protective wall and put her on edge.

"But you're going to tell me?" His tone was teasing, but Morgan's heart raced. Andrew smiling at her warmed a freeze deep within she hadn't even acknowledged existed. Somehow, though, keeping that ice in place felt safer than risking a thaw.

So, rather than answer, she bit into her lower lip.

"Great kid you have," he continued, obviously not fazed by her refusal to answer. "He is yours, isn't he?"

"He's mine." And how very blessed she felt. Greyson was the best thing that had ever happened to her.

"I like him."

"Thanks." Morgan's heart swelled with pride. "He obviously likes you, too."

Andrew's brow arched. "I get the impression you wish he didn't, though. He told me you weren't into firefighters."

Greyson had said that? Ha. Based upon her reaction to Andrew, she was definitely into firefighters. What was it about her that was attracted to men who thrived on danger?

"We're not that bad, you know?" Andrew said.

The man's grin was lethal. So much so that Morgan fought to tamp down welling-up emotions. He was cute and knew it. Just like Trey. But she wasn't interested in any man, much less one who thought it was a good idea to run into burning buildings for a living.

"I never said you were. I appreciate you taking the extra time with my son," she replied, carefully choosing her words.

"You're welcome. I meant it when I said you have a great kid."

"He is, only..." her voice trailed off, then she made herself smile. Just because this man had shaken up her world didn't mean

31

she should be rude. She shouldn't, especially when he really had been kind to Greyson.

"Sorry. The last thing you want to hear about is our personal issues." She kept the smile in place, because it wasn't his fault she got all flustered by him. "My name is Morgan. Morgan Morris, and thank you again." Because what would telling him her name hurt? "Greyson's excitement while talking to you is priceless. It's good to see him smiling."

Andrew's gaze bore into her. "Doesn't he smile much?"

Morgan didn't want to tell this almost-stranger about how her son had gone from a full speed ahead kid to a quiet, subdued child, or that she was in Pine Hill to put the sparkle back into his eyes that had been missing for too long. She planned to surround him with so much love that his little heart healed from the ache they were both suffering from. Slowly, he was coming out of his shell and Morgan thrilled at every smile, laugh, and seemingly carefree moment. They were precious.

"He smiles, but just hasn't as much since...well, for a couple of years."

Andrew's brows raised. "What happened a couple of years ago?"

Taking a deep breath, Morgan whispered words that tore at her heart. "His dad died."

Andrew felt like a complete heel for pushing. When he'd noticed that Morgan didn't have a wedding ring, he'd figured divorce, not death. Then again, it was hard to imagine any man willingly walking away from her and Greyson, so maybe he should have suspected something more had happened.

"I'm sorry," he said and meant it.

"Me, too," she said, glancing away as if she might be fighting tears.

Helplessness and a need to make things better hit him. His grandma would've said she needed a hug. She certainly looked as if she could use one. But she didn't know him and likely wouldn't welcome his comfort. He'd never risk her taking his desire to comfort the wrong way.

"Greyson was so excited the fire department was coming by today," Morgan continued, sounding nervous and as if she were chattering to distract herself from where her thoughts had gone. "I think he has a case of hero worship."

"I'm no hero," Andrew quickly denied. "Just doing my job, ma'am, and grateful I have the health and skills to be able to do so."

She eyed him as if trying to decide how

to take his response. "I suppose it's a matter of opinion, but to most, firefighters are heroic. Some jobs are inherently more heroic than others." She nodded over to where Suzie and all the kids had lined up. "They're ready for you. Thanks again for being kind to Greyson. I truly do appreciate it and am positive he'll be talking about it for weeks."

And with that she walked away.

"Reindeer. I definitely need reindeer."

Rosie, a vivacious, neon blue-haired woman in her late sixties, elaborated on her over-the-top Christmas wedding plans. She and several other women, including Morgan, had gathered at The Threaded Needle quilt shop to prepare supplies for an upcoming sewing event. As Morgan unfolded a bolt of red fabric onto the cutting table, she suppressed a grin.

Rosie smoothed the material. Her manicured nails perfectly matched her hair, and her huge diamond engagement ring flashed with her movements. "Reindeer pulling a sleigh driven by Santa and delivering me to my lucky groom," she continued, her well-preserved face lighting up with excitement as she shimmied her body a little. Morgan and her cousin Sophie shared an amused look.

"Your wedding is less than two months away. Where are you going to find trained reindeer to pull a sleigh?" Morgan's Grammy Claudia asked, frowning at her lifelong friend who kept upsizing what she wanted for her wedding.

"The North Pole might have a few to spare," Sophie replied, obviously unable to resist getting into the spirit of things.

Sophie and her sister, Isabelle, owned the quilt shop on the town square. They were avid supporters of an organization that made quilts for military servicepeople, past and present, to thank them and welcome them home. Morgan had never heard of Quilts of Valor Foundation prior to moving to Pine Hill, but as the daughter of military parents, she had the utmost respect for all those who served, so she had volunteered to help prepare for the upcoming event. Plus, she enjoyed being with her family and their friends.

"You should have gotten married on the Fourth of July, as you'd led your so-called lucky groom to believe," Maybelle Kirby said drily as she cut a strip of the stretched-out material. The older woman was classically beautiful. Likely in her seventies, she took great care with her appearance and overall presentation. She'd always reminded Morgan of an older Grace Kelly. If Pine Hill had royalty, Maybelle would be queen. Despite lacking an official title, there was a perpetual regal aura that clung to the woman. Even as a little girl, during her holiday visits, Morgan recalled being a bit in awe of Maybelle.

"If we'd gotten married in July, the ice sculptors refused to guarantee that the candy cane carvings would hold up throughout the ceremony. And then where would we be?" Rosie asked with an *isn't it obvious?* expression.

"In deep water," Isabelle suggested with an amused eyeroll from where she leaned against the shop's counter watching them. Sophie was all Christmas sunshine but her sister was usually all business, so Isabelle's joke had Morgan smiling.

"You'd be married," Maybelle deadpanned as she handed Sophie another stack of cut material strips. Sophie was going to run them all through a special cutting machine that had dies to cut particular patterns.

"Not doing more last-minute wedding planning," Grammy Claudia added, shaking her head as she laid perfectly cut fabric squares onto a growing stack. Her gray hair was tucked so securely in a bun that it didn't even wobble. "Maybe you and Lou should elope and be done with this wedding business."

Her heavily-but-tastefully made-up eyes widening, Rosie gasped. "And deprive Pine Hill of the privilege of attending our winter wonderland wedding?" She ran her fingers through her azure hair. The punk rock shade of blue fit the feisty woman.

"Go ahead. Deprive us," Maybelle encouraged.

Rosie pouted. "Why, Maybelle Kirby, you should be ashamed of yourself for even suggesting such a thing. You know perfectly well that our friends and family would never forgive us."

"We'd forgive," Maybelle assured her, cutting more material strips. "Forgive and be grateful the hoopla had ended. That poor man doesn't realize he's getting coal this Christmas."

Morgan's gaze met Sophie's again, and she fought to keep from laughing at the older women's bickering.

"Coal is just immature diamonds, and this girl has always been all sparkles," Rosie informed in her most Southern accent, gesturing to her blingy poinsettia sweater and gold leggings.

"You are a bit rough around the edges," Ruby teased as Rosie strutted her stuff at the end of the cutting table.

"Oh, phooey on you old biddies," Rosie

fussed at her friends. She shooed them away and picked up the rotary cutter she'd been slashing material strips with before her latest wedding discussion distraction. "We're talking about my wedding day. I want it to be special, something the town will always remember." Rosie fluttered her lashes. "I mean, how many times does a girl get to marry the man of her dreams?"

Maybelle cleared her throat and the other women in the room all avoided making eye contact. Rosie shot her a narrow-eyed look but continued on as if there had been no unsubtle reminder that this wasn't her first walk down the aisle.

"Y'all are such Scrooges. But no matter. I'm going to have the most Christmas-y Christmas wedding in the history of Pine Hill," Rosie declared. "So much so that people will be talking about how marvelous it was for years—no, decades—to come." Rosie's raspberry-pink lips curled upward. "And you ladies are going to help make my day special with no more complaints."

"I've not heard any complaints." Ruby said, glancing around at the other women. "You heard any complaints, Claudia?"

Morgan's grandmother shook her head. "Butterflies do not complain."

Morgan smiled at the name the women had given to their group of friends. She wasn't sure why or where they'd come up with the name, but they'd been known far and wide as the Butterflies for decades.

For all their good-natured squabbling, with Greyson in school, there was nowhere Morgan would rather be than here with these women at her cousins' sewing shop. Her childhood had been full of wonderful memories of them during every holiday vacation to Pine Hill from wherever her parents had been currently stationed. These ladies had always been around, making life interesting, and always making Christmas magical.

This, she thought, was why she'd moved to Pine Hill two months ago. In Pine Hill, she had her grandparents, aunts, uncles, cousins, and these ladies. Morgan was in Pine Hill to make a new start for her and Greyson. One that was filled with family, love, and community.

And Christmas.

She was determined to give Greyson the best Christmas of his young life to make up for the previous two years when they'd barely celebrated. That first year after losing Trey, they'd been in shock. Last Christmas, the lights and decorations had just seemed to open wounds.

"Okay, sleigh pulled by reindeer," Ruby said. "Got it. We can talk to Mr. Harvey and see if he can make arrangements for his horses to be replaced by reindeer. Does one need to have a red nose just in case it's a foggy night?" Obviously amused at her own question, she giggled in the cutest old lady way.

"Laugh if you will, but I'm being serious. I want our wedding to be straight from a fairy tale. Like something you'd see in the movies and think, Oh, I wish I were there."

In the short time Morgan had been in town, she was convinced Lou was so crazy about his bride-to-be he'd do his best to give her whatever she wanted. Especially since she'd put off the wedding several times already over various concerns, some real and some not so real. No way would he give her any excuse to put their wedding off yet again. If Rosie insisted on reindeer, Morgan suspected he really would book a flight to the North Pole if it came down to it. Anything to get Rosie headed down that aisle to him.

"If you're marrying the right man, the wedding itself doesn't matter so much." Ruby smiled, obviously thinking of her own wedding. "My Charlie and I had a simple church wedding in the middle of June. Nothing could have been more perfect than seeing that precious man waiting at the front of the church for me. Fifty years later and not once have I regretted marrying him."

Morgan thought back to her own wedding six years ago. She'd been in the early part of her nursing school education, but they'd been young and in love when they'd stood before the justice of the peace and recited their vows. And they'd kept them—until, as promised, death did them part. She'd not thought that would be so soon. She swallowed back the emotion clogging her throat at the memories that threatened to assail her.

She'd come to Pine Hill to make a new, positive, happy life. Positive and happy, that was her from now on. Most of the time, she really was a glass-half-full person. It was just since Trey's death that she felt as if life kept tipping her glass over and draining it, and her. But coming to Pine Hill was refilling her cup, and every day seemed better than the one before.

"What about you, Morgan? Do you have plans to remarry?" Ruby asked.

Channeling positivity and happiness, Morgan settled for wrinkling her nose instead of frowning—or worse, crying. "No. I don't plan to date, much less get serious enough to consider marriage." Now why had the fireman from Greyson's class just popped into her head? Probably for the same reason she'd not been able to stop thinking about him as she'd drifted off to sleep the night before. "I just want to be a good mom to Greyson."

"Nothing says a woman can't be a good

mom and date, too," Maybelle pointed out in a no-nonsense tone.

Morgan considered pointing out that Maybelle herself had never remarried after losing her soldier husband at a young age, nor had the woman had children. But she decided there was no reason to remind Maybelle of her loss. Over the years, Maybelle had dedicated her life to the betterment of Pine Hill. Morgan wanted to do the same. Positive and happy, she reminded herself. She had this.

"True, but Greyson's been through so much. The last thing he needs is for me to get distracted by a man." The last thing she needed was to be distracted by a man, which was why she needed to quit thinking about Andrew. "Currently, my top priority is to give my son the most amazing Christmas ever," Morgan said, knowing the women would be all over that as Christmas was their thing. "That's one of the reasons I agreed when Grammy Claudia suggested I move to Pine Hill. I want him to know the love of being around family and the enchantment of Christmas. He needs that."

They both did.

"I'm so glad you moved here, and not just because there's no place better to show a child Christmas," Grammy Claudia said, reaching over to pat Morgan's hand. "This town always goes above and beyond. No doubt this year will be something else with Rosie's wedding on top of the other festivities." She cast a skeptical glance toward her friend, then stage-whispered, "If the abominable bridezilla doesn't delay her 'Winder Wonderland' wedding again."

Morgan, Isabelle, and Sophie exchanged looks, then smothered their laughter.

"I heard that, Claudia," Rosie fussed from across the cutting table. "You, especially, should be grateful I changed the date, since it meant you got to travel to Montana rather than sit here all summer." Morgan's grandmother had longed to travel her entire life, but it was only over the past couple of years that she and Grampy had started doing so. The travel bug had bitten them both hard, and now they were constantly heading out on one trip or another. "Plus," Rosie continued, "we had all this extra time rather than having to have everything done by July fourth."

"Yeah, yeah," Maybelle said drily, waving the rotary cutter. "We know you got cold feet and you're just going to find some other reason why you and Lou can't get married this Christmas because you've suddenly realized a Christmas in July wedding was what you really wanted, after all."

"Well, with the rate you're going with getting fit for your new bridesmaid dresses, it'll probably have to be a Christmas in July

Janice Lynn

wedding," Rosie complained with an impatient eye roll.

"Why bother getting fitted again for a dress I may never need? You still have over a month to change your mind again," Maybelle accused, cutting more material. "Besides, I didn't like the gleam in your eyes when you said you'd found new dresses for us. There was nothing wrong with the bridesmaid gowns we already have."

"Well, you didn't think I was going to have you wearing those strapless silver tinsel numbers in December, did you? You'd all turn into popsicles!"

"My Charles liked the silver number. Of course, he liked the red gown with the furry white collar, too," Ruby mused, her expression saying she hadn't been so sure about either one. "He's looking forward to seeing what you choose next, as he says I'll look lovely no matter what I'm wearing. That man is just the sweetest."

All the Butterflies rolled their eyes at Ruby's comment.

"Of course, you will look lovely because Rosie would never put us in something unflattering." Maybelle gave Rosie a look that said she'd best not, if she knew what was good for her. "But sleigh-pulling reindeer?"

"Are you saying you can't do it?" Rosie asked, obvious challenge in her eyes.

"We could improvise," Ruby suggested.

"I could have my Charles ask the local taxidermist if we can borrow some antlers. Mr. Harvey could strap them onto his horses. You know, like that cartoon where an antler was tied onto a dog's head?"

Grammy Claudia, Maybelle, Sophie, Isabelle, and Morgan all covered their mouths to hide their smiles, while shaking their heads.

Rosie wasn't smiling. "Real reindeer, ladies. I'm not starting my marriage with imposter caribou."

Grammy snorted. "Next thing you know, she's going to insist we find ones named Donner, Blitzen, and Comet."

"Cupid would be kind of cute since it's for a wedding," Ruby added.

"Do not encourage her," Maybelle warned.

Morgan giggled as the older women continued arguing back and forth over whether or not Rosie would delay her wedding yet again over the reindeer. Then again, maybe there were other reasons Rosie kept putting off her wedding. Things that Morgan would understand all too well—such as the idea that Rosie didn't want to risk marrying again, and possibly losing another husband.

The morning flew by, and the conversation turned to questions about Morgan's new job at the Pine Hill Assisted Living Center.

"I've only been there six weeks and it's

a lot different from the hospital, but I really do like my job there," she told them. Mostly, she was grateful to be working again. "I'm doing three twelve-hour shifts per week. On those days, Greyson stays with Grammy when he's not in school. I feel so blessed for the wonderful coworkers and patients I've met and for Grammy and Grampy." She smiled at her grandmother. "Coming to Pine Hill was the right move for Greyson and me."

"No place better," Maybelle said.

"Agreed, but I'm enjoying the opportunity to decide for myself," Grammy said, referring to her and Grampy's recent trips. Their brief visit to Georgia last year had been the highlight of her and Greyson's holidays.

"Oh, I meant to ask you," Sophie said to Morgan. "How did Greyson like Santa visiting his class yesterday?"

"He was certainly a big hit with the kids," Morgan said. "But Greyson was more excited over meeting real-life firefighters." She shot an apologetic look Sophie's way. "Don't tell Cole."

"My grandson is a firefighter," Ruby said proudly. "He is such a joy. I don't know what I'd do without him. He's always swinging by to help Charlie and me with things around the house. Or maybe it's just to grab some home-cooked dinner." Ruby laughed. "Andrew was working yesterday, so he didn't come by, but called to check on us." She beamed with pride. "He mentioned that he'd been at the school with Cole and Ben."

Andrew was Ruby's grandson? That must be why he'd seemed vaguely familiar. No doubt their paths had crossed at some point during one of her holiday visits. She wasn't surprised that he hadn't remembered, either. He wouldn't have taken notice of a kid several years younger than him.

"Did Greyson get to meet Andrew?" Ruby asked.

Trying to keep her expression nonchalant, Morgan nodded. "He did. Andrew was giving out plastic fire helmets and was a big hit with the kids, especially Greyson." And her, unfortunately, based upon how much she'd thought about him since. Ugh. She didn't want him in her head messing with her new positive and happy life. "It was all I could do to convince Greyson to take his helmet off when I put him to bed last night, and he insisted upon wearing it right up until the point he got out of the car at school this morning."

"He looked adorable. You should have let him keep it on," Grammy said. "He was so excited to show me and his Grampy his helmet and firefighter goodies."

"Sounds just like Andrew when he was a kid," Ruby mused, smiling with nostalgia. "I think I still have the plastic helmet he used to wear around my house. I certainly have numerous photos of him wearing them in my scrapbooks."

"It's hard to picture Andrew as a little boy," Morgan said, then—realizing what she'd done—shut her mouth and hoped the Butterflies had missed her slip.

No such luck.

"Oh?" Maybelle looked at Morgan over her reading glasses. "Why is that?"

She gulped. "Um, well, just he's so... grown up now."

Yeah, she wasn't fooling anyone. But it was the best excuse she could come up with since five sets of eyes were trained on her. As the only one who hadn't caught Morgan's blush, Ruby saved her.

"I understand. I have the opposite problem. It's hard for me to remember he's a grown man, now, rather than that sweet little boy running around my house and always getting into something. Those were the days."

Grammy eyed Morgan curiously. "Did you ever met Andrew when you visited before?"

"I don't recall meeting him." See, she sounded as if he wasn't memorable to her. Maybe that would throw the women off the scent. While she trusted their good intentions, she didn't welcome the idea of interference when she wasn't sure what was going on in her head in the first place.

She doubted she'd be able to get them to back down, though. According to what Sophie and her new friend Sarah had told her, Butterflies were like hound dogs when it came to the possibility of romantic interest.

"Mom and dad were stationed overseas during my teen years," she went on to say. "So I spent my school holidays exploring Europe rather than returning stateside during those years. If I did meet him, it would have been when we were small."

"I was so glad when you decided to come back to the states for college," Grammy admitted. "We sure missed seeing you during the holidays."

Guilt hit Morgan that she'd rarely made it to Pine Hill during college or in the years after. She'd met Trey and had been all caught up in life with him. She'd only visited her grandparents a couple of times, and those had been rushed holiday visits of no more than a day, giving her little chance to socialize with others in town.

"Andrew's a few years older than you, so you might not remember if you met when you were younger," Ruby pointed out, still seeming oblivious to the others' curiosity. "I'll have to ask him if he recalls meeting you."

Morgan's face heated. Ready to escape, she glanced at her watch. "Sorry, ladies, but I need to pick Greyson up from school.

I'll see you soon to help with wedding plans or making ornaments or whatever y'all need me for." She went to her grandmother and kissed her cheek. "I'll see you at home this evening, Grammy. Love you."

And *I'm so sorry I didn't come home more*. She'd make up for that.

Chapter Three

" *T*HANKS FOR DRIVING US TO the fire hall, Sophie," Morgan said. ""I know it's not easy for you to sneak away from the quilt shop on a Saturday morning"

She smiled at the battery-operated Christmas light necklace her cousin wore over a red sweater dress she'd matched up with green tights and black boots. Her dark ponytail was tied with a red and green ribbon, and she looked as if she could be one of Santa's elves.

Morgan glanced down at her own jeans and boring fuzzy blue sweater. If she wanted to give Greyson the best Christmas of his life, she was going to have to get her Christmas on and dress the part.

"No need to thank me." Sophie practically bubbled with an excitement brighter than her outfit. "You know I love any excuse to see Cole."

The couple had been dating for about a year and Sophie admitted to being hopelessly in love with the Marine turned firefighter. She'd even referred to him more than once as her "real-life hero." From what she'd seen when she'd met Cole at Grammy's, Morgan was convinced the feeling was mutual.

"You should have seen him in his Santa suit," Morgan whispered, glancing at a headphoned Greyson to make sure he wouldn't overhear. "He was adorable with his ho-ho-hos and trying to make his fake belly shake like a bowl full of jelly. He was so convincing that I wouldn't have known it was him had I not recognized his eyes."

"He took over for another, much shorter, fireman, Bob, last year. Andrew told me there were several wardrobe malfunctions after I left the fire hall." Sophie shook her head with a soft smile. "I'm not sure how he managed to pull that off since I fitted that suit perfectly for him and made a few upgrades this year for increased authenticity. But from what I heard, the issue was with the padding. It's not easy to make such a strong, in-shape man look as if he's not."

Sophie's expression became a bit dreamy, as she added, "But you're right. Cole is absolutely adorable as Santa."

"Of course, you're a little biased." Morgan was glad her cousin was so happy. She remembered that totally in love feeling, the "walk on air because the world is all sunshine and rainbows" euphoria. She wanted her cousin to enjoy it, so she wouldn't point out that all that happiness sometimes came with a high price.

"A little," Sophie agreed, smiling. "But you have to admit, he pulls Santa off very well, especially with the makeup I picked up after Halloween this year." Her expression grew dreamy again. "He certainly makes every day feel like Christmas to me." Then glancing at Greyson in the rearview mirror, she asked in a much louder voice, "Hey there, Champ. You excited to go to the fire hall?"

Lifting one side of his headphones away from his ear and looking up from the computer tablet he held, Greyson answered, "Yes! I hope Firefighter Andrew is there today. I like him."

Sophie's gaze cut to Morgan in question. Earlier, Sophie had cornered Morgan to ask about why she'd blushed when Andrew's name had come up. Morgan hadn't seen her cousin since then, and she'd hoped Sophie would've forgotten or not thought much of it, but she should've known better. Her cousin had been raised around the Butterflies, and apparently, that rubbed off.

Morgan shrugged. "Andrew gave him a firefighter helmet and they bonded."

"So much for those books and crayons Col—er, Santa gave out."

"No worries. Greyson has been coloring in his Santa book, too. He hasn't started his contest sheet, though." It was a page-sized ornament that each child was supposed to decorate however they wanted, just using crayons.

"I'm practicing," Greyson piped up, having kept his earphones at an angle to be able to hear his game and their conversation. "My ornament has to be really good because it will hang on the fire hall wall."

"That's great. If you need any help coming up with design ideas, I've got tons of Christmas books we could look through for inspiration," Sophie offered. She pulled into the fire hall and parked her car. "The guys are going to be excited to get those brownies. Thanks for making them."

"Greyson did most of the work," Morgan praised. "He helped me pour the batter into the pan and put candy on top of them after they'd cooled."

Morgan had loved the time in the kitchen with her son that morning. Greyson had talked nonstop about the firefighters and wondering what the fire hall would be like, and whether or not Andrew would like a few candy sprinkles or a lot. He'd made the full gamut from nearly plain to heavily sprinkled to be sure his hero would get something to his taste. Although she was a bit nervous over how excited he was about going to the fire hall—and a little anxious for herself over possibly seeing Andrew again—she'd smiled and answered his questions as best she could. Seeing Greyson so animated about the trip was worth her bout of momma nerves over his love of firefighting.

That was almost certainly why her insides were all jittery.

It was because of Greyson, and not the prospect of seeing Andrew again.

Whether or not Andrew was at the fire hall didn't matter. Not one little bit. And definitely wasn't why her stomach had gone from quivery to twisted.

When Sophie had parked, Morgan got Greyson out of his safety seat, then got the container of brownies.

"Can I carry them?"

"Sure," Morgan answered, smiling at how her son looked in the plastic helmet he'd insisted on bringing with him. He'd also donned a cloth firefighting vest that was left over from his Halloween costume. Yep. He was adorable.

"I want to make sure Firefighter Andrew

gets to pick one first," Greyson announced, holding onto the box as if it held precious and fragile items. "I hope he's here. If he is, I think he'll pick lots of sprinkles, don't you, Mom?"

Morgan ignored Sophie's speculative glance and focused on her son's question. "Lots of sprinkles is what I'd pick."

"Me, too. That way you get a brownie and candy," Greyson agreed, holding the box with great care.

"Somebody was seriously impressed by Cole's bestie," Sophie whispered when Greyson got just enough ahead of them to not overhear. "He should be here today, by the way. He and Cole work the same shifts."

There her belly went, starting its shaken-snow-globe thing again.

Trying not to look Sophie's way, Morgan watched Greyson stop at the stretch of sidewalk leading into the fire hall to wait on them and smiled that in spite his impatience to go inside, he'd still followed the rules.

Sophie obviously took her smile to mean something else. "What about you? Were you seriously impressed, as well? Based on that look on your face, I'm thinking you were."

She was saved from answering by their reaching Greyson's side.

"Today is the best day ever," he told them and looked one hundred percent convinced it truly was. "I can't wait to give him a brownie."

Neither Morgan, or Sophie, had to ask who he meant.

"Cole, your honey is here," Jules called over the Christmas music Chief was already insisting upon, her tone teasing.

A few of the firefighters groaned at the merry tunes continuously playing, but it didn't bother Andrew. He never got tired of Christmas music and was all for rocking around the Christmas tree at any time of year. Grandma Ruby was just as likely to have her favorite Elvis Christmas soundtrack playing during July as she was in December. Andrew knew most of the tunes by heart, as some of his favorite memories were belting the tunes out with pretend microphones with her as they danced around.

"Unlike present company, Sophie is sweet as honey," Cole called back to the female firefighter from where he worked next to Andrew cleaning their gear. He always took the gentle mocking in stride, obviously seeing nothing wrong with the way Sophie had him wrapped around her finger. Setting aside his work, Cole stood, smiling in the direction of the door. "And it looks as if she's brought sweets with her."

That got Andrew's stomach's attention and it growled in eager anticipation. Sophie brought treats to the fire hall on a regular basis and Andrew was usually one of the first in line to grab a few—and to tease that his buddy didn't deserve her cooking, sewing skills, and bubbly Christmas goodness.

Andrew looked toward the door leading into the truck deck, expecting to see Sophie, dressed in some incredibly Christmassy outfit, bearing baked gifts. And indeed, Cole's girl was there, Christmas personified, but it wasn't just Sophie who had come for a visit.

Cole glanced toward him and grinned.

"You remember Morgan?" his 'friend' teased, turnabout being fair play.

"Um, yeah. From our visit to the school." He coughed to try to cover how seeing her again had thrown him off his game. "She's Greyson's mom. I really like that kid. It's good to see him again."

"Right. That's why you remember Morgan. Because she's Greyson's mom," Cole joked.

"It's why she was at the school," Andrew defended. "And I'm guessing it's why she's here today. Greyson sounded really excited about coming to see the fire hall." He tried to keep the focus on the boy to make it seem as if it was no big deal that Morgan was at the fire hall. It wasn't a big deal. The reason he was happy was that he was glad to see Greyson.

He'd thought about the kid a lot that week. He'd wondered at how much the boy remembered of his father, since Morgan had made it seem as if it had been a few years since his death. Greyson couldn't have been more than three at the time. He'd also thought about how rough it must have been for Morgan, raising Greyson alone. Not that any of it was any of Andrew's business.

"That's right." The corner of Cole's mouth hiked up a few notches. "He was why your line got backed up."

Andrew watched as Sophie spotted them and headed their way, Morgan and Greyson at her side. Greyson's firefighter helmet had him grinning.

"My line got backed up because Greyson is an awesome little dude, and we were talking. You're just bummed that he recognized my fine firefighting skills over your lackluster ones."

Spotting him, Greyson's eyes lit up. After a quick glance up at his mom for permission, the kid took off skipping toward him.

Andrew recalled that skip. It was the one where he'd known he'd get in trouble if he ran, but a fast walk wasn't nearly good enough, and so he'd go for a quick skip.

"Since I was in a padded red suit, sporting caked-on make-up with fake wrinkles, and walking around saying 'ho-ho-ho,' I can understand how he'd make that mistake. I won't hold it against him." As the women arrived, Cole bent to let Sophie peck his cheek. Despite his bluster, Cole's cheeks pinkened at her quick kiss. Or it could just be her bright Christmas sweater reflecting off his face. Either way, Andrew made note to call him out on it later. He was anticipating more Morgan comments and at least he'd have some return ammo.

"Hi." Greyson said as he came to a halt a few feet from Andrew. His beaming smile was replaced by a bit of hesitance as he asked, "Remember me?"

The uncertainty in his eyes tugged at Andrew's heart. *Oh, kid, how could I forget?*

"I never forget a future firefighter. Especially one who's such a good secret keeper," he said, glad the boy's expression relaxed. "I'm digging your helmet, by the way. And the vest."

"I brought you something." He held the box out toward Andrew. "Mom and I made them for you."

"They're for everyone as a thank you to the fire department for coming to visit with his class," Morgan clarified, joining them. She wore jeans and a fuzzy blue sweater with a cream-colored scarf around her neck.

Her hair was loose and hung just over her shoulders.

"And here I was thinking they were all for me," he teased, once again struck by how big her eyes were. Big and mesmerizing. Plus, there was something hypnotic about that shade of green. It just sucked him in and made him want to keep looking. Or maybe that was just Morgan in general. She was the prettiest thing he'd ever seen. Why would he want to look at anything else when she was there?

"I can make you more," Greyson said, drawing Andrew's attention back. "Some just for you."

"Nah, bud. I'm good." He patted his flat belly beneath his navy T-shirt with its gold fire hall emblem. "Based on how good that box smells, it's probably better if you don't or they'll be making me do Santa auditions for the next community Christmas play."

"They're brownies." Greyson stared up at Andrew with eager eyes that were so similar to his mother's—except in how they looked at him. Greyson's were full of adoration. Morgan's, not so much. "With red and green candy sprinkles. They're the best."

Andrew gave an impressed nod. "Sounds it. I'm all about the red and green candy sprinkles. The more, the better."

Beaming, Greyson glanced toward his mom. "I told you."

"You going to share?" Ben fussed at Andrew, joining them. "'Cause my nose is telling me I need some of what is inside that box."

Tightly holding onto the brownies, Greyson said, "Let Firefighter Andrew get his first."

"Figures." Ben laughed. "Remind me to hand out helmets next time instead of stickers."

"You could hand out the helmets, the coloring books, and the stickers and it wouldn't help your ugly mug," Andrew teased, eyeing the now-opened box Greyson had sat on the table. "Little Man, those look good."

"They are," Greyson assured him. "I taste-tested them before we came."

"Taste-tested them eh? Good to know. Let me check you to make sure they aren't magic Christmas brownies meant to turn me into an elf." Andrew lifted the plastic helmet off the kid's head and pretended to look behind his ears. The boy's laughter made Andrew's insides feel warm and squishy. "Good news. I think we're safe to have some, Ben."

"They won't turn you into an elf." Greyson giggled. "My mom taught me how to make brownies, but they're just plain, not magic."

"Also, good to know since I like plain

brownies, especially ones with red and green candy sprinkles."

"She could teach you how to make them, too," Greyson offered. "Or if she is busy with work, I could teach you. My Grammy Claudia has a big kitchen."

Claudia, as in his Grandma Ruby's friend? That would explain how Morgan and Sophie knew each other. Sophie's mother was Claudia's much younger sister. Andrew didn't see a lot of similarities between Morgan and brown-haired Sophie, but come to think of it, there was a resemblance between Morgan and Isabelle. Possibly it was more obvious because Sophie's older sister had blond hair, too, but there was something about the high cheekbones and dimples that said "related." Maybe the shared traits with Isabelle was why he'd been struck with the sensation that he knew Morgan when he'd first seen her at the school. Looking at Isabelle had never made him feel hot beneath the collar, though. So maybe it was more likely that, at some point in the past, he'd seen her when she'd been visiting Pine Hill. It was hard to imagine that he wouldn't remember her, but if she'd been a kid at the time, he might not have paid much attention.

"I'm glad you like to learn new things. It's always good to gain new life skills," he told Greyson, smiling as memories of mak-

Janice Lynn

ing various items with his Grandma hit. She'd insisted he learn everything within her power to teach him and he'd been an eager pupil.

Ben cleared his throat and gestured to the open box. "You going to pick one of those so the rest of us can partake? Man's starving here."

Andrew eyed the brownies and chose the one that was most smothered in red and green, earning an approving look from Greyson. "This one looks like it has my name written all over it."

"Cause you're so sweet?" Ben teased, looking to Greyson for permission to grab a brownie. When the boy nodded, he chose one.

"Nah," Cole said, coming over to eye the box's contents. "It's 'cause he needs to be sweetened up. Let's let him have two in hopes it works."

Andrew rolled his eyes, then glanced toward Greyson. "You see what I have to put up with? Are you sure you want to be a firefighter and deal with the likes of these clowns?"

Greyson nodded. "I like Firefighters Cole and Ben. Just as soon as I'm big enough, I'll come help you."

Andrew held out his hands as if measuring Greyson. "Won't be too much longer because I think you grew an inch from when I met you the other day."

His comment earned a big grin from the boy, which he found even sweeter than the delicious, still-warm brownie practically melting in his mouth. Glancing up, his gaze met Morgan's and a whole new sweetness spread through him.

One that had everything to do with the tenderness in her eyes as she watched him and Greyson.

He got the sense that she didn't want to like him. But she did. And that might be the sweetest thing ever. Because even though it went against his not dating a single mom rule, he liked her and Greyson, too.

Morgan gave a nervous glance toward the man she was now alone with—if one could call standing next him in the middle of the fire department dayroom with four other guys and one female firefighter finishing off the remaining brownies there, "alone." She'd counted on Greyson being by her side for the whole visit to the fire hall. Or at least, she'd thought that if he left her side, it would be to stand with his new favorite person, meaning that she or Andrew would be chaperoned at all times. But Cole and Sophie had lured

Greyson away with the promise of a drive around the block in the fire truck, and now here she and Andrew were.

"Did you miss me?"

At Andrew's question, Morgan blinked. "Pardon?"

"You heard me," he pointed out, his hazel eyes sparkling with humor. "I asked if you missed me. I think you did."

Feeling self-conscious and wishing there had been room for her to go with Cole, Sophie, and Greyson out in the fire truck—why had they taken the smaller truck, anyway?—Morgan folded her arms over her fuzzy sweater, then arched her brow. "Why would I have missed you?"

He'd been on her mind almost continuously since they'd met. Did that mean she'd missed him or that he'd confused her by making her feel things she'd not felt in so long?

"Because you haven't seen me since Monday," he pointed out, hooking his thumbs in his pants pockets and rocking back on his heels.

Morgan rolled her eyes. "Oh, the horrors. However did I survive?"

"I know, right?" His lips twitched. "We should do something about that to make sure you aren't deprived of my presence for so long next time."

Once upon a time she'd have dived into

the fun she saw reflected in his eyes. But not these days. These days that fun terrified her as much as it attracted her. But he was good with Greyson and her heart had practically melted at how he'd giggled at being checked to see if he was turning into an elf.

"Sure of yourself, aren't you?" she asked, keeping her voice wry, despite how much her lips threatened to curve upward. She wasn't even sure why she wanted to smile, she just did.

He shrugged. "Life's too short for self-doubt."

That got her attention.

"You never doubt yourself?"

"Not that I'll admit to." He grinned sheepishly. "Women don't like wishy-washy men."

"I heard that you rarely dated. Guess now I know why," she teased, surprising herself. And, Good Lord, why had she just said that she knew he rarely dated? That was as good as admitting that she'd been talking about him. Which she had been, but she didn't want him to know that. Next thing you knew she'd be telling him she missed him, and she hadn't.

His grin was positively wicked. "I date."

Everything within her lit up at his claim. *Don't read too much into what he's saying,* she reminded herself. He's just flirting. That's what guys did, right? Although, if Suzie was to be believed that wasn't Andrew's usual as he was normally straightforward.

"Good for you," she managed to say. "I don't."

She added the last part as much for her benefit as to make sure he understood he was wasting his time if that was what he wanted.

"I get that you're not into firefighters. Truth be told, I'm not into dating single moms," he continued, his gaze not leaving hers. "Since I'm not interested in anything serious or long term, I don't feel it fair to Greyson, or any kid, to allow them to get attached and hope for something more."

So, he really did tell women upfront that he wasn't interested in commitment. Morgan respected his honesty.

"But, I am always on the lookout for new friends. A man can never have too many, especially with the lot I'm stuck with," he continued, his eyes friendly. "I think Greyson would enjoy it if we all went to lunch at Lou's next Saturday and then made a day of it."

"Greyson, huh?" Greyson was at the top of the reasons why she shouldn't say yes. She didn't need to encourage her son's fascination with Andrew. She could only hope that he'd come back from his ride in the fire truck and be totally into Cole rather than the man eyeing her as if he could read her every thought.

He grinned sheepishly. "I'm positive you'd enjoy it if we went to lunch at Lou's next Saturday and made a day of it, too, Morgan. Surely, being new in town, you're on the lookout for new friends, too?"

Andrew was asking her and Greyson to spend the day with him. Why did that make her want to do cartwheels and air high-fives and funny little dances of excitement? And smile. She really wanted to smile. But at the same time, the invitation also scared her as she wasn't ready to even begin to consider spending the day with a man, not even as friends. So why did a part of her want to say yes? Her conflicted feelings were proof of why she had to say no. She wasn't going to go to lunch with him. She opened her mouth to tell him so, but he continued before she got out the first word.

"I should remind you that we've already established that you shouldn't go too long in between seeing me."

She arched a brow. "'Too long' being five days?"

He faked confusion. "Is that all it was since I met you at the school? It seems so much longer."

It had to her as well, but she wasn't ad-mitting to that, either. Or to how his sparkly eyes, frequent grins, and humor made her wonder what would happen if she said yes to his invitation.

69

"After lunch, we could take Greyson to Harvey Farms. It's the first weekend of their transformation for Christmas. There's a sleigh ride—actually, it's a decorated wagon—and a bonfire with hot cocoa afterwards." He painted a picture that was tempting. "Greyson would like that."

A sleigh ride did sound fun. No doubt Greyson would love it. And the time spent with his firefighter idol, though that would be draw enough.

Morgan eyed Andrew and couldn't resist pointing out, "You do realize that next Saturday is a week away? That's seven days. Your premise that I was deprived when I had to go five days without seeing you was your argument on why I should say yes. Now you're suggesting I go a full week. You're really going to have to get your story straight."

She couldn't argue with him that seeing him again did feel like a privilege, though. One that filled her insides with excitement and anticipation and a lot of awareness of everything about him. Things like the way his frequent grin made her want to smile, too. And the way Greyson smiled around him. Not that she was going to go, but if she did, she suspected he was right and that she'd have fun. She knew Greyson would. Maybe she and Greyson could go to Harvey Farms on their own or with some of her family.

"Good catch," Andrew admitted, his grin cocky as ever. "Beauty and brains. I like that." The admiration in his eyes suggested he really did. "Seven days." He shook his head as if the time frame were unfathomable. "Just imagine how horrible it's going to be if you have to go longer?"

"It boggles one's mind," she stated with mock solemnity, reminding herself that no matter how cute his grin was, no matter how much Greyson would enjoy the outing, she wasn't ready for such an event to occur.

Even if it was only as 'friends,' she couldn't, wouldn't, go with him.

He was the first person she'd met since losing her husband who'd made her even think about dating or feel aware that she was still a young woman capable of enjoying a man's attention. Spending time with him just felt too dangerous.

"Okay," he gave an exaggerated sigh, eyes still sparkling with that hint he knew her every thought. "You convinced me that I shouldn't make you wait that long." His gaze held hers and he leaned a little closer. "How about I take you and Little Man to dinner at Lou's on Monday evening, only two days away, and then we'll make a day of it on Saturday still, too? Maybe grab something to eat at the sandwich shop at Harvey Farms before going on the sleigh ride?"

She had to admit, Andrew kept pulling

off the perfect requests, as he included Greyson in both invitations.

"I work a twelve-hour shift at the Pine Hill Assisted Living Center on Monday," she said. Then realizing what she'd done, she quickly added, "Not that I would have said yes, but it's a moot point, because I can't."

He regarded her for what felt like an eternity but couldn't have been more than a few seconds. His eyes filled with compassion she didn't need or want. "Tell me, Morgan. Why wouldn't you have said yes to doing something we both know you want to do when it truly would be just as friends?"

Her breath caught at how he was looking at her, at how the warmth in his eyes made her insides feel alive again, at how he was so close to her she'd swear she got a whiff of spicy aftershave that had her wanting to deeply inhale, and at how he was calling her out on the fact that she did want to say yes. If she spent time with him, would she be able to remember that 'just friends' part?

"That might work if we were friends," she finally answered, glancing around the fire hall to see if anyone was paying them the slightest bit of attention. They didn't seem to be. Too bad. She was ready for an interruption. Why weren't Sophie and Cole back with Greyson yet?

It was almost as if...as if her cousin had

purposely left her alone with Andrew. No doubt that's exactly what So-in-Love Sophie and her boyfriend had done.

"We could be friends," Andrew suggested, his expression both pulling her in and annoying her. How could he be so arrogantly self-assured and yet have such kindness in his eyes at the same time? "All friendships start somewhere. Why shouldn't ours start right here, right now?"

Because so many things about you terrify me.

"I'm not sure we have anything in common," she said instead, glancing toward the doorway.

"Maybe not," he admitted. "Too bad though because we would have had a good time."

Morgan was sure she would have. There was that whole being attracted to the wrong kind of man thing she had going. It was all fun and games in the beginning and then... and then, it wasn't.

Andrew, with his motorcycle, plane-jumping, and firefighting was definitely not what she needed if she ever decided to date again.

"I'm a fun guy."

"And a modest one," she added, emotions torn in a thousand directions. Why did he have to be so likeable?

He grinned. "Glad you noticed that about me."

"How could I miss it? Your humility was the first thing I noticed." What was she doing? "Seriously, I appreciate the offer, but like I said, I work twelve hours on Monday. Sorry."

"If you insist upon depriving yourself of the pleasure of my company, maybe I could still take Greyson?"

That had her pausing and staring at him in shock. "You want to take my son to dinner by yourself? Absolutely not."

"I guess that didn't come out exactly right. Sorry. I meant on the sleigh ride, but I understand why you said no."

"Even if I was crazy enough to allow a stranger to take my child out for the day— which I'm not—I still wouldn't think it's a good idea. Please respect my decision on what's best for my son."

He regarded her for a moment, then nodded. "I won't mention it in front of him, but that doesn't mean I don't want to spend the day with him—and you. And, for the record, I'm not really a stranger since our grandmas have been best friends most of their lives. That makes us practically family."

"This is how you're trying to convince me to go to dinner with you?" she couldn't resist asking. "By saying we're practically family? Seriously?"

He chuckled. "Is it working?"

She shook her head.

He reached over, picked up another brownie from an almost empty box, and took a bite, still looking at her with a sparkly Santa twinkle in his eyes. "Okay, if that's what you want, Morgan. Thanks for the brownies."

Chapter Four

"*I* GUESS SOMEBODY GOT SHOT DOWN."

Losing focus on the gruesome aliens he was destroying on the video game monitor screen, Andrew winced. Ben had overheard his conversation with Morgan? He should have known his buddy wasn't nearly so absorbed with cleaning his equipment as he'd pretended to be.

"Your hearing must be messed up."

From the chair next to Andrew's in the fire hall's dayroom, Ben snorted. "Nothing wrong with my hearing. Major crash and burn—I couldn't miss it, kind of like that alien kicking your butt there."

Andrew made hash of the alien in question. "Crash and burn makes it sound like I was trying to get her to date me, and that's not true. I asked to be her and Greyson's friend. That's all. Can you blame me? She made me brownies. Who wouldn't want to be friends with someone who makes you brownies?"

"The kid made you brownies," Ben argued as another round of aliens arrived to prevent them from moving on to the next game level.

"Exactly. I want to be his friend, too. Future firefighter and he bakes me brownies, which makes me like the kid all the more. You, not so much," Andrew said, never taking his gaze off the game.

"Because you know you're never going to oust my top scorer position on our favorite video game?" Ben teased.

Andrew snorted.

"You asked Morgan out?" Cole asked, coming near where Andrew pretended great interest in the video game. "How did I miss that?"

"It was when you took Greyson out in the fire truck," Ben supplied.

"And when you were eavesdropping but seem to have missed the part where I asked her just as friends," Andrew added.

Ben gave him a knowing look. "Man carries on a conversation in my house, that's not me eavesdropping."

"Since when is the fire hall your house?"

"Isn't it yours?" Ben questioned.

"You have a point," Andrew conceded. "I'm here almost as much as I am my place, and you guys and Jules are family."

"Don't let him send you off on a wild rabbit chase while he completely avoids fessing up to having asked Morgan out," Cole warned, kicking the leg rest out on the chair he'd settled into to work on a crossword puzzle.

"Is that all you want? A confession I asked her out?" Andrew shrugged. "I asked her out as friends."

"And she said no," Ben finished. "Our boy was cracking me up with all his lines. Never known him to get shot down before a woman even got to know him. Usually, they're asking him out rather than the other way around."

"Even if I had been asking her out on a date, which I wasn't, it wouldn't have been the first time I've been told no." Although it had been a few years since the previous time that had happened. "It's unlikely to be the last."

It was the one that bothered him, though. For so many reasons. Greyson's clear loneliness and desire to be a firefighter called to him, made him want to reach out to the kid. And, Morgan, well, he'd like to be her friend, too.

"Can't blame her for saying no to the likes of you," Cole teased, grinning, then his expression turning more serious, he added, "But to be fair, from what Sophie has told me, Morgan isn't interested in dating anyone."

Andrew was having more and more difficulty focusing on the video game. He wanted to pick Cole's brain and learn everything he could about Morgan and Greyson.

"Why's that?" Ben replied, saving Andrew from having to be the one to ask.

"She's had a rough time the past couple of years. First, she lost her husband. Then the hospital where she'd been working downsized this past summer and she lost her job. Sophie says Morgan felt overwhelmed, and that's why she moved to Pine Hill—she thought being close to family would help."

"That is rough," Ben admitted, then cut his gaze to Andrew. "Sounds as if you're wasting your time with that one."

Had she said yes, spending the day with Morgan and Greyson wouldn't have been wasted time. Of that, he was certain.

"She's not really your type, anyway," Cole pointed out.

"I have a type of friend?" He wasn't ready to give up yet on their being friends. Especially not now that he knew she needed his help to move past her grief and start living life fully again. Couldn't she see that he was

someone safe? Neither of them were looking for a relationship, so he could help her
and Greyson heal and have fun until she
was ready to find the right person to settle
down with. Although, the thought of her
with someone else didn't sit well and he took
out a line of aliens to appease his frustration
with the entire situation.

Cole eyed him over his folded back
crossword puzzle book. "Give her time.
Maybe she'll see things differently after she
gets settled into Pine Hill life."

"Like you did with Sophie?" he asked,
hoping to put his friend on the defense rather than the offense. Andrew much preferred
to deliver the punches than to take them.

"That was a completely different situation. Sophie deserved better than me. Still
does. But I'm a lucky man because she loves
me, anyway."

Andrew disagreed. Sophie was lucky to
have his pal's heart. Still, he made a gag-
ging noise, then elbowed Ben. "Reach over
and divest that syrupy sap of his man card,
please."

Cole harrumphed. "Man card or no, I
can take your sorry self."

"In your dreams," Andrew countered,
although he wouldn't want to put it to the
test. Cole had been a highly trained member
of a special forces unit during his Marine
days. Andrew had taken years of Ishin Ryu

Ju-Jitsu, but he'd never used his skills in real life or death combat, not the way Cole had. Based upon the nightmares his buddy used to have when he would sleep at the station, Andrew knew Cole had seen and done things he'd rather forget.

"By the way, you have two weeks to work on your next comedy routine," Cole added, causing Andrew to look his way again.

"Watch it!" Ben warned as an alien side-swiped him on the video screen.

"Comedy routine?" Andrew asked, his gaze back on the monitor but his attention divided. At the rate he was paying attention to the game, earth was doomed.

"Asking Morgan out again," Cole supplied.

"Why two weeks?"

"'Cause that's when you'll be seeing her again. Sophie said Morgan was volunteering at the Quilts of Valor Foundation Sew-In. That thing the quilt shop is hosting at the church." Cole settled back in his chair to study his crossword puzzle. "I signed us up. As long as no calls come in, Chief says we can volunteer all day."

Andrew could believe it. Chief was all about volunteering, as was Cole.

Ben grimaced. "We're sewing, aren't we?"

"Yep."

"Great." Ben sighed. "Santa Cole has

struck again, going around spreading Christmas cheer."

"Look at it this way, maybe your 'the one' will be there and you two can knit a life together," Cole suggested.

"Stitch, not knit. Two completely different things," Andrew corrected him. With Sophie running a quilt shop, Cole should know better.

"Whatever," Cole said, shrugging. "It's for a good cause."

Ben was still fussing. Not wanting to seem too eager, Andrew mumbled some complaints, but only half-heartedly as he didn't mind helping to make quilts for veterans.

Seeing Morgan Morris again would be an added bonus.

Maybe he'd get lucky and she really would have missed him. And, if so, maybe she would have decided that she was ready to be friends. Fourteen days...it could happen.

"Never heard you humming before," said the eighty-year-old man lying in his hospital bed.

"Was I humming?" Morgan asked.

John Harper had only been at the assisted living facility for a week, but he'd quickly become her favorite patient. She'd admitted him on the day of his transfer from Pine Hill General Hospital. He'd been wearing his Korean War Veteran ball cap, as he did every day, and they'd bonded when she'd thanked him for his service and told him she'd grown up a 'military brat' whose parents still proudly served their country overseas. John's quick wit and positive attitude during his intake assessment had kept her smiling.

"Like a songbird," he told her, eyeing the pills she held out to him in a small plastic cup. "Do I have to take those?"

John pushed right through the pain that she knew his physical therapy caused him, but he made no bones about not wanting to take his medications.

"I'd recommend it if you want to keep your blood pressure and sugar under control. Of course, it's up to you on whether you want to slow that fractured hip from mending so you can go home."

Sighing, he took the cup. "What you're saying is that they're never going to let me out of here if I don't take these so I should take them."

"Did I say that?" she teased.

He gave her a wry look and tilted the pill cup, popping the medication into his mouth.

Then he took a sip from the water bottle Morgan kept near him.

"I didn't mean you had to take them all at once," she pointed out, shaking her head as she watched to make sure he got them down okay. "It's all or nothing with you, isn't it, John?"

"If I'm going to take them, there isn't a reason to mess around with it. Just take 'em and get it over with. Now, tell me what had you humming? That boy of yours finally find something to talk about other than the fire-fighters who came to visit his school?"

Morgan always chatted with her patients while she was providing their care, hoping to give them a look at the world outside the facility and to help them feel connected. Greyson was her favorite subject.

"He may still be talking about it when he graduates high school," she admitted as she tossed the empty medicine cup into the trash. She worried she might still be think-ing about a certain firefighter when Greyson graduated high school, too. Andrew seemed unforgettable. Then again, it had only been two days since she'd seen him at the fire hall.

"You don't sound overly excited about it."

"I'm hoping he'll decided on something less dangerous by then."

"Nothing wrong with being a firefighter."

84

"Except for the whole running-into-a-burning-building part," Morgan countered.

"There is that," John conceded.

"What am I saying? You ran into bullets being fired and here I am fretting over my five-year-old wanting to grow up to be a firefighter." She wrapped the blood pressure cuff around his upper left arm, making sure to line the arrow up with his artery. "You probably think I'm silly worrying about such things."

He shook his head. "Nothing wrong with worrying about your son. It just means that you love him."

"That I do. With all my heart."

The old man smiled. "A mother's love is precious."

"Tell me about your mother," she prompted after she'd finished taking his blood pressure, glad to see normal numbers, and wanting to keep him talking. "What was she like?"

Memories obviously flooded him as his eyes shined and a smile toyed on his lips. "She was a tough old bird."

"So that's where you get it," she accused, smiling.

He laughed. "It's been a few decades since anyone found me tough."

She shook her head. "I can't imagine that's true. I've watched you during your therapy. You're tough, John." She could tell her words pleased him. "Way tougher than I'll ever be, for sure."

His old blue eyes met hers. "You're tougher than you give yourself credit for."

Surprised and touched by his comment, Morgan looked at him curiously. "What makes you say that?"

Although she talked with him a lot, even opting a few times to take her lunch break while sitting in his room and chatting while she ate, she'd only told him highlights of the past couple of years of her life. She didn't see how he'd concluded from that that she was tough. Her insides were pure mush and most of the time she felt like a silly worry-wart.

"Some things a man just knows when he meets a woman."

"I'm going to take that as a compliment."

"I meant it as one." A bushy white brow rose. "Now, I know I'm old, but I'm not so senile as to miss that you haven't answered my question."

But she was apparently senile enough to have forgotten what he'd asked. "Which question was that?"

"What, or who, was responsible for the humming? Not that you're not always a smiley little thing, but there was an extra little glimmer in your eyes when you walked in here today, and I'm not buying that seeing this old face was responsible."

Morgan wanted to hug him. She was delighted that he'd called her a smiley little thing when, not so long ago, finding smiles outside of Greyson had seemed impossible.

"For the record, seeing your 'old face' does make me smile. But to answer your question..." She shrugged. "Life is finally starting to feel normal again. Moving to Pine Hill was a good decision for me and Greyson. I always enjoyed visiting my grandparents, but living here, well, it feels as if I belong."

"Nothing like the feeling of coming home to Pine Hill," he mused, apparently thinking back to when he'd come home himself after his time in the service. "But your answer is boring."

Morgan laughed. "Boring? How's that?"

"Because it is." He sighed, pushing his arms through the clean shirt Morgan was helping him put on. "I was hoping you were going to tell me a man had put that hop in your step."

"The only man I need in my life is five years old and lets me read him a couple of stories each night when I tuck him into bed." She grinned, then gave a mischievous look. "Plus, you, of course."

"Of course," he agreed, shaking his head. "A shame, though, that you're raising that boy alone. He needs strong male role models."

Morgan tsked. "You're showing your age,

John. That's an outdated thought. You just complimented me on being tough, which hopefully makes me a strong role model for my son." Lord, she hoped so. She was trying so hard, had gotten knocked down when she'd lost her job, but she'd gotten back to her feet, just as she had when Trey died. "For those times Greyson does need a masculine role model, I can't imagine a better man than my Grampy."

She'd eternally be thankful to her grandparents for taking them in while she figured out her next step. Losing Trey, then her job in under a two-year span, had shaken her very foundation, but with each day she'd been in Pine Hill she'd felt more like her old self. Happy. Positive. Increasingly confident she could take care of her son.

John frowned and asked in a serious voice, "Did you just accuse me of being old?"

Morgan gave him a sheepish look. "I did. Sorry. I mean, you're what? Twenty-nine?"

He snorted, then cracked a grin. "A few lifetimes ago, maybe."

"Speaking of strong male role models, I'll have to bring Greyson to meet you sometime soon. I think he'd find you fascinating." She certainly did.

"Lying in a hospital bed at an assisted living facility isn't fascinating for any kid." He shook his head, obviously full of self-disgust at his current situation. "I'm glad he has your grandfather, but he needs younger role models than the likes of me and your Grampy. Sign the boy up for sports this spring. Scouts or a camping club, too."

"Maybe." If Greyson wanted to play sports, be in scouts, or go to camp, she'd make sure he got the opportunity to do so. She wanted him to be involved with the community and to have different life experiences. Just so long as they were safe ones. "But you really needn't worry. He's found a few younger role models to hero worship, too."

The man's brows drew together in question. "The firefighters?"

"I brought him to the fire hall on Saturday for him to tour it with my cousin Sophie's boyfriend. Too bad Greyson is so taken with another firefighter."

She'd thought Cole and Sophie taking Greyson out in the fire truck might win Greyson over, but when they'd gotten back to the fire department her son had immediately searched out Andrew and given a play by play of riding in the truck.

"Oh?" The old man's brow quirked up. "What's so special about this other firefighter?"

His eyes. His smile. His laugh. His sense of humor. His modesty...Morgan swallowed, not liking any of the responses that popped into her head.

"He spent extra time with Greyson

when he visited the school. Apparently, that means they bonded for life. Andrew gave him a plastic fire helmet that Greyson has worn almost non-stop. It's all I can do to get him to take it off to take a bath or go to bed at night. I have to admit, he does look super cute in it."

Smiling, John's expression became wistful. "I'd like to see that."

She got out her phone and pulled up the photo she'd taken of Greyson at the fire hall wearing his hat. "Isn't he cute?"

The older man nodded. "Looks like you."

Everyone said so. Probably because his eyes were the same color. Morgan mostly saw Trey, though. Sometimes Greyson's expressions or the way he tackled problems were so similar, it was eerie, leaving her worried that he'd inherited all of her husband's daredevil tendencies.

She scrolled through a couple of photos, showing John. But she should have scrolled faster or stopped with the first one, as she couldn't help pausing when she reached one Greyson had requested she take. One of him with Andrew. She stared at the image of Andrew kneeling next to Greyson. Both wore big smiles. The next photo was one she'd snapped as Andrew had stolen Greyson's plastic helmet and put it on while Greyson giggled up at him.

If she hadn't had to work and had said

yes to his offer, she and Greyson would be seeing him for dinner at Lou's that evening. It had been two days, so according to his silly story, she should be going into withdrawal by now. She wasn't missing him, though.

"Which firefighter is that with Greyson? He looks familiar."

"His new BFF. Andrew Scott."

"Ah, Charles and Ruby Jenkins' grandson. Good kid." John smiled. "Well, you were just telling me the other day how you were worried Greyson wasn't making new friends."

"For the record, I meant someone closer to his own age and not so…" her voice trailed off as she searched for words to describe Andrew.

"Not so what?" John prompted, then chuckled. "You're blushing. Perhaps Greyson isn't the only one smitten with the firefighter?"

Morgan wasn't touching that one with a ten-foot pole.

"Now that you're dressed, are you ready to go to the community room? Pastor Smith arranged for some church members to sing Christmas carols at ten to kick off our Christmas season. Your therapist won't be here until one today, so going might brighten up your morning."

John perked up. "Maybelle Kirby going to be there?"

Surprised by his question and the way his shoulders had straightened, Morgan's eyes widened. "Maybelle? I'm not sure. Do you hope she's there?"

He gave Morgan an *of course* I do look.

"My Carla was a looker, and Lord knows not a day goes by that I don't miss that woman. She was a good one, for sure. But Maybelle..." He attempted to whistle, and it came out a low phwwwhht phwooooh. "She was the prettiest girl these eyes ever beheld. When Maybelle came to town, we all stopped what we were doing to pay homage."

Thinking of what a classically beautiful woman Maybelle still was, Morgan could only imagine what a beauty she would have been back in her heyday. Those Butterflies sure made an impact on all they met in one way or another.

"Had a bit of a crush on her, eh?"

"We all had a crush on her," he admitted, wiggling his way to the edge of the bed and using the trapeze bar so his upper body could do most of the work. "But she only had eyes for Gary."

"That was her husband?" she asked, hating the pain she saw on John's face from his movements. Morgan always wanted to help, but she knew that it was better if she let him continue to build his strength and work it out on his own. He preferred it that way, anyway. "Maybelle's one of my

Grammy's dearest friends. I knew she was a widow, but I don't really know a lot about the circumstances. Just that her husband died while serving in the military."

"We all went to war. I came home. He didn't."

His voice held survivor's guilt even all these decades later. It was something she'd encountered with military patients in the past, and even with some of her parents' friends. That strong emotional burden so many carried always left Morgan's heart achy.

"She never remarried, but not for the lack of us trying." A look of determination on his face, he continued to edge off the bed. "It didn't take long after I got back stateside to realize I couldn't sway Maybelle with my lackluster charms. And then I met Carla. She was a bright girl with a smile that you could feel all the way to your core." He smiled at the memory. "We loved each other and had a nice life. She was a good wife and mother to our boys. I miss her and feel blessed to have shared over forty years with her by my side. I've no complaints on how my life turned out. It's been a good one."

Despite the pain his movements were causing, he wasn't a complainer. Except about taking his medications. He took them, he just never wanted to.

"But this old noggin still works well

enough to not pass up an opportunity to see Maybelle. The sight of her always brings me back to my teenage years." Gritting his dentures, he swung his legs off the edge of his bed. "Did you say they'll be singing? She has a good voice. An alto."

Morgan had heard Maybelle sing at church. The woman did have a lovely voice. She was impressed that John commented on it and wondered if church was where he'd heard her sing, as well.

"Here, take my hand while you get into your wheelchair," she offered, making sure the brakes were locked so the chair wouldn't roll.

"Getting to see Maybelle and you trying to hold my hand?" John teased. "Today must be my lucky day"

Morgan smiled. "It must be."

"Or maybe not." He gave the wheelchair a disgusted look. "If I thought I wouldn't embarrass myself worse, I'd take my walker. Being in that thing is humiliating. Not that the walker is a lot better, mind you, but still."

There wasn't anything embarrassing about using a wheelchair or a walker, of course, but her heart went out to him. "We can try the walker, if you want, but then we'd have to find a seat for you in the community room. If you take the wheelchair, I can park you anywhere you'd like," she pointed out. "I bet I can situate you where Maybelle is directly in your line of sight, so you can look at her the whole time without getting a crick in your neck." She waggled her brows. "There are advantages to having wheels on your seat."

"Smart thinking." John's eyes twinkled as he made his way into the wheelchair. "I knew there was a reason I liked you."

"And here I thought it was because I kept delivering your medicines so you can get better and bust out of this place," Morgan teased and was still smiling when she rolled him into the assisted living's community room. But when she saw the group standing to one side of the room near a tall, heavily decorated tree, her jaw dropped. Why was Andrew there?

"Isn't that your firefighter?" John asked loud enough that it wouldn't have surprised Morgan if Andrew had heard. Eek.

"Shhhh," she hushed, instantly regretting that she'd shown him that particular photo. It wasn't as if she hadn't looked at the picture dozens of other times. Had she really needed another peek? It had only been two days. "He's Greyson's firefighter, not mine."

Whatever he was, he made breathing difficult and her cheeks hot.

"You sound out of breath, Morgan." John cackled. "Did I gain a few pounds in the last minute, or are you struggling to-day?"

She was definitely struggling, but not from pushing John's wheelchair, and he knew it.

"Keep that up, and I'll turn you to where you have no view of Maybelle," she threatened.

He didn't sound too worried as he said, "You wouldn't."

He was right. She wouldn't. But, making her voice as fierce as she could pull off, she said, "Try me."

He sighed. "Here I thought you were sweet."

Morgan's lips twitched. "Looks can be so deceiving."

She sure hoped hers were and that she looked as if she was unaware that Andrew was there, when in reality everything in her was focused on his presence. Was he there to help with the singing? Well, duh, of course that's why he'd be there. Why else would he be? And he was holding a guitar. Did he play?

John laughed. "That they can. Find me a spot with a pretty view and my lips are sealed."

Smiling despite how shaky her insides felt, Morgan parked John's wheelchair to where he had a direct, unobstructed view of where Maybelle and the other Butterflies had claimed seats by hanging their jackets over some chairs. The women were talking to Pastor Smith, his daughter, Sarah, and a few others who'd come to help with the singing.

Catching her Grammy Claudia's eye, Morgan waved. Having noticed the movement from his periphery, Andrew glanced her way.

She wasn't surprised when he grinned and nodded his head in her direction in acknowledgement. *Oh, my.* If breathing had been difficult before, it was outright impossible now.

"You have a fan," John pointed out, sounding amused.

Morgan snorted. "Maybelle looks especially lovely in that blue sweater, don't you think? It matches her eyes perfectly," she said, hoping to distract him from additional Andrew comments. Then, leaning close to his ear, she whispered, "You owe me."

"Fine. You win," he conceded, but his face crinkled with a smile. "I'll put in a good word for you if the firefighter comes near."

Suppressing a laugh at his comeback, Morgan rolled her eyes. "Do it, and I'll call your doctor and request extra therapy for tomorrow. Or better yet, I'll return the favor and tell Maybelle what a great patient you are and that you're currently accepting visitors."

John laughed but settled back into his

wheelchair, looking happy with his view. Giving him one last look, she turned to go.

"Morgan," Grammy Claudia said, coming up and kissing her cheek. "I was hoping I'd get to see you while we were here. Will you get to stay and listen to the carols?"

"If all my patients are here, I'll be able to. If not, then, I'll be in and out." She glanced at her watch. "Speaking of which, I need to go check to see if another patient wants to come down here before the singing gets started."

After saying a quick bye in case she didn't get a chance to talk to her again, Morgan went to her patient's room. The lady wanted to join the others and Morgan stayed at her side as she slowly made her way down the hallway.

When she stepped back into the community room, Andrew was with the Butterflies, talking to Ruby. Morgan arrived just in time to see the woman reach up and pinch his cheeks as if he were a little boy rather than a grown, handsome man. Andrew didn't seem to mind, though, just smiled indulgently, and seemed to eat up his grandmother's attention. He turned, caught Morgan watching them, gave a little shrug of his shoulders, and grinned.

Lord help her, the man's smile sent her heart into a reindeer stampede.

Unable to stop her traitorous mouth,

her lips turned upwards. Which he seemed to take as permission to cross the room.

"Want a turn?"

"At what?" she asked, confused.

"Pinching my cheeks."

"Um, no. You keep your cheeks to yourself."

"Your loss," he said, his smile not wavering as he teased her. "How's my little buddy doing?"

"Still thinks you're the greatest thing ever."

Grinning, he rocked back on his heels. "Now, if we could just convince his mom of that."

"Greyson's young and easily impressed." Unable to drag her gaze from his, she added, "His mother is a harder sell. It takes more than a helmet and flashy red truck to impress her."

His expression growing thoughtful, he ran his hand over his jaw. "I should probably mention that flashy red truck has sirens. That's sure to impress, right?"

Morgan shrugged. "You could try that angle, but you should know that she's not really into men who toot their own horn—or sirens."

Now why had she said that? He'd asked her to be his friend, so what did it matter what type of man she was into? Especially since she wasn't into any type?

He laughed. "Touché."

Morgan fought smiling again. Why did he have to be so likeable?

"Good thing I have Greyson on my side," he added.

Morgan couldn't argue with him there. Greyson would have been upset if he'd known Andrew had invited them on the sleigh ride and that she'd said no. Still, it had been the right thing to do.

"Think he would like to watch Cole and me jump? There's an airfield nearby where friends and family can watch. Cole's a pro from his military days, but I've only been jumping a few years. We could make it a day we're off work when Greyson's out of school. If you ask me nicely, you could come, too."

"No." Horrified, she shook her head. "Absolutely not."

His brows drew together, and he gave an exaggerated sigh. "I take it jumping out of airplanes doesn't impress you, either?"

"No." Her husband had parachuted a few times with Morgan firmly on the ground, praying the entire time that his chute would open properly, that he'd make it safely back to the ground and to her. He'd loved it so much that she hadn't had to the heart to try to talk him out of it. She'd hoped, though, he'd decide on his own to slow down his adrenaline junkie ways after Greyson had been born. If anything, Trey had just kept pushing himself further. Eventually, he'd pushed too far.

"Mind giving me a clue what does impress you?" Andrew asked.

"About you?" That he'd smiled at his grandmother when Ruby had pinched his cheeks. That he'd given extra time and attention to Greyson at school. That he'd included Greyson in his dinner invitation. That he was there, volunteering his time at the assisted living. "Professionally, I appreciate what you do. Fighting fires to save others at your own risk is admirable. But as far as personally," she shrugged. "I'm not interested in a friendship with you. The sooner you accept that, the better for us both."

"Ouch." His disappointment was palpable. "Guess that puts me in my place. Again."

Guilt hit, but not enough to make her change her mind. This was for her and Greyson's good. They didn't need another adrenaline junkie in their lives. "I'm sorry."

"Don't be. No harm done. I just thought you could use a friend. That, and I thought I saw something when our eyes met that day at the school. Maybe I only saw what I wanted to see."

"You apparently have a vivid imagination." He hadn't imagined anything, but there was no point in telling him that. He fought fires for a living, rode a Harley, and jumped out of airplanes for fun. Could there be a worse fit for her as a friend...or otherwise?

"Apparently," he agreed, studying her. "Because I also thought you missed me and were glad to see me today."

"Why in the world would you think that? Like I said, vivid imagination. I've got to get back to work," she said, knowing he wasn't buying a word of what she was saying. "One of my patients may need me."

"They look pretty content." Andrew glanced around the community room. "You should stay. After the usual carols are sung, I'll be taking requests. My grandma wants me to play some Elvis Christmas songs. Have anything you'd like to hear?"

"Nothing," she denied, wondering if he'd be singing solos or leading the group while he played his guitar. "How do you know my patients are the content ones?"

"I watched you bring them in, Morgan. Look," he gestured to them one by one. "This is the best time they've had all day."

He was right. Doris was smiling and chatting to anyone who would listen. Lucille was humming along to music that played over the intercom system. John was sitting in his chair and watching Maybelle, looking happier than he had since his admission. The others watched the activities with interest.

"I still need to get back to work. I'm on the clock. I should be with my patients, not talking to you."

He held up his hands. "Sorry. I didn't mean to get in your way at work."

Ugh. She was coming across as such a fuddy-duddy. That wasn't who she wanted to be, but how did she explain that a friendship with him scared her?

"You're not," she relented. "It's just... nothing." Heat flooded her face. "Have a good day, Andrew."

As she walked away, she could feel his gaze and fought turning around to tell him to stop.

"Tell Greyson I said hi," he called after her.

Without turning, Morgan gave a thumbs up.

"And if you have any fires you need put out," he continued, "you know who to ask."

The only fire Morgan needed put out was the one that blazed in her cheeks.

Chapter Five

"We don't really have to sew,
do we?" Ben asked as Andrew
drove the fire truck into Pine
Hill Church's parking lot for the local Quilts
of Valor Foundation Sew-In. So far it had
been a slow Saturday, but just in case they
needed to get somewhere fast, they were
ready.

"There will be volunteers to teach you
anything you're willing to learn," Cole answered from the passenger seat.

"Don't we need machines?" Ben continued, not sounding sure about spending the
day at a sewing event.

"The machines are already there. I
helped Sophie and a few other volunteers

set up most of the day yesterday. Her quilting machine alone took me about six hours to get moved and set up." Cole tapped his fingers on the dashboard. "There are plenty of extra sewing machines. I thought Sophie just had so many because she owned a quilt shop, but apparently lots of folks have two, or more, in this town and were happy to share them."

Andrew had loaded his grandma's machines into her car for her a couple of nights ago. She'd upgraded a few times over the years, but she never let her old faithfuls go as long as they still worked. There would be plenty of extra machines for anyone wanting to jump in to help.

Ben shrugged, then glanced at where Andrew watched them, his hands on the steering wheel still despite having killed the engine. "You're being suspiciously quiet."

Eyes narrowing, Cole eyed him. "He's right. What's up?"

Andrew shook his head. "Just listening to you two."

"Oh, wait, I get it now." Ben nudged Cole's arm. "Our friend is saving his breath for all the hot air he's going to blow toward Morgan Morris. He's hoping third time's a charm, am I right?"

Andrew rolled his eyes, then got out of the truck to head toward the church's community room entrance. The wind whipped at his jacket, but the temperature was mild for November. It would have been a great day for taking Big Bertha on a spin through the Kentucky hills if he hadn't had other plans.

"Since things didn't work out with Lisa, maybe I should ask her to dinner," Ben suggested as he caught up with him.

Pausing, Andrew frowned. "Not that I want to date her, but what makes you think you'd have any better luck than I did?"

"'Cause I'm a lot prettier than your ugly mug," Ben countered, doing a little shimmy, as if to put himself on display.

"He has a point," Cole agreed, looking amused.

"I need new friends," Andrew huffed, not that either of them appeared worried.

"Nah. You're stuck with us," Cole told him, then waved at Bodie Lewis who'd just gotten out of his sheriff's deputy SUV and was waiting for his dog Harry to jump down. Harry leaped onto the pavement and ran over to Cole, who immediately bent to give him a good scratching behind the ears. Harry, an Australian Sheppard and Blue Heeler mix, was the smartest dog Andrew had ever encountered and had played a huge role in helping Bodie deal with his PTSD from being the sole survivor of an enemy attack during his military days. Andrew suspected the dog had taken to Cole for similar reasons and vice versa. These days, both men seemed to be doing great.

"Sarah got you quilting today?" Andrew asked Bodie. The pastor's daughter had donated several quilts to the Quilts of Valor Foundation over the years. One of them had been given to Bodie, who had come to Pine Hill to thank her. He'd ended up staying as Sarah's handyman as she renovated her late aunt's house to turn it into a bed and breakfast. The two had married last Christmas and were making a success of the B&B.

Bodie shook his head. "Sheriff Roscoe needed me on patrol duty today so I'm just here to drop off Harry. I mentioned that he seemed restless while I was on the phone with Sarah a bit ago and she asked me to bring him by. Lately, he doesn't want to be away from her for more than a few minutes." Bodie gave his dog a wry look. "I think it's because she plies him with those special treats she gets at Carrie's pet shop."

"Harry is a great dog. Aren't you, boy?" Cole asked, giving Harry another scratch behind the ears.

Seeming to understand, Harry gave a single bark answer that Andrew guessed was in agreement. Andrew reached over to pet Harry as well. He'd always loved dogs, but had never felt right about the idea of adopting one. Not when he planned to leave someday to fight wildland fires, and would be gone for weeks, possibly months at a time.

Janice Lynn

"You guys volunteering?" Bodie asked.

"I promised Sophie that we'd help with whatever she needed," Cole answered.

"Sophie has him wrapped around her finger," Ben accused, shaking his head.

"You're just jealous you're not wrapped around someone's finger," Andrew pointed out, earning a nod of agreement from Ben, who was more than ready to settle down.

Cole's expression had turned serious, though. "Today isn't about Sophie."

While Andrew knew his friend would have come just because Sophie asked him to, this particular cause was also one that was near and dear to Cole's heart. While he'd gotten better about accepting his past and coming to terms with the self-proclaimed 'bad things' he'd done prior to coming to Pine Hill, Cole was still committed to volunteering and helping others—especially other veterans. That was why Cole had taken a particular interest in the organization Sophie championed. She'd wrapped him in a Quilt of Valor, and Andrew knew how much both Bodie and Cole's quilts welcoming them home meant.

Today's sew-in was intended to create quilts to be presented to local veterans. Andrew was proud they were there and able to give back in a small way to those who had given so much for their country. Had fire-

108

fighting not been so entrenched in his blood, he might have joined the Marines himself.

"I plan to sew," he volunteered.

"Get out of here," Ben said, his face showing that he was grudgingly impressed, while also a bit disbelieving.

"You think my grandma let me grow up without learning to sew?" He wouldn't mention he'd been an eager student in more recent times for reasons of his own. "She insisted I know all the 'basics of life,' as she put it."

Cole gave him a wry look. "Too bad she didn't teach you to cook."

"I can cook." Cooking was definitely a Grandma Ruby 'basics of life' skill.

"Not like Grandma Ruby," Cole pointed out.

"No one cooks like my grandma," Andrew conceded. "She has a magic oven. Whatever she puts in comes out tasting like heaven."

"That's true," all the men agreed.

Harry with them, the men entered the bustling church community room. There were about twenty or so people already there helping with any last minute set up needs. Morgan was putting out supplies with Sarah and Sophie. Wearing jeans and a red Christmas sweatshirt that looked as if it had come straight from her cousin's closet, she was laughing at something the two women were saying. She looked relaxed and as if she'd been a part of Pine Hill forever.

Andrew glanced around, searching for Greyson, and was disappointed when he didn't see him.

Spotting them, Sarah and Sophie ascended upon their group. Morgan reluctantly moved with them. Sarah and Sophie each smiled at their special men and kissed their cheeks.

Andrew's gaze met Morgan's and, hoping he'd at least get a smile, he gave her an expectant look and tilted his chin toward her. Making a little noise that was a mix of humor and surprise, she shook her head.

Chuckling, he asked, "Miss me?"

She shook her head again, but something in the way she looked at him made him think she had. Plus, while she wasn't smiling, her lips were twitching as if she wanted to.

"Don't say I didn't warn you about going too long in between seeing me. It's hazardous to your health."

"Is that like a black label warning? A cautionary tale?" Now her eyes were sparkling with humor. "If so, maybe it should say to avoid at all costs."

"Nah," he countered. "I'm harmless."

"That's doubtful."

"Guess that depends upon who you ask." He laughed. "Where's Greyson? If I'm going to have to take all this abuse, I want him around to defend me."

Not that he bought that Morgan didn't like him. She did. She just didn't want to.

"He's with Isabelle. They'll be here a little later."

"Good to know. I wanted to ask how his entry for the coloring contest is going. He told me at the fire hall that he hadn't started it yet."

"He still hasn't. He says he's still thinking about how he wants to decorate it." Morgan's eyes lit up as she talked about her son. Then she gave him a wry look. "I imagine once he sees you're here he's going to want to be right beside you. You'll be happy to know he had me print out the photo of you two." She shook her head as if she didn't get why Greyson had wanted that. "His hero worship is still in full force. If he gets in your way, let me know. I don't want him to be a nuisance to you."

Why did it make him feel so good to know Greyson liked him? That the kid had felt the connection between them? That he might be able to make a positive difference in the kid's life?

"He may not have any time for me today with Harry here," Andrew mused. "But, if he does, he won't be in my way. I'm glad I'll get to see him today."

"Thank you."

"You're welcome, Morgan." He glanced around the room at the sewing machines set up, the stacks of precut material, the ironing boards, and cutting boards ready to go if they needed more material. Hopefully, before day's end, they'd have several quilt tops made, sandwiched, and ready to be machine-quilted at Sophie and her sister's sewing shop.

"Sophie's been busy," he said.

"Yes, she and some others have been meeting at The Threaded Needle to make sure we had everything prepared for today. I've helped, but not as much as I'd like to."

"You're a seamstress?"

Morgan snorted "That's a joke. I couldn't sew a straight line if my life depended upon it, but not because my Grammy Claudia didn't try to teach me. I'm assigned to kitchen duties and ironing. You?"

"Eye candy," he said with a straight face, hoping to get another glimmer of a smile from her. "It's a tough job, but someone has to do it."

Morgan snickered, making Andrew's insides warm. She did need his friendship even if she didn't realize it.

"Oh! I need to go help Rosie." She pointed to where Rosie was coming in and carrying what appeared to be a heavy box. Morgan took a step in her direction, then paused to meet his eyes. "Um, bye, although

I guess we'll be seeing each other for however long you're here."

"You're going to get your quota of me today." At least, Andrew hoped no calls came in so he and the guys could volunteer for the full event. "And I'll go help Rosie get her things."

Together they met a flustered Rosie. It was surprising, since there usually wasn't much of anything that could fluster her, outside of going through with her wedding. Andrew was more accustomed to seeing her vivacious and full of flirty life that was envious at any age. He smiled at his grandma's dear friend.

"Hey, Rosie. Can I take that for you?"

The blue-haired woman shifted the box onto her hip, then held her hand out for him to take and kiss. Ah, there was the Rosie he knew and loved.

"Hello, Andrew, and yes, please do take this ole heavy thing."

Andrew reached for the box, taking it from her and easily balancing it to one side, then eyed her hand. "Lou know about us?"

Obviously delighted at his comment, Rosie giggled. "Why do you think he's trying to rush me down the aisle, dear boy?"

Andrew laughed, took her hand and gave a gentle squeeze rather than bringing it fully to his lips. "Where does this box go?"

"To the kitchen. I made goodies for

snacks and Lou sent over a batch of his special chili, too. It's still in my car if you want to be a dear and go grab it after you drop this off," Rosie told him. When he headed to the kitchen and she thought he was out of hearing range, she told Morgan, "You should have called, honey child. I could have whipped up some of my grandmother's cinnamon bread."

Andrew harrumphed. He knew all about the Cupid-effect rumors associated with Rosie's grandmother's famous cinnamon bread. It was said to be an infallible tool for winning over a sweetheart.

But Rosie had it all wrong if she thought Morgan needed to give the bread to him. It was him in need of the bread. A dozen loaves. Maybe more. Not that he wanted to win Morgan's heart. He didn't. But he'd like to be her friend and spend time with her and Greyson.

A batch of match-making cinnamon bread might work better than the luck he'd had thus far in convincing her he had the best of intentions.

"You seem to really enjoy your job at the assisted living."

Morgan smiled at Rosie's comment.

They had gotten everything ready in the kitchen and were taking a shift at the ironing boards, pressing seams, along with a few others. There was something rewarding about flattening the seams.

"I do love it," she admitted, running her iron over the sewn block and pressing the seams all in the same direction. "I'm so glad Grammy convinced me to apply."

"Girl, Claudia's talked of nothing else since you agreed to move here. Well, that and the trip she and your grandfather took to Montana earlier this year. That woman does love to travel."

"I'm so glad Grampy is finally taking her places. I hope having Greyson and me staying with them doesn't slow them down."

"It won't. They had that weekend trip to Charleston last month," Rosie reminded her. "Plus they have the Grand Canyon tour planned for next summer. So, don't you worry your pretty head about that. If anything, they'll rest easier knowing you're at the house keeping an eye on things whenever they're away."

Next summer. Would she still be living with her grandparents then? Technically, she could move out now that she was working again, but they'd convinced her she shouldn't start looking for a place until after the holidays, and she'd agreed that the idea made sense. Spending Christmas with her grandparents would be good for her and Greyson, and they seemed to enjoy having them there.

"I hope so. I never want to be a burden, but them taking us in while I get back on my feet has been a lifesaver." *Emotionally and financially,* she thought.

"It's what grandparents live for," Rosie said, smiling.

"Why, Rosie, I wouldn't have thought you old enough to be a grandma," Morgan said, knowing the compliment would tickle the woman.

Beaming, Rosie stuck a finger over her painted cherry red lips. "Shhh, let's not let my secret out."

As Rosie had lived in Pine Hill all her life, it wasn't much of a secret that she had kids and grandkids, even if none of them lived locally, as far as Morgan knew. Still, Morgan nodded and placed another pressed piece of material in a growing stack at the end of her ironing board. She and Rosie continued to chat while they ironed, but Morgan's gaze kept wandering to where Andrew sat at a sewing machine and ran material beneath the footer. She'd been so surprised when he sat down at the machine and seemed so at ease with its use.

"That man is positively scrumptious!"

"Rosie," Morgan scolded, her cheeks going hot with embarrassment that Rosie had noticed where Morgan's gaze kept going. "He's Ruby's grandson. You shouldn't say such things."

Rosie huffed. "Ruby would be the first to brag on what an amazing young man he is—and she does so all the time. She's very proud of him."

"That's not exactly the same thing as you saying he's scrumptious," Morgan pointed out.

Rosie waved off her comment. "My friends may be old, but I'm still young"—she gave a conspiratorial smile—"even if it's only at heart, though I'll deny that last bit if you tell Maybelle."

"Tell me what?" Maybelle asked, joining them to pick up the ironed pieces. She looked as lovely as ever with her dark fitted pants and cream-colored blouse topped with a red, white, and blue scarf. No wonder John had carried a crush on her all these years.

Rosie gave Morgan a look of warning and she suppressed a smile.

"We were talking about how much my patients enjoyed the singing at the nursing home this week. I'm glad Pastor Smith plans to arrange another visit prior to Christmas to sing carols for the residents again."

"The singing was a hit, wasn't it? Ruby's grandson does such a great Elvis impersonation. He always gets lots of requests for his numbers," Maybelle said, smiling.

"I've never seen so many happy old people," Rosie added, then turned to Maybelle. "I guess you felt right at home, eh?"

Maybelle's gaze cut to Rosie's and she gave a dismissive shake of her head.

Suppressing another smile, Morgan disregarded the comments about Andrew. It wasn't as if she needed any reminders of how appealing his voice was. She also diplomatically chose not to point out that both women were likely every bit as old as many of the patients at the center. More so than some. John, certainly, was a contemporary of Maybelle's, and he wasn't the youngest man there. She didn't think either would appreciate that tidbit. Fortunately, both women appeared to be in great health and had no need of assistance.

Ignoring her friend's comment, Maybelle focused on Morgan. "I saw where you spent quite a bit of time with John Harper. I assume you're his nurse. He's recovering well from his fall?"

Was Maybelle just asking to be polite, or was there a little something extra to her question?

"Oh, silly woman." Rosie scolded. "She can't tell you. Did you forget about that medical Hippo stuff?"

"HIPPA," Morgan automatically corrected.

"HIPPA," Maybelle repeated. "Sorry. For

once, Rosie's right. I guess you can't tell me how he is doing?"

Reluctantly, Morgan shook her head. "Unless a patient specifically gives permission to discuss their case with someone, then I can't share any information."

"No worries," Maybelle assured her. "I'd meant to get over to say hello, but was busy helping Pastor Smith, then with singing, and John didn't stick around long after it was over."

No, he'd wanted to go back to his room and had seemed a bit down the rest of the day. Although he'd never have admitted it, Morgan had sensed his frustration with his body not cooperating with what he wanted it to do. Seeing Maybelle likely made him all the more aware of his inability to walk without the aid of a walker. She'd reminded him more than once that he was getting stronger every day and that, Lord willing, he should fully recover with time and continued therapy. Besides, she very much doubted Maybelle would think less of him just because he used a walker...but logic rarely won out in a battle against pride.

"After the singing, a few of us were talking and we've decided all the quilts from the sew-in are going to military residents at the assisted living facility." Maybelle's smile was positively radiant. "I nominated John for a quilt."

Morgan's eyes widened. "For a Quilt of Valor?"

Maybelle nodded. "I should have done so years ago, but just never thought to. He definitely deserves one." She gave a little shrug. "All our military men and women do, of course."

Happiness filled Morgan. "Oh, Maybelle, that's wonderful! He is going to love that."

Maybelle didn't look so sure. "Maybe. Maybe not."

"What do you mean?" she asked, confused.

"You have to keep in mind that many of our veterans don't see themselves as heroes deserving of something special. They did their job and proudly served. Most, especially of John's generation, don't want to be recognized for what they see as their honor and duty."

Both her parents had desk jobs, but she'd always thought them heroic for their choice to serve. She'd never wondered whether or not they, or any military personnel, questioned their heroism. She'd just assumed they saw themselves as she did—heroes she was so grateful for.

"You're right," Morgan admitted. "As deserving as he is of recognition, I could see John not wanting attention brought to himself."

Maybelle nodded. "He's a humble man,

and the last one to expect any kind of recognition for all that he's done by serving our
country and making us so proud with his
sacrifice. But that's exactly why I want him
to have a quilt. Especially right now while
he's dealing with his fractured hip, he needs
to be wrapped up with some healing and
love."

"Who doesn't?" Being wrapped up in
healing and love sounded good to Morgan.
Where did she sign up? And why did her
gaze immediately go back to the man bent
over the sewing machine, chatting with the
others at his table, and obviously keeping
the entire group entertained? His table was
the noisiest by far, breaking out in loud
laughter every few minutes. She found herself wondering if laughter really was the best
medicine ever, because she couldn't seem to
prevent the giddy happy feeling inside when
he was near.

Not to mention how she had checked
the days off between each time they had
interacted and was grateful the counter had
reset.

Not because she missed him. She
hadn't.

Except…if she was honest with herself,
maybe it was, maybe she had. If so, what did
that mean?

"This is humiliating," Ben groaned, staring at the crooked seam he'd just sewn. "Who knew there was anything you could do better than me?"

Running another two pieces of material beneath his sewing machine's footer, Andrew said, "Hate to break it to you, pal, but everyone knows I'm the better man."

Ben snorted. "Not sure being able to sew a perfect quarter-inch seam makes you the better man."

"Listen to you spouting off about a quarter-inch seam," Cole teased as he delivered a freshly ironed stack of material ready to be sewn together. "At least we know you learned something today."

Beginning to rip out the scraggily seam, Ben sighed. "A lot of good knowing does me."

"Quit trying to go so fast," Andrew reminded him. "Take your time and keep the material lined up with the piece of tape I put on the machine for you to use as a guide."

Ben finished getting the material back apart, tossed it onto the machine, and let out a loud sigh.

"Maybe you need a break to clear your head and stretch your legs," Andrew suggested. "How about taking fifteen, going outside, and getting some fresh air?"

Ben considered a moment, then shrugged. "Yeah, I think I might do that. Want to go with me?"

"I'll step out with you for a bit," Cole said.

Andrew glanced back toward his machine and the stack of material waiting to be sewn together. "Let me finish up these, then I'll head that way."

"Next thing you know he'll be making curtains for the fire hall," Ben mumbled to Cole as they walked away.

Andrew chuckled and sat back down at his sewing machine. After a few minutes, the door opening caught his eye and he glanced that way, expecting to see his friends coming back inside. Instead, Isabelle came in with Greyson holding her hand. The boy was chatting with her but didn't look thrilled to be at a sewing event.

No doubt it wasn't the most exciting place for a five-year-old kid.

Andrew finished up his stack, then stood. He rotated his shoulders and rolled his neck, which had gotten stiff from having sat in the same position for so long. Glancing around, he spotted Greyson again, now with his mother. Seeing him standing, she must have pointed him out as the boy looked his way, then smiled.

Andrew's heart jerked at the realness of that big, happy smile. The boy ran over to him and without thought, Andrew knelt and hugged the kid.

"I didn't know you'd be here!" Greyson told him, not hiding his surprise.

"You think I'd miss out on being a part of something so special? I'm smarter than I look," he teased.

The kid's nose crinkled. "Sewing is for girls."

Andrew shook his head. "Not hardly, bud. It's a necessary life skill." Listen to him sounding like his grandma. "Plus, if you ever decided you wanted to be a smokejumper, you'd need to be able to sew."

Greyson gave him a confused look.

"Smokejumpers sew their own parachutes, harnesses—you name it. They always make their own. Base camps are set up with rooms for sewing equipment."

Greyson's eyes widened. "Really? You're sure?"

"Absolutely."

"Do you sew?"

Andrew nodded. "My grandma started teaching me when I was about your age."

Greyson regarded him thoughtfully. Then, a hopeful look in his eyes, he asked, "Will you teach me?"

Andrew felt something big. Gigantic. Colossal. It was incredible how humbled he felt at Greyson asking him to teach him to sew. It was as if he'd been granted some awesome privilege.

"As long as your mom is okay with it and you promise to listen closely. I don't want to have to make an emergency room run because of Frankenstein fingers." Andrew wiggled his fingers back and forth and made a funny face.

Giggling, Greyson imitated him. "I promise."

Man, he really liked this kid. "Then let's go ask your mom."

Pride hit that he was hopefully going to teach Greyson a useful new skill while also opening the kid's eyes to the fact that he shouldn't be so quick to judge what was or wasn't considered manly. Who would have ever thought he'd be the one steering a kid in, hopefully, the right direction of seeing beyond preconceived ideas to accept new life experiences?

He kind of liked the feeling. A lot.

"Greyson sure is infatuated," Grammy pointed out as she helped press a seam. She'd relieved Rosie about five minutes earlier. Morgan wasn't surprised by the direction the conversation had quickly taken. Everyone

125

kept 'casually' mentioning Andrew in some shape, form, or fashion.

Not looking up from where she ran her iron over the material, Morgan nodded.

"Andrew's good with him, getting down to talk with Greyson on his own level. And you can just see the patience on his face as he is working with him. I love it." Grammy beamed, Cupid arrows and hearts flashing every which way in her eyes, as she swapped material under her iron. "Plus, he comes from a good family. Ruby and Charlie are the best. That's a nice bonus."

Privately, Morgan had to admit that all the same thoughts had run through her mind. Unbidden, unwanted, but still there. She turned toward her grandmother. "Please don't."

"Don't what?" Grammy asked innocently, avoiding eye contact by placing her iron on the wool mat she'd sat on her end of the ironing board and checking the seam, as if something was off on how it lined up.

"Don't match-make."

"Pointing out that young man's plusses isn't match-making," Grammy defended, not looking the least deterred. "Unless you object to me thinking he's a good role model for your son, since that's what I was talking about."

Morgan gave her a *yeah, right* look. "Okay, but I don't want you or your Butterfly friends getting any ideas. I've heard stories of how you ladies like to, um, nudge, relationships in the direction you want them to go." Sarah and Sophie had both told Butterfly matchmaking tales. "I'm not interested or ready for a relationship."

Her Grammy just smiled. "Sometimes the right person comes along before we think we're ready."

"Even if I'm wrong about the timing"— which she wasn't—"Andrew's not the right person." Why did the words feel so heavy on her tongue? "Besides, I barely know him."

Grammy Claudia shrugged, her face taking on a grandmothers-are-wise-and-all-knowing expression. "I didn't say Andrew. I said 'the right person.' You made that connection, not me."

Ugh. Grammy was right. How had Morgan fallen into that trap?

"Only you know if the two are the same."

Morgan considered what her grandmother said. Grammy had certainly implied Andrew might be the right person, even if she hadn't said it directly. But Morgan wasn't going to argue with her since she knew her grandmother had her best interests at heart. She didn't want to dig herself deeper into a hole she couldn't climb out of.

"I don't think there is another right person for me," she said.

Grammy gave her an empathetic look,

the one that was often followed by a big hug, and sometimes tears on Morgan's part.

"I know you loved Trey, dear, but you can love again."

"Maybe."

"Definitely. You're young, you have a big, beautiful heart, and you have so much life ahead of you outside of your work and your role as Greyson's mother. When the right person presents himself, you will love again."

"I'm not sure I want to," she admitted so softly she wasn't sure her grandmother heard, especially when Grammy didn't immediately respond.

When she peeked in her direction, her gaze collided with her grandmother's shiny one. Grammy was fighting back tears and one had slid down her cheek.

Regret hit. Morgan never wanted to hurt her grandmother or make her sad. Not ever. "Sorry. I'm obviously feeling sorry for myself and shouldn't have said that."

Grammy immediately shook her head. "I'm glad you did, Morgan. You're allowed to voice the things that are heavy on your heart, especially to me."

"But I didn't mean to make you cry," she argued.

"Oh, Morgan. I'm sad that my granddaughter felt such loss and pain that she doesn't want to risk love again, but I'm also happy that she trusted me enough to share it with me." Another tear escaped Grammy's eyes. "And best of all, there's happiness in my tears, because you want to know what else I heard?"

Morgan waited.

"Hope. As heart-wrenching as your words were, as much as they make me want to take you in my arms and hold you close the way I did when you were a little girl, I also heard that you hoped I was going to tell you that you were wrong to believe you won't love again."

Her grandmother was reading way too much into her admission. She'd been admitting she was scared of loving again. Nothing more. But she decided not to argue. She'd already made her grandmother cry and she didn't want to draw attention from the others. They might not be the first women crying over ironing boards at a sew-in, but today was supposed to be fun, positive, and about giving back to others, not her own emotional admissions.

"I love you, Grammy," Morgan said, smiling at her grandmother. "I'm so glad I'm here."

"I love you, too, but am disappointed in myself for taking so long to respond to you a moment ago. I was searching for the right words, wanting to say something profound to help you cling to that hope, to nurture it, and let it blossom to heal your heart."

Grammy gave her a defeated look. "I blew it, didn't I?"

Morgan gulped. "I, um." She didn't want to disappoint her Grammy, who was waiting for an answer, or make her feel as if she'd failed in any way. "You didn't blow it, Grammy. And, maybe you're right, and when the right person comes along, I'll feel otherwise."

There. She'd pointed out that the right person hadn't come along yet, but had left the possibility open. How was that for diplomacy?

Her efforts were rewarded with a smile and a hug. "Oh, honey. Of course, I'm right. I didn't get this old without learning a few things along the way."

"You're not that old, Grammy."

"Old enough," she admitted, laughing, then picking her iron back up to press the next seam so they didn't fall behind on helping to keep the assembly line of sewing activities going. "I'm curious. How did you know Trey was the right person for you? What was it about him that drew you in and made you know he was the one?"

She thought back to the first time she'd met Trey.

"I'm not sure if I ever told you, but we met in the emergency room. I was still a student, doing a clinical rotation, and he'd gashed his arm while rock climbing." She shuddered at the memory of the cut. "I should have known right then that he was a daredevil. Actually, I did know. He wasn't afraid of anything and made every moment count for something. Being with him made me feel more alive, partially because next to him, I felt dull in comparison and couldn't quite believe someone as exciting as him wanted me."

"Phooey on whoever made you feel dull," Grammy said. "You're a shining star, and any man with half a brain would want you in his life."

"That's a very grandmotherly thing to say," Morgan pointed out, smiling. "But what I meant was that next to Trey's, my life felt dull. I was in school, studying—and whenever I wasn't in class or studying, I was working. Life had become routine, but Trey changed all of that. He dazzled me and made every breath count. I think I fell for him that first time I saw him there in the emergency room. He smiled at me and I was a goner."

"I recall that he wasn't hard to look at, either."

"Grammy!"

Her grandmother smiled. "You think Rosie is the only one with eyes?"

"Apparently not."

"Trey was a handsome man," Grammy paused, ran her iron over another seam, and then added, "as is Andrew."

Morgan was saved from responding by Greyson skipping over to the ironing table.

"Slow down," she warned, gesturing to the irons. "These are hot."

He came to a screeching halt about five feet away from where she stood. "Is it okay if Firefighter Andrew teaches me to sew?"

Of all the things she might have guessed Greyson was coming to ask so excitedly, that wouldn't have made the list.

"You want to learn to sew?" He'd shown absolutely no interest in it up until now. In fact, he'd begged her not to have to come, which was why she'd let him spend part of the morning with Isabelle.

His head bobbed up and down. "Please."

Stunned, Morgan just stared at him.

"He must take after me," Grammy said, sounding proud. "Wanting to learn at such a young age."

Andrew stepped up next to Greyson, placed his hand on his shoulder.

Morgan's heart squeezed with a bazillion emotions she refused to label as she eyed him suspiciously. "What have you done to my son?"

Confusion flickered in his eyes. "Pardon?"

"He didn't do anything," Greyson began, having taken her seriously, too.

Laughing, Morgan held up her hands. "Sorry. I was teasing since I'm surprised you wanted to learn to sew when you hadn't seemed interested earlier."

"Oh." Greyson gave her a sheepish look. "Well, I am now."

Because Andrew had been sewing, and anything the firefighter did must be cool?

"Sewing is a basic life skill everyone should know, right?" Greyson looked up at his hero for confirmation.

"Absolutely," Andrew agreed, smiling proudly down at him.

"That's my boy," Grammy beamed.

"Um, well, if you want to learn, then it would be great if Andrew taught you." She doubted he'd be interested otherwise. "Just be careful not to catch your fingers."

Because no matter how much she tried not to worry, she couldn't help wanting to wrap him in a bubble.

Greyson looked up at Andrew and, wiggling his fingers, grinned. "No Frankenstein fingers for me, right?"

Andrew winked at him. "Right."

Not sure what he meant, she shifted her gaze to Andrew's. "You'll make sure he's careful?"

"Are you kidding? Little Man knows the importance of safety first. That's Firefighting 101."

Not what she necessarily wanted to hear, but Morgan nodded. "Make sure to put it on a slow setting. He's never sewn before."

Greyson's cheeks pinkened. "I'm not a baby, Mommy."

"I know. It's just…" That she worried about him using the high-powered equipment and wanted him to be careful. How did she let him do things where he might get hurt without worrying? Was that even possible? Was it because she'd lost Trey in an accident? Or would she have been an overprotective mother regardless?

"It's okay, Morgan." Andrew's gaze said it really was, and that he'd keep a close watch on Greyson without her having to say another word. "We got this, don't we, kid?"

First giving her a frustrated look, Greyson glanced up at Andrew, nodded and mouthed, "Moms."

A bit hurt by Greyson's reaction, but knowing that she needed to give her son this space, Morgan took a deep breath. "I'm glad you want to learn. I'm just doing my mom part and reminding you to be careful." She smiled. "Have fun and learn lots."

Seeming relieved, Greyson smiled, then looked over to the machines as if he was anxious to get to them as quickly as possible. Probably in case she changed her mind or something else that he viewed as her making him appear babyish in Andrew's eyes.

Greyson tugged on Andrew's hand. "Let's go, please."

"Thank your mom for saying yes," Andrew said, no doubt earning bonus points with Grammy—as if he didn't hold the high score with her already.

"Thank you, Mommy," Greyson said, meeting her eyes and looking a little embarrassed as it dawned on him that he shouldn't have had to be reminded. He really was a great kid, and his manners were usually point on. "I love you."

Talk about earning bonus points. Greyson had just racked up a few of his own.

"I love you, too," she said, feeling squishy and emotional inside. Goodness. Her conversation with her Grammy must have turned her into a basket case.

"Good job. Now, take Ben's seat, but wait for me before you touch anything, okay?" Andrew told him. "I'm going to talk to your mom just a minute."

Greyson hesitated when he realized Andrew wasn't immediately coming with him, but then nodded.

"Okay," he promised, then fast-walked over to the chair Ben had previously occupied. When he sat down, he tucked his hands beneath his thighs, as if to emphasize that he wasn't going to touch anything.

Morgan swallowed, then met Andrew's hazel eyes.

"I'll watch him close and make sure we keep the needle moving at a snail's pace. I can't promise that nothing will happen, but I can promise that I'll do everything within my power to keep him from getting hurt." His gaze bore into hers and held a steely gleam she'd never seen in them as he added, "Always."

His promise rocked through her, making emotions wash over her and threatening to fill her eyes with tears.

"Thank you. I'm sorry I embarrassed him by being such a worrywart. I just don't want him getting hurt, you know?"

Andrew's gaze held hers, and for once his expression was totally serious as he said, "It's okay, Morgan. I'll make sure he knows how cool I think it is that you love him so much. He's a lucky kid."

With that, he headed back over to where Greyson sat patiently waiting, hands still tucked under his little thighs. That is until Andrew said something to him and the two fist-bumped, looking in complete camaraderie.

Grammy cleared her throat. "Ahem. Did I mention how good he was with your son?"

"A time or two," Morgan mused, her gaze not leaving where Andrew had pulled his chair over next to Greyson's. Her son's face was intent as he soaked up every word Andrew said.

"He's good with you, too."

"Not interested," she reminded Grammy,

although...no, she wasn't. Really. "But I am impressed with how he is with Greyson."

As Andrew touched and pointed out various parts of the sewing machine, Morgan could tell he was giving Greyson a lowdown of how every part worked prior to letting him actually start stitching. Andrew's expression suggested the unveiling of the mechanics of the machine was some great secret being shared and Greyson should pay close attention. Greyson's face was intent, clearly soaking up every word Andrew said. Andrew was obviously giving Greyson this information so he'd know how to use the machine safely, but Greyson didn't seem like he resented it because Andrew wasn't a worrywart like her.

Ugh. She was really going to have to be careful. She wanted to keep Greyson safe, but not make him feel as if he was trapped inside a protective bubble.

"Want a break so you can go watch?" Sarah asked, coming over to where the irons were set up.

Morgan glanced toward her friend. From the moment she'd met Sarah the first Sunday Morgan had gone to church with Grammy, she'd thought her the kindest person she'd ever met. "I couldn't. I want to do my part to help."

"Are you kidding me? You've been here since we unlocked the door this morning and have been back and forth between the iron and the kitchen all day, serving others. All of Lou's chili is gone, but there's plenty of soup left. Grab a bowl and some of the butterscotch bars Ruby made because they are melt-in-your-mouth good, and have a seat for a few."

As if to add input, Morgan's stomach growled. "Um, yeah, maybe I will get some soup. Every time I'd serve a bowl I'd think how wonderful it smelled. You made it, right?"

"Bodie and I did," Sarah beamed. "It's a Spicy Chicken Tortilla. We enjoy experimenting with easy recipes to serve our guests at Hamilton House. Cooking together can be such fun." She gave a happy newlywed smile. "Be sure to let me know what you think."

"You heard her," Grammy Claudia said, beaming at Sarah's suggestion. "Go eat, then get over there and see if Andrew has had better luck teaching your son to sew than I did you." She laughed. "You remember that time I tried to get you to help me hem your Sunday School dress?"

Morgan didn't, but she smiled at her grandmother.

"I've never seen a kid look as happy as you did to see your grandfather walk in and ask if you wanted to go fishing. You couldn't get outdoors fast enough."

"Sorry about that." Because she did remember going fishing with her grandfather on several occasions during her holiday visits and looked forward to Greyson getting to make similar memories.

Grammy Claudia waved her hand dismissively. "Don't be sorry. Differences in tastes and skills make our world go around. It just means that there's someone for every task. I couldn't do half the things you do, Morgan." She turned her attention to Sarah. "Now, has Maybelle talked with you about these reindeer Rosie is insisting upon for her wedding? And what about these bridesmaid dresses she's having us fitted for this week? Has she mentioned them to you?"

Smiling, Morgan went to the kitchen. She soon decided Sarah and Bodie's Spicy Chicken Tortilla soup tasted even better than it had smelled as she stood in the doorway, eating and watching Greyson and Andrew.

"For a man who says he doesn't want any of his own, he's great with kids."

Uh-oh. Here came another Butterfly matchmaking attempt. This time from Andrew's grandma.

"It sure looks that way," Morgan agreed, taking another bite of her soup as she braced herself for whatever Ruby had come over to say. "Greyson adores him."

"It appears the feeling is mutual." Ruby glanced her way. "How about you?"

She'd known Ruby seeking her out wasn't coincidence, but Morgan still fought wincing. She gave Andrew's grandmother a tight smile that she hoped conveyed that she wasn't interested in having this conversation and particularly not with her. She finished off the last bite of soup, then tossed the plastic bowl in the nearby bin.

"Let's go see how things are going with their sewing efforts," she suggested, changing the subject. She knew Ruby meant well—they all did—but meaning well didn't make her any happier about their interference.

"Yes. Let's." Ruby's smile said she knew what Morgan was doing but was going to let her get away with it. This time. Butterflies were like that, choosing their battle strategies carefully.

She and Ruby came to stand just to the side of where Andrew had pulled a chair over next to Greyson's. He leaned in and closely watched Greyson's every move.

"Now, take your time, keep the material along the edge of the tape," Andrew said patiently. "I'm going to work the peddle for now."

Morgan wanted to hug him for that as the foot peddle was what controlled the pace at which the needle went up and down. He could keep the speed at a minimum and make sure it stayed consistent.

"Like this?" Greyson asked, gently gliding the material along the blue tape Andrew had apparently placed on the machine.

"Exactly like that. You're a pro," Andrew said. Ben and Cole had just come back inside, and Andrew called over, "Hey, Ben! Get over here and let this five-year-old show you how it's done."

"Say what? You showing me up, kid?" Ben teased, coming up behind them to stand next to Morgan and Ruby.

"Firefighter Andrew is a good teacher," Greyson bragged, never taking his gaze away from where his fingers slowly pushed the material beneath the needle. "I bet if you asked nicely he could show you how to sew, too."

"Yeah, Ben, you should ask nicely." Andrew covered his mouth, probably to hide his laughter, but his gaze never left Greyson's hands.

"I don't know, kid," Ben mused. "He tried earlier, and my seams didn't look anything like yours. Either he was holding out on me or you're just a natural."

"He's a natural." Andrew sounded proud. "Kid's got skills."

Greyson beamed, sitting up straighter as he guided the material and looked happier than he had since...well, since the last time he'd been with Andrew.

Lord, everyone was right.

He was great with Greyson and her chest was doing silly things in response.

Perhaps sensing her gaze on him, Andrew turned for the briefest second, caught her watching him, and winked, his gaze then immediately returning to what Greyson was doing.

Morgan couldn't breathe. She wasn't sure if she'd forgotten how, or if the shock had made her physically incapable of pulling air into her chest. Either way, lack of oxygen had her head feeling woozy.

It was definitely lack of oxygen that made her lightheaded and not the realization that Grammy was right about something else, too.

Andrew was great with her.

Chapter Six

*A*NDREW HELD HIS BREATH AS Greyson guided the ten-inch square's side through the machine, maintaining the proper seam allowance at all times. As the boy came to the end of the material, Andrew lifted his foot, stopping the needle.

"Fantastic," he declared. "Now, let's backstitch just a bit so the stitches don't easily pull out."

Greyson looked to him for instructions on what to do. Andrew gestured to the backstitch button. "Press that, keep the material positioned correctly, and let the machine move the material back."

Greyson did as asked, and they added

a couple of backstitches to the connected squares.

"You remember when I showed you how to cut the thread?" he asked, knowing the kid probably did. He'd been all ears, soaking up every word said.

Greyson nodded and pointed to a button with a scissors emblem on it.

"Do it."

Greyson pushed the button, and the machine clipped the thread.

"Nice job." He held out his hand for a fist bump.

Returning the gesture, Greyson then asked, "Now what?"

"Now we work on another one while someone irons the seam you just created flat. Then we can connect the two pieces of fabric."

"I'll do it," Morgan spoke up from near them. "I should be helping, anyway, but couldn't resist witnessing what a great job Greyson did. I knew he would. He's very good at learning new things."

Greyson sat up a little taller in his chair, obviously pleased at his mother's compliment.

"Sounds good." Andrew handed over the material and noted that her hand trembled as she took it. His gaze met hers in question, but her only response was to shake her head and turn to go to the ironing board she'd been working at earlier.

Andrew wanted to go after her, to ask if she was okay, but knew it would be best if he stayed with Greyson to make sure he used the machine properly. So, he stayed and helped the boy to sew another two squares together.

"For once, Ben's right. You're a natural, kid," he said, then turned to Ben. "Isn't this quarter-inch seam my kindergartner friend here just sewed perfect?"

"Great job," Ben told Greyson, fist bumping him, too, before shooting Andrew a dirty look. "Don't think I didn't catch that you just implied I don't have the skills of a kindergartner."

"Implied?" Andrew teased.

Ben snorted, picked up a paper with their block pattern printed on it, wadded it up and tossed it at Andrew.

Laughing, Andrew caught the paper and tossed it right back.

"Act your age, boys," Grandma Ruby told them, but her eyes danced with merriment at their fun.

"Yes, ma'am," they both said at once, causing Morgan to laugh as she handed over the freshly pressed piece of material. The sound of her laughter warmed his insides and had him grinning.

"Ready for me to iron that one?" she

asked, pointing to the square he and Greyson had just finished.

Ben and Andrew exchanged looks, then Ben mouthed, "You owe me," and took Greyson's second piece.

"Shown up by a kindergartner," Ben shook his head. "I can tell where I'm not needed. I'm going to try my luck at something else." He waggled his brows at Andrew's grandmother. "Grandma Ruby, you want to show me how to use an iron without burning the building down?"

Andrew doubted that his grandmother had missed the look he and Ben had exchanged. Obviously, she approved of his desire to be Morgan's friend as she placed her hand on Ben's shoulder and, laughing, led him over to the ironing boards so they could tackle a fresh set of seams needing pressed.

Andrew patted an empty chair near them. "Have a seat, Morgan, and Greyson and I will teach you how to sew."

"My son may be a natural, but I assure you that he didn't get that from me."

"His dad sewed?"

Greyson's ears perked up at the mention of his father.

"No, Trey was a talented man, but to my knowledge he didn't sew."

The man must have been amazing to have won Morgan's heart and fathered an awesome son such as Greyson.

A pang of envy hit.

Which didn't make sense. Andrew didn't want a wife and kids. But Morgan and Greyson were enough to make a man second-guess what he inherently knew, apparently.

"Grammy was just telling me about the time she tried to teach me to sew," Morgan said, obviously wanting to change the subject. "From what she said, Greyson's seams are much prettier than mine ever were."

Morgan smiled at her son.

"Firefighter Andrew and I can teach you," Greyson offered, looking as if he was eager to show off his newly learned skills.

"I'd like that." The pleasure in Morgan's eyes at the offer about undid Andrew. And the warm feelings inside of him only grew as he and Greyson tutored Morgan to complete a single block.

"Good job, Mommy. You did it." Greyson patted her hand, looking proud.

"Woot, woot," Morgan cheered, dancing around in her chair as she examined where she'd sewn the material together. "Not bad if I do say so myself."

Andrew laughed. "Not bad at all."

Her gaze met his and she smiled. "Thank you."

Her smile reached her eyes and some-how managed to make its way inside his chest and slap his heart around. At least, that's the explanation Andrew was going with for the acrobatics going on in his chest.

"Harry is such a great dog. Why don't you have a dog?"

Andrew should have known Greyson would ask that question when he'd suggested they take Bodie's dog out. Greyson had completed a full section of ten squares, but there was only so long a five-year-old could be expected to sit still. Meanwhile, Harry had been laying with his head on his paws, taking in all the day's activities and keeping a close watch on Sarah.

Andrew had thought both dog and boy would enjoy stretching their legs on the church's playground. Morgan had approved the outing so long as Greyson agreed to wear his coat, hat, and gloves. Harry had seemed a bit hesitant to leave Sarah's side. But once she'd assured the dog she was fine, Harry had headed toward the exit.

"It's really cool that Harry can catch a Frisbee," Greyson said, tossing the plastic disk across the yard the way Andrew had shown him. He'd been stunned that Greyson hadn't known what to do with the iconic toy.

"If I had a dog, I'd want him to be able

to catch a Frisbee, too," the boy continued. "You need a dog."

"What would I do with a dog when I go to smokejumper training?" Applying was something he'd been thinking about more and more lately. He'd pulled up the site and stared at the application form for longer than he cared to admit. If he knew his grandparents would be okay without him, he'd be gone in a heartbeat. At thirty-five, he'd no longer be eligible to apply. He was only twenty-seven, but the clock's countdown ticked louder and louder in his head.

"I could keep your dog for you," Greyson offered. "I would take really good care of him while you were away, and you wouldn't have to worry at all."

Andrew smiled. "I imagine you would, kid. With having you for a friend, I may have to rethink my reasons for not having a dog."

Greyson beamed. "I could help you pick one."

"You have something in mind?"

Greyson shook his head. "Mom says when we get on our feet and move into a house of our own, that maybe we can go to the shelter and adopt one."

On her feet. Had Morgan's husband left her in a financial mess? Andrew had assumed Morgan had moved in with her grandmother to have help with Greyson until she found a place. He'd not considered that there might have been financial motivations as well. But thinking back on it, he remembered Cole mentioning that she'd lost her job and hadn't been able to find another where they'd been living. What kind of man left his wife and small child without having made sure they were taken care of?

Then again, he was making big assumptions. Other than the little bit she'd told him, and that Cole had told him, he knew nothing regarding Morgan's former husband and marriage.

"But if you needed us to watch your dog, I know Grammy would let us keep him at her house," Greyson said. "She's nice that way."

The *your dog* had Andrew smiling. The kid already had him owning a dog.

"She is, isn't she?" he agreed. He'd always liked his grandmother's friend Claudia. "Your mom is nice, too."

Greyson nodded. "She reads me stories. I get two a night."

"Two? That's awesome." Andrew made sure to look impressed. Actually, he truly was impressed at what a great job Morgan did. "What type of stories does she read?"

"One Bible story," the boy held up one gloved finger, then a second, "and one story I get to pick."

Andrew could see that about Morgan:

that she'd want her son to have a strong sense of faith.

"Have a favorite?"

Taking the Frisbee Harry had returned to him and giving it another fling for the dog to go chasing after, Greyson told him about the story of a hungry caterpillar.

"Mommy reads it like it's me who is hungry and eating everything." The boy giggled, obviously recalling some special memory. "It's really funny when she does that."

An image of Morgan making the boy laugh popped into his head and had him trying to see himself there with them. He didn't fit into the picture...and it astonished him how much he wished he did.

"This week we've been reading Christmas stories. Grammy really likes Christmas books and has bunches on her shelf." Greyson took the Frisbee from Harry and patted the dog on the head. "Good boy."

Andrew knew what the kid meant. His grandma had lots of Christmas books on her bookshelves, too. He had fond memories of her having read him many, if not all, of them.

"I like the one about the snowman and a magic hat. I've never built a snowman." Greyson glanced toward him. "Have you?"

"Oh, yeah." Andrew grabbed hold of his jacket collar and straightened it in a cliché move. "I'm practically an expert snowman builder."

"Maybe, if it snows, you can teach me how," Greyson suggested, his eyes big and full of hope. "Like you did with sewing. Building a snowman is a basic life skill, too, right?"

Something happened in Andrew's chest again. Something that had him wishing he could drive Greyson and Morgan to the nearest place with snow, so they could build a snowman together right away.

"Definitely a necessary basic life skill." Taking the Frisbee from Harry, Andrew gave it a long fling and said, "I'd like that."

As he watched Harry take off after the Frisbee and catch it mid-air, it stunned Andrew just how much he really would like to teach Greyson how to build a snowman.

And a bazillion other things, too.

Grammy carried a stack of material she'd sewn and set it down at where Morgan was helping pin blocks together.

"Morgan, darling, you should get Greyson home. The poor thing is completely tuckered out."

Morgan glanced at where Greyson had fallen asleep while lying on a blanket on the floor next to Harry. Boy and dog were curled next to each other and Greyson's arm was flung over Harry.

"You're right, but he looks content there, doesn't he?" Morgan's heart squeezed. Once they were in their own place, adopting a dog into their family would be a top priority. "Plus, I hate to leave when there's still so much to be done."

"There's always more to be done, but just look at how much we've gotten accomplished today." Grammy gestured to the multiple finished quilt tops, sandwiched quilts, and fully completed quilts. "You've been here all day. Go home, get Greyson ready for bed, and relax for a while. Maybe take a bubble bath. You worked a lot of hours this week and deserve a bit of a break."

A bubble bath sounded heavenly, and she probably should get Greyson bathed and to bed so he wouldn't be falling asleep during church in the morning. Morgan smiled at her grandmother.

"Thanks, Grammy." She kissed her cheek. "I'll see you at home later."

Morgan gathered up all of Greyson's things, put them in her car, started the engine so it could warm up, then went to where he was asleep.

Harry's eyes opened and he peered up at her in question.

"I know, Harry. You're quite comfy, and

153

I'm about to disturb you. Sorry, but it's time for me to get this little guy home."

Kneeling down, she contemplated on how best to get him up. She hated to wake him, but lifting his sleeping body from the floor by herself wouldn't be an easy feat. He was growing up so fast. Too fast. Time be still.

"Want some help?"

Morgan glanced up at Andrew and gave a wry smile. "You implying I don't have enough muscle for the job?"

"I'd say you probably spend your work days lifting and assisting patients, and that would make this a piece of cake in comparison."

True, but fortunately she'd never had to get any of her patients up off of the floor without assistance—or while they were sleeping.

"However, if you're willing to let me," he continued, "I'd be happy to carry Greyson out for you. He's my buddy."

That he was. All day, wherever Andrew had been, so had Greyson. Several times Morgan had encouraged him to come help her, but he'd not wanted to be far from his new best friend. Andrew had never seemed to mind, had repeatedly assured her that he was enjoying having Greyson as his sidekick, and had even taken Greyson outside to play Frisbee with Harry. More than once she'd caught Greyson glancing up at Andrew with complete adoration, had heard her son

154

giggling at something just between them, and had even seen Andrew hoist Greyson up onto his shoulders and walk around the room with Greyson's arms spread out as if he were flying a plane. They'd both had huge smiles on their faces.

That morning she'd worried her son would be bored at the sew-in. Instead, he'd had a great time. Because of the man who'd just knelt down beside her, looking at her with kindness and something more in his hazel eyes. She'd be eternally grateful for the impact his kindness was having on Greyson, but as for how he made her feel…

Oh, Andrew. She didn't need him looking at her this way when she already felt so weak where he was concerned…not only because he knew how to bring Greyson out of his shell, but also because he made her want to smile and laugh, too.

"Thank you," she said.

"No problem." He took her appreciation as permission to scoop Greyson up as if he weighed nothing. "Come on, Little Man. It's time to get you to your car."

Greyson mumbled something, wrapped his arms around Andrew's neck, his legs around his waist, and held on as if he worried someone was going to pry him away.

"I need to put his coat on him."

Reluctantly and without opening his eyes, Greyson cooperated on pushing his arms into his jacket sleeves, immediately snuggling back against Andrew's chest.

"Greyson, honey, I need to zip you. When I started the car, the wind had really picked up and had a cold bite to it."

Greyson made a noise but this time, he didn't loosen his hold around Andrew's neck. Morgan hesitated. He'd probably be fine going out with his coat unzipped. Andrew's body would partially shield him from the wind and the car wasn't that far from the door.

"Grab my jacket and throw it over him."

Morgan's gaze cut to Andrew's. Did he think she was being overly protective? She probably was, but she didn't want Greyson getting cold.

"It's over on that chair." He gestured with his head to where his uniform jacket was draped over a chair back. "Put it over him and I'll make sure he stays warm."

"Thank you, but won't you get cold?"

Andrew grinned. "If I say yes, will you offer to keep me warm?"

Morgan rolled her eyes. "No."

"Then, I'll admit that I'll be fine. I'm hot-natured."

"Seems like that would be problematic when fighting fires," she said as she wrapped Andrew's jacket over Greyson. With his little body plastered to Andrew's, it covered him almost completely.

"The gear does get hot, but it's a small price to pay for staying protected," he said as they headed toward the door.

"Your grandmother told me you've always wanted to be a firefighter."

"You talked about me with my grandma? I knew you wanted to be my friend, Morgan Morris. Did she tell you how amazing I am, or just offer to show you my baby pictures?"

Oh, heavens. That grin.

"Both, actually. It was right after you'd come to the school to talk to the kids and she asked if I met you," she rushed out. Then her face flamed. Why had she said something so revealing to him? "We were talking about how excited Greyson was to meet the firefighters, and she asked if I'd met you, and she told me how Greyson reminded her of you and—"

"It's okay, Morgan," he assured her, his tone teasing. "You don't have to explain why you were talking about me with my grandma. I don't mind."

"But we weren't really talking about you," she said. "We were talking about Greyson and him wanting to be a firefighter and then she said—"

"Morgan," Andrew interrupted, his eyes dancing, "you do realize you're protesting too much, don't you?"

Morgan paused, realized he was right and then clamped her mouth, saying nothing aside from a quick goodbye to the others. Four sets of Butterfly eyes were on them as they headed toward the exit. When they stepped outside, the wind bit into Morgan's face, cooling it and whipping at her hair. She shivered beneath her jacket and felt a twinge of guilt that Andrew was coatless.

"I should have pulled the car up next to the door," she said, wishing she'd thought to do so.

"I'm fine. Greyson in my arms is warmer than a coat, anyway."

Morgan smiled. She agreed that cuddling with Greyson's warm little body was better than a jacket. She opened the back door of her car and stepped aside so Andrew could place Greyson into his car seat.

"Need me to buckle him in?" she asked.

He shook his head. "I got this." And he proved that he did.

"Okay, you did that like a pro."

"Don't sound so surprised," he said with a laugh, checking to make sure the latches had properly caught.

"I just didn't imagine you having any reason to know how to buckle a kid into a car seat," she admitted.

"I've not, but I've unfortunately had reason to unbuckle a few while working motor vehicle accidents."

Morgan had forgotten that the fire department was often called to help with more serious wrecks and that they used the Jaws of Life tool. The solemness in his tone suggested he'd worked some he wished he hadn't. With how great he was with Greyson, Morgan suspected he was phenomenal when working with scared, hurting kids during an accident, too. Her admiration for him kicked up yet another notch.

Andrew straightened and turned to face her. Morgan hadn't realized quite how close she still was until she found herself pinned between the open car door and his six-foot frame. Her gaze lifted to his and she gulped as she stared up at him.

His gaze searched hers. "When am I going to see you next, Morgan?"

Dragging the cold air into her lungs felt difficult. Or maybe it was breathing at all that was difficult with how close Andrew was, and the way he was looking down at her.

"I'm not sure," she admitted.

"We need to make it soon. Friends shouldn't go too long in between seeing each other and we can't have you missing me."

She bit into her lower lip. "No, we can't have that." Because she suspected she would be missing him, the moment she got into her car and drove away from the church.

At her soft reply, his brow lifted. "You softening to me, Morgan?"

She shook her head. "No."

"You sure?"

There was such a mixture of teasing and sincerity in his question that Morgan's head spun. She reached out to ground herself by touching the car, but the world still seemed to be shifting beneath her feet.

"No," she admitted, barely above a whisper. "I'm not sure of anything where you're concerned. How I feel when I'm with you, and when I watch you with Greyson, scares me."

Morgan's soft reply sent Andrew's pulse pounding.

Between the moonlight and the glow from the church's parking lot lampposts, Morgan's face appeared ethereal. Hadn't he always found her angelic, though?

"I'd never hurt you or Greyson," he promised. Quite the opposite: he wanted to protect them and make them happy, to somehow make up for all the bad things they'd gone through.

Her eyes wide, full of so much emotion, she nodded. "I believe that you wouldn't intentionally hurt us, but that doesn't mean you wouldn't hurt us accidentally, Andrew. Greyson has been through so much. It worries me how attached he is becoming to you. I couldn't bear to see his heartbreak if...well, if you got bored with him."

He couldn't imagine any circumstances within his control in which he'd do so.

"Greyson is a great kid, Morgan. I'd never get bored with him." Unable to resist, he reached up, brushing his thumb across her cheek he heard himself say, "Or you."

"Andrew, I..." she gulped as she stared up at him with her green eyes glittering in the moonlight. Looking into them made him feel as giddy as if it was Christmas morning.

He lifted her chin, tilting her face just so as his gaze dropped to her lush mouth—the same mouth that was likely going to tell him to stop any moment. And whether she said anything or not, he knew he needed to not give in to the desperate urge to kiss her. He'd said he wanted to be Morgan's friend. Nothing more.

"I like you," she said so softly he could have imagined it.

Yes! He mentally shoved a triumphant fist into the air, but in reality, he just smiled down at her and tried to play it cool when his insides felt at war. Because she wasn't looking up at him with I want to be your friend eyes. What he saw there was so much more which meant he should take a step back. Yet, he couldn't.

"I like you so much," she continued, not

sounding happy about it at all. "You make me smile and feel alive inside, but—"

"Why does there have to be a but?"

"Because there is one," she insisted. "Let me finish because I need to say this." Her face took on a worried expression and he longed to soothe out the worry lines that appeared along her forehead. "Greyson's crazy about you. That's part of the problem."

Confused, Andrew asked, "Why is that a problem? Why wouldn't he like me? What's not to like?"

"There you go not being serious," she accused, her chin trembling.

"Morgan," he cupped her face, the warmth of her skin seeping through his palms and radiating all the way to his core, "anyone ever tell you that you worry too much?"

"All the time. But Andrew…" Her lashes fluttered, her lips parted, and when her gaze met his, what he saw had his legs quivering. He'd like to blame the cold, but truth was, he couldn't have said what the temperature was as the warmth in Morgan's eyes drew him in.

"I like you, Morgan," he repeated, admitting to himself that his feelings for her went beyond friendship. "I never date women with kids. Not ever. But I think you may be the exception." He paused, heart racing, then repeated, "You are the exception."

She was. In so many ways. Ways he wasn't even sure he understood.

"What if I don't want to be the exception?"

Understanding what she meant, he gave a low laugh. "It doesn't seem to matter what either one of us wants, does it? I can't be in the same room with you without needing to talk to you and see your eyes brighten when I tease you. They do brighten, Morgan. They light up as beautifully as that big moon in the sky."

She closed her eyes, then opening them, shook her head.

"I can't do this," she breathed, but even as she said the words, her hand left the car and pressed against his chest, pressing flat against his uniform shirt. "I shouldn't do this."

For a moment he wondered if she was going to push him away despite the feelings for him that he saw swirling in those big green eyes, but instead she seemed to be absorbing the beat of his heart with her palm and letting it guide her.

Barely able to breathe, he dropped his gaze to her parted lips, then lifted it back to her eyes.

Staring up at him, she nodded ever so slightly.

With a burst of adrenaline that rivaled any he'd ever experienced, he lowered his head to close the short distance between his mouth and hers, anticipating the softness of her lips against his.

"Mommy?"

"Greyson." Andrew took a step back so fast that he stumbled and almost fell.

"Oh," Morgan jerked away at the same time and bumped against the car door prior to bending down to where Greyson could see her more easily. "Yes, baby?"

Seemingly oblivious to what he'd interrupted, the boy yawned. "Are we going home?"

"Yes. I'm sorry. Andrew helped carry you to the car and I was just thanking him and..." she stopped talking and Andrew could tell she was struggling to find words.

"Hey, buddy," he said, bending to peep into the car. "Sorry I distracted your mom. I'll see you soon."

"Tomorrow?" Greyson asked, looking hopeful.

"What's tomorrow?" he and Morgan asked simultaneously.

"Church," Greyson said, glancing toward his mom as if she should have known that. "Can Andrew come to church with us?"

Morgan's expression reminded Andrew of a cornered animal, and he teetered between frustration and guilt as he came to her rescue.

"I'm not sure. I'll be at the fire hall all

night and sometimes we don't get much sleep." Truth. He never knew what a shift would bring, and even though it had been a slow day with no calls, that didn't mean he and the guys wouldn't be up all night should a call, or several, come in. There were times when a whole shift would be quiet, just for chaos to strike right at the very end. Fires didn't come on schedule.

"But if you get sleep, you'll come?" Greyson implored.

Guilt tipped the scale and Andrew glanced toward Morgan. She averted her gaze as if she didn't want him to see what was there. Whatever that magic bubble had been, it was gone.

"I don't want to make a promise I might not be able to keep."

Greyson nodded as if he understood. "It's okay if you can't promise. But I hope you're able to come. I'd like that."

"I always like seeing you, too, but it's unlikely I'll be there." Very unlikely, as he hadn't been to church in some time. Occasionally, his grandma would convince him to go for some special occasion or other, but it was rare. And yet his hesitance now was mostly because he got the impression Morgan was torn on whether she'd want him there. "Night, Greyson. Until we meet again."

He held up his fist and Greyson bumped

his little fist against it. Andrew's insides smiled.

"Night, Andrew."

Andrew stepped back and Morgan closed the car door, then faced him.

"I need to get him home," she immediately said.

"I know."

"I...about what happened a few minutes ago," she began.

"Nothing happened, Morgan."

"Okay, then, about what almost happened," she corrected. "I'm sorry. I shouldn't have said what I did."

It took him a second, but then the penny dropped. "That you like me? That's what you wish you hadn't said?"

She nodded.

"You're overthinking this, Morgan," he suggested. "Why can't we just like each other, be friends, and not slap any other label on it?"

"You make it sound simple, but it's not." She glanced through the car window to where the boy appeared to have gone back to sleep. "I have to protect Greyson."

Andrew suspected that even though she was saying "Greyson," the person she was really trying to protect was herself.

Which made him wonder if maybe he was under-thinking the whole thing, be-

cause maybe just being friends with Morgan
was impossible.

Chapter Seven

"**W**HAT'S HE SAYING TO HER?"

"They just moved closer."

"Come on, Andrew, kiss her," Rosie said, peeping out the dark classroom's window where they had a clear view of Morgan's car and the couple standing to the side of it in the church parking lot.

Maybelle cut her gaze to her friend. "Now, now, he shouldn't rush things."

"Especially not with my Morgan. She's as skittish as a newborn colt when it comes to romance," Claudia reminded them.

"You sure about that? Miss Skittish just put her hand over his heart," Maybelle pointed out.

"Way to go, Morgan!" Rosie cheered.

"What is taking that boy so long? His grandfather didn't have a problem making his move for that first kiss," Ruby mused, shaking her head.

Three Butterflies' gazes shot to her.

"Why, Ruby Jenkins, I do believe you're blushing bright enough to give our position away," Rosie teased, looking impressed.

Ruby put her hands over her cheeks.

"Fifty years of marriage and thinking of her first kiss still makes her blush," Maybelle mused, smiling. "I remember my first kiss."

"Way back in the Dark Ages?" Rosie teased, never missing a chance to rib Maybelle about her age. The two women had been going back and forth at each other for over five decades, and yet Ruby never doubted that they loved each other dearly. They all did. Theirs was a sisterhood that had withstood time and tribulations.

"Ooooh, he's leaning!"

Leaning was good. Ruby had been beginning to think she was going to have to have a talk with him. Then again, she had no doubt her grandson was usually much more confident when he dated.

But Morgan was different.

Whether Andrew recognized that yet or not, Ruby and the Butterflies most certainly had noticed the looks passing between the couple. For all his dating, she'd certainly never seen Andrew look that way at anyone else.

When he looked at Morgan, his face shown with a protectiveness Ruby had never seen there, as if he'd take on the world to make it a better place for her. And, there was uncertainty, as well, that was just as unfamiliar on her brave, confident grandson's face. The looks from Morgan were hesitant, and yet she seemed unable to resist stealing a look.

"Oh no! He just jumped back."

"Did he trip over something?"

"What happened? Did she push him away?" Ruby asked, trying to get a better view through the window without being spotted.

"Shhh," Maybelle ordered. "She's bending down now. Greyson must have woken up and said something."

Ruby let out a heartfelt sigh. "Kids have the darnedest timing."

Feeling flustered, Andrew watched Morgan's car pull out of the church parking lot and drive away.

He'd almost kissed her.

He'd wanted to kiss her.

She'd wanted him to kiss her.

But it was best that they hadn't kissed. Amongst other reasons, that would have been difficult to explain to Greyson had he awakened to Andrew kissing his mother.

A gust of wind knocked into him, cutting through his clothes. His gaze dropped to the coat he held, but he didn't bother putting it on, just headed back toward the church community room's entrance.

He and the guys would help finish up anything the remaining Quilts of Valor volunteers needed from them, and then they would head back to the fire hall.

Warm air engulfed him as he stepped back into the building. Just as he got fully inside and the door behind him had closed, a door to his right opened, and four Butterflies fluttered into the room in a rush.

Four Butterflies with guilty eyes. What had they been up to?

"Grandma?"

"Hello, Andrew," she said all innocent-like, letting him know they'd definitely been up to something. "Morgan and Greyson gone?"

Nodding, Andrew eyed the women. Looking over at the room they'd exited, thinking of where those windows faced, he realized that he had a pretty good idea of exactly what they were guilty of. "Where were y'all?"

The women exchanged looks, then Maybelle said, "We took a quick break to calm

171

this one down." She pointed to Rosie. "The closer we get to her wedding, the more and more skittish she gets."

Why had Morgan's grandmother just covered her mouth? Was she trying to keep him from seeing her smirk?

"You needed to go somewhere private to discuss Rosie's upcoming wedding?" he asked.

"I can't have anyone overhearing about the surprises I have in store for my big day," Rosie retorted, following Maybelle's lead.

"Although, we may need your help with one of the surprises, Andrew," his grandma added, not that he bought her innocent look. "We still haven't tracked down eight reindeer to pull Santa's sleigh. Do you think you can find some?"

"Eight sleigh-pulling reindeer," Andrew said, rocking back on his heels.

"Nine works, too, if you find one with a red nose," Rosie added, laughing. "My wedding is going to be a winter wonderland with snow and—"

"Will there be snow at your wedding? How are you managing that?"

"Will there be snow?" Rosie laughed. "Dear boy, you underestimate me. I've got snow machines coming in from Snow-to-Go. I found them online. Five-star rating. They're going to have Harvey Farms absolutely gorgeous."

"Snow," he mused. "Greyson's never built a snowman."

All four women's eyes widened.

"Never?"

"Oh, dear. My great-grandson has never made a snowman?" Claudia shook her head. "That will never do."

Rosie clapped her hands together with excitement. "Why didn't I think of this before?"

Andrew and three Butterflies stared at her, waiting for her to elaborate.

"We're going to build snowmen at the reception."

Maybelle frowned. "Aren't you spending a fortune to have an ice-skating rink set up?"

"Yes, but not everyone ice-skates."

Maybelle's expression said it all as she asked, "But everyone builds snowmen?"

Rosie ignored Maybelle's sarcasm. "We'll go down to the Goodwill and buy up all their scarves and hats for decorating them." She clapped her hands together. "Oh, this is going to be fun."

"You're crazy," Maybelle vocalized what Andrew was thinking.

"Not that I don't want Greyson to have the opportunity to build a snowman, but building snowmen at your wedding reception? Are you sure?" Claudia asked, eyeing her friend with uncertainty. "I mean, we don't even know that we won't really have a blizzard. Maybe you should plan something on the indoors."

"The weather will cooperate. It wouldn't dare do otherwise on my wedding day," Rosie declared. "Besides, if it really becomes a blizzard, we'll move the ceremony inside that big, beautiful barn the Harveys built and we'll still have our outdoor fun, too. What could be better than a white Christmas Eve wedding and reception?"

"What, indeed?" Maybelle asked, shaking her head.

"Poor Lou," Grandma Ruby sympathized. "With all the things you have planned for your wedding day, he'll never get to go on his honeymoon."

"Poor Lou nothing. He's getting the wedding of the decade and me. What more could he want?"

Maybelle snorted. "I could make a few suggestions."

"A wedding with less drama?" Grandma Ruby asked.

"If he wanted boring, he wouldn't have proposed to Rosie," Claudia pointed out.

"That's true," Andrew's grandmother agreed.

Knowing none of them were going to admit to the fact that they'd been spying, Andrew said, "I'm going to go see if I can help the guys finish up that stack of material they're working on before we head back to the fire department."

Maybe it would be a crazy busy night and Greyson's invitation would be a moot point.

"Do you think he'll come?" Greyson asked as he undid the buckle to the built-in car seat in Grammy's minivan.

Morgan shrugged as she handed him his Bible. Hadn't she wondered the same thing long into the night? Would he show up for church? Would he get calls and have to work dangerous fires? Would he have kissed her had Greyson not awakened?

"Who?" Grammy asked from the front passenger seat as she gathered her things.

"Andrew. I invited him." Greyson got out of the car and took his Bible.

"Andrew is coming to church today?" Grammy gave Morgan a questioning look. A questioning, pleased look. "Will he be coming to lunch afterwards?"

"I hope so," Greyson answered before Morgan could find words. "I can show him my toy fire station. He would like it and think I did a great job putting it together."

"You did do a great job," Morgan agreed.

"It looks terrific—anyone would be impressed."

He bobbed his head back and forth, watching as his breath made a visible puff of air from the cold. Morgan smiled at the image her son made in his slick black shoes and dark dress pants with his overcoat, scarf, hat, and gloves. She was biased, but he was a cutie.

He was also full of excitement over the idea that Andrew was going to be at church. So much so that Morgan fought wincing. She didn't want him to get his hopes up when it was unlikely that Andrew would attend.

She didn't want to get her hopes up, either.

"Greyson, remember that Andrew worked all night," she said, taking his hand as they headed across the church parking lot. Why did her gaze go to where she'd been parked the night before? To where she'd been standing while they talked? To where he'd been touching her face? To where she'd placed her hand over his heart? Morgan gulped. "It's possible he didn't get much rest. He may be sleeping and not able to come this morning."

Was she trying to convince him or herself?

"Do you think he had lots of fires last night?" Greyson asked, glancing up at her as they stepped up to the church door.

"I didn't hear anything come over the scanner," her grandfather answered as he opened the building's door and held it for them.

Greyson perked up. "I bet he'll be here, then."

"Good morning, Rosie," Morgan told the blue-haired lady coming over to tell them hi, glad for the distraction from more Andrew talk. "How are the wedding plans going?"

Rosie grunted. "No reindeer yet."

"Reindeer?" Greyson asked. "For a wedding?"

"Rosie wants to arrive at her wedding in a sleigh pulled by reindeer."

"Like Santa?" he asked, looking confused.

Rosie laughed. "Exactly like Santa, dear boy, because being married to me is going to be like Lou getting Christmas twenty-four-seven for the rest of his life."

Morgan and her grandmother exchanged smiles. Greyson just continued to look confused.

"What Rosie is saying is that Lou is a lucky man because getting to share your life with someone you love is the best gift," Grammy explained, patting him on the shoulders. "Now, let's get you to your Sunday school class and see what Sarah and that other gorgeous granddaughter of mine,

Annabelle, has in store for you to learn about today."

Morgan followed along behind her grandmother and Greyson, unable to get her grandmother's words out of her head. Unable to get her own words from the night before out of her head, either. She'd told Andrew she couldn't do this.

But what if her heart wasn't giving her a choice?

For the first time in the history of forever, Andrew's truck wouldn't start. He fiddled with the battery cable, but nothing. Not even a sputter of a crank. Glancing at his watch, he grabbed a battery jumper cable box and attempted to jump the battery. Still nothing.

Maybe it would work if he let the battery charge a few minutes.

"Okay, God. I know Easter Sunday was the last time I made it to church, but I'm trying to get there today and need a little help."

Leaning against the truck, Andrew took out his phone, played a quick mind game, then checked to see if the engine would crank yet.

Still nothing.

He glanced down at his church clothes and shook his head. "I'm all slicked up in these fancy shoes Grandma gave me for Christmas last year, dress pants, and a button-down beneath my coat. Plus, it's fifty-five degrees outside. Not exactly a great temp for riding Big Bertha."

He could give the charger a few more minutes and still maybe make it on time, but if he didn't leave soon, he'd be cutting it close. Maybe he should just forget the whole thing, go change, and spend the morning figuring out what was wrong with his truck. It was probably what he should do.

But he kept thinking of Greyson's invitation. Could he really disappoint the kid by not showing?

He looked at his watch. He'd either have to take Big Bertha or not go. He'd be late if he went to change, but he at least needed to swap jackets or he'd turn into an icicle on the short ride over to the church. He ran back into his house and got his jacket and helmet.

Donning his helmet, he straddled the Harley. "Looks like you're going to church, Ole Girl."

One kick start of his leg and her engine purred to life. Purred? More like roared to life. Guiding the motorcycle out onto Main Street, Andrew squeezed the handlebar, revving the engine and taking off toward the church.

Cold wind hit him in the face and cut

through his clothes as he made short work of the distance between his place and the church. It wasn't that far, and he knew he had enough time, but he still breathed a sigh of relief when the church's steeple came into view.

No doubt Bertha's roar meant that everyone inside the church building would know he was there even prior to his pulling into the parking lot.

So much for his making a good impression.

Had that been what he'd been trying to do? To make a good impression on Morgan? Well, at least, he was there. At church. Not early, but not late, either. That had to count for something, right?

Ben was a churchgoer and would be there. Sophie likely had a spot reserved for Cole in a near-the-front pew. They'd know that he was there, and they wouldn't buy that he was there for Greyson. His friends would give him plenty of grief over this one, but he didn't care.

This wasn't about Ben or Cole, or even Morgan, really...although his pulse raced at the thought that he'd see her in a few minutes.

This morning was about Greyson.

Greyson had invited him, and the kid had had enough disappointments in life. Andrew wouldn't be another.

Not over something as simple as giving the kid an hour of his time.

Chapter Eight

GREYSON WIGGLED IN HIS SEAT, turning to look at the back entrance yet again. Morgan wanted to tell him to face forward, but she didn't. She understood why he was doing it. It was all she could do not to turn to look, as well.

Which was silly.

She didn't really expect Andrew to come to church just because Greyson had invited him and they'd almost kissed...did she?

Immediately, she scolded her subconscious, because what did their almost-kiss have to do with anything? Hadn't she decided during the long hours of the night that she was glad Greyson had interrupted them? The last thing she needed was to get further involved with Andrew.

Outside the sanctuary, a motorcycle thrummed. From the pew in front of where Morgan sat with her grandparents, Ruby turned, her eyes bright with excitement, and a big smile on her wrinkled face.

"Did you invite Andrew to church?"

The motorcycle was Andrew? Morgan's breath caught. Of course, it was. Hadn't Suzie mentioned that Andrew rode a motorcycle?

"I invited him. I hope he comes," Greyson piped up from where he sat between Morgan and Grammy. He'd been telling an attentive Grammy about what he'd learned in Bible class that morning, but at the prospect of Andrew arriving, everything else was forgotten.

"Good job, Greyson," Ruby beamed, looking as if she were about to pop with excitement, "because that sure sounded like Big Bertha."

"Big Bertha?" Morgan asked.

"His motorcycle," Andrew's grandmother told her, an indulgent look on her face. "I don't really approve of such things, but boys will be boys, and he's always had a penchant for bikes."

"Motorcycles are cool," Greyson said from beside her.

Ruby laughed. Morgan didn't.

Greyson practically jumped up and down in the pew he bounced so much as he waved toward the back of the auditorium.

"There he is. He's here." He turned and grinned at Morgan, then bounced and waved more. "Andrew, here we are!"

"Shhhh, Greyson, we're in church. You can't yell," Morgan said, placing her hand on her son's shoulder in hopes of calming him down a bit. Ha. She needed someone to calm her down a bit.

What was it about adrenaline junkies that affected her so much?

Greyson frowned. "How is he supposed to find us?"

"He's a smart man. I think he'll be able to find you."

Giving her a quick look that said he wasn't taking any chances, Greyson stood and turned toward the back, waving again, just to be sure.

"Someone sure is happy to see my grandson," Ruby said, exchanging a look with Grammy. Both women turned smiling, expectant faces toward Morgan.

She wanted to set the Butterflies straight, but remembered Andrew's comment from the night before about her protesting too much. Sometimes saying nothing at all was the wisest course of action.

Plus, anything she said could and would be held against her.

"Andrew!" Greyson said, looking toward the end of the pew.

He was there. He'd come to church because Greyson had invited him.

"Hey, buddy," Andrew said.

Morgan couldn't not look and when she did, he flashed the grin that set her insides off like a pinball machine. She'd always found him handsome in his firefighter uniform, had never seen him in anything else. But in dress pants and a button down with his leather jacket draped over his arm and his helmet in his hand... Wow.

Men like him were why firemen ended up on calendars.

His cheeks were pink from the cold. His hair was a little flattened from where he'd had his helmet on, and a little mussed from where he'd tried to fix it by running his fingers through it. The style should've detracted from his attractiveness, but it seemed to just add to his many charms. And his smile should be classified as a lethal weapon because it sure wreaked havoc on her insides.

"Good morning, Morgan."

"Good morning," she managed to reply, despite how her tongue seemed stuck to the roof of her mouth.

"Sit by me," Greyson requested, motioning to where he had been sitting. "There's plenty of room, isn't there, Mommy?"

Morgan didn't know about plenty, but as

her grandfather had stood to let Andrew into the row and Grammy was telling Andrew how good it was to see him and Greyson was about to pop with excitement that Andrew was there, she didn't really have a choice but to scoot over as close as she could to Maybelle.

Only Maybelle didn't budge, so there was only so far Morgan could go to make room without climbing up into the woman's lap. Which would serve her right, since Morgan had a sneaking suspicion on why Maybelle hadn't moved.

Ugh. Butterflies!

Taking his cue from Greyson, Andrew sat down on the pew between him and Grammy, then turned toward her, looking as if he was about to say something else. But between them, Greyson held up the ornament he'd previously been showing his great-grandmother. His little face was so animated and full of excitement at Andrew's arrival that despite her jitters, Morgan just smiled as she watched her son show off his wares.

"I made this in my class this morning. My big cousin Annabelle and Mrs. Sarah helped me. Annabelle sits with the high school kids," Greyson barely took a breath as he continued, "My ornament is made from colored plastic wrap, but it looks like stained glass. See?"

Andrew took the ornament, turning to look at it from both sides. "That's really cool. You did a great job."

Greyson smiled. "Mrs. Sarah helped me. She's a good teacher and nice. Plus, I love her dog. We should play Frisbee with Harry again. Sarah says we can anytime, because Harry likes playing Frisbee." He gave a proud look as he added, "She said Harry loved playing with me, too."

Harry was hard not to love. The dog made it difficult to not want to give in to Greyson's pleas for a dog right away. Maybe soon they'd be out of her grandparents' house and could start looking.

"You're lucky to have Sarah teaching your class. That stern-looking woman to the other side of you was my Sunday school teacher when I was about your age," Andrew said loudly enough Maybelle couldn't help but overhear.

Morgan imagined that had he whispered, the four Butterflies would have still heard. She had no doubt that they were all tuned in to the conversation and most likely even Rosie, who sat on the opposite side of Maybelle, could recite every word that had been said from the moment Andrew had arrived.

"Had you behaved, I wouldn't have had to be stern," Maybelle retorted, leaning forward to cut her wise blue eyes toward Andrew. "Good thing you were cute when you were Greyson's age, or you'd have stayed in the corner."

"Aw, now, Maybelle, you know you think I'm cute now, too," Andrew teased, giving the older woman his signature grin.

To Morgan's surprise, Maybelle blushed. Apparently, Andrew had that effect on women of all ages.

"You're not too old for me to send to the corner, young man," Maybelle scolded, and Morgan had no trouble envisioning Maybelle taking Andrew by the shirt sleeve and marching him to the nearest corner for time out.

"Yes, ma'am," Andrew said, sitting up a little straighter in the pew.

Greyson stared up at Andrew in wonder. "You went to church here when you were my age?"

"Don't make it sound as if it was eons ago, kid," Andrew ruffled the boy's hair. "But, yes, I've run up and down and around these pews quite a few times during my day."

"Mom doesn't let me run in church," Greyson pointed out.

"No one 'let' him do it, either," Ruby said from in front of them, reaching around to pat her grandson's knee and bestow a big, happy grandma smile on him. "Good to see you here this morning, dear."

He waggled his brows and gave a look

that probably always worked on his grandmother as he asked, "Think it'll earn me a
batch of your Christmas cookies?"

Morgan wasn't surprised by Ruby's happy little laugh. Eyes twinkling, Ruby said, "It
might just so long as you behave back there
and don't make me have to turn around to
straighten you up."

"Grandma's threatening to withhold the
cookies." Andrew sighed. "Guess there'll be
no running in church for me today."

"Lord forbid," Maybelle intoned, and
tsked at him. "Don't you go teaching Greyson your bad habits."

Andrew leaned over and stage whispered, "Don't listen to them, Greyson. I was
actually a great kid and always did what I
was told."

Maybelle cleared her throat. Ruby
laughed and patted him on the knee again.
Rosie snorted from the other side of Maybelle. Grammy just smiled as her gaze
stayed on Morgan, making her feel as if she
shouldn't look directly at Andrew for fear of
putting the women in a tizzy.

"Well, most of the time," he amended,
winking at Greyson.

Morgan took in the back and forth,
self-conscious that she and Andrew were
surrounded by Butterflies and even more so
that the conversation was going on around
her, with her quietly taking it all in.

"No running in church, Greyson," Andrew told him. "Can't have the ladies saying I was a bad influence. There are cookies on the line here."

Greyson shook his head. "I wouldn't run here anyway. Mommy says I might bump into someone and if an older person falls, it might hurt them."

Morgan beamed, happy that he'd been paying attention.

"One of her patients has a broken bone from where he fell—but not from anyone running and bumping into him." Greyson's face squished with thought. "Well, I don't think anyone bumped him."

He looked to her for confirmation and she shook her head. John had slipped on ice and lost his footing. Not that she'd say that in front of Maybelle since the woman knew him. John was entitled to his privacy, especially in front of someone Morgan knew he'd want to impress.

"Yet another reason not to run in church," Andrew agreed. "I'm glad you're considerate of other people, Greyson. That's a good trait to have."

Greyson lit up at the compliment. "Do you want to come eat with us after church? Grammy made pot roast. It's really good. Mommy and I want you to come, don't we?"

Morgan's cheeks flamed. "Greyson, Andrew's barely sat down and here you are trying to get him to go somewhere else. Be thankful he accepted your invitation to come to church rather than pushing for more of his time. He worked all night and may want to go home and rest after services."

Andrew shook his head. "Nope. It was a slow night. I got plenty of rest."

"Oh. Well, you may have things you need to do."

He shrugged. "Got to eat, regardless of whatever else I do."

If he wanted off the hook from going to her grandmother's for lunch, he wasn't helping. Then again, he probably didn't want off the hook. She was the one who got all anxious and uncertain around him. And he, well...he'd said he wanted to be her friend. Was that all he wanted? Their almost-kiss must've meant something more.

"Oh, Andrew, you definitely should. Claudia's pot roast is heavenly," his grandmother urged, turning around from the pew in front of them again. "It's one of your grandfather's favorite things Claudia makes and he always raves about it anytime we get a chance to have it. You'll love it."

"You think?" He sounded amused. "If Grandpa raves about it, then I shouldn't pass up an opportunity to try it."

Morgan just shook her head. She wasn't sure if the Butterflies and Greyson had railroaded Andrew into agreeing, or if he was in

on the meddling and had somehow orches-
trated the whole thing to keep her world
off-kilter,

He definitely made things feel topsy-
turvy. Things such as her good sense.

Because when her gaze met his, even
knowing all the reasons why she shouldn't
give in to the urge, she couldn't prevent the
smile on her face that he was there.

And coming to Grammy's for lunch.

Andrew had noticed Morgan when she'd
been across a classroom in jeans and a
sweatshirt and he'd thought her the prettiest thing he'd ever seen. Little had he known
how absolutely gorgeous she'd be in her
green dress with her hair clipped up and
a touch of makeup. Her eyes looked even
greener than usual.

The color was that of garland, wreaths,
pine trees, and everything Christmas.

She was everything Christmas. Right
down to the glossy red lipstick coating her
lips. Her kissable lips.

Nope. He'd better not be thinking about
kissing Morgan or he'd get tossed out of the
church building. Probably by Maybelle. Even
his grandma might take hold of his ear and
march him out of the building for that one.

Besides, the best thing about his sweet Morgan's lips was that they were curved in a smile. At him. That alone was worth getting slicked up for church. The woman had an amazing smile and she needed to bring it out more often.

He wanted to make her smile all the time.

"Hi," he heard himself say even though it made no sense since he'd already said good morning. Not much about the way Morgan made him feel made sense. Because who would have ever thought he'd be sitting in church next to her young son and feeling as happy as a lark? Especially considering his truck had something wrong with it? That's what he should have said he needed be doing that afternoon. But even if the temperature dropped to arctic, he'd keep riding Big Bertha rather than give up the opportunity to spend the afternoon with Morgan and Greyson.

The song leader went to the podium, made a few announcements, then gave the song number for the first hymnal. Greyson snuggled in between Morgan and him on the pew, glancing up at him and smiling repeatedly as he held his song book over for Andrew to look at as well. Although it triggered different emotions within Andrew, there was such a sweet innocence in the boy's adoration that made Andrew want to never disappoint him.

If he felt that way after knowing Greyson for such a short time, it was no wonder Morgan was so protective of her son.

"Amazing grace, how sweet..." he began singing, earning another pleased look from Greyson.

He stretched his arm out around the boy, accidentally brushing his hand against Morgan in the process. The dress's silky green fabric was soft against his knuckles, reminding him of how her skin had felt when he'd almost kissed her at the sew-in.

And making his gaze drop to her hollyberry red lips again.

Yep. His true green Pine Hill blood was coming through, what with his mental descriptions using Christmas terms.

Or maybe, he admitted, it was just Morgan making him think that way, rather than having grown up in this Christmas-loving town.

"I bet you didn't realize you'd be forced into helping put up Christmas decorations when you said you'd come to lunch today," Morgan teased as she and Andrew trimmed the seven-foot Blue Spruce tree her grandfather had picked up the day before from Harvey Farms.

"I don't mind," he said, clipping another wayward branch and placing it on a growing pile. "I've got lots of experience thanks to helping my grandma. She goes all out with lights and yard blow-ups and the like. You'll have to drive by and show Greyson. He'd like that."

"I'll make a point to bring him by one evening to see them."

"Just this past week she had me up on her roof hanging a strand of lights around her chimney and putting a plastic Santa up there while she was in the yard directing me this way and that. You'd think using more kilowatts than the state of Texas would assure her that she has enough decorations," he grinned, "but not my Grandma. She's always having me put up a few more."

"She's very lucky to have you."

"It's the other way around. I'm the lucky one. My parents were—are—workaholics and I practically lived at my grandparents' house growing up. It's thanks to them that I had such a great childhood. There's not much I wouldn't do for them."

Morgan's gaze cut to his from where she held the clippers next to another branch. "You're a good person, aren't you?"

His brow arched. "Not sure how you deduced that from what I just said, but the real question is, why you're just now figuring it out despite how I keep shouting it from the rooftops?"

Smiling, Morgan shrugged. "I suppose I had a case of selective hearing."

He paused from clipping the higher branches into shape to look at her, obviously intrigued. "You didn't want to hear what I was saying?"

"When you were tooting your own horn?" She wrinkled her nose at him. "Not really."

His hazel eyes sparkled. "Whether I'm tooting my own horn or not, you like me."

Although she'd been the one to tell him that very thing the night before, she gave him her best *you're crazy* look. "Who told you that?"

His lips twitched. "A little birdie."

"Ha. In this town, a little 'butterfly' would be more believable."

He chuckled. "True that."

"Mommy, look at this ornament that Grammy found," Greyson said, coming back into the living room from where he'd been helping her grandmother. "She said you made it when you were a little girl."

Morgan smiled at the clothespin angel. "That was a long time ago. I can't believe she still has it."

She suspected she'd be that way and someday she'd be pulling out handmade ornaments from decades ago, possibly the 'stained glass' church that Greyson had made, to show his children. Her heart skipped a beat at the thought of how quickly time was slipping by. That "someday" would be here much too soon. The thought made her a little light-headed. Good thing she wasn't up on the stepladder.

"Grandmas keep those kinds of things," Andrew said as he admired the angel. "For-ever."

Thankful for the distraction from her runaway thoughts, she asked, "Ruby has ornaments you made?"

He gave her a look that said, *You're kidding me, right?* "Dozens. She has a tree dedicated to the ornaments her kids and grandkids have made for her over the years. It's not the prettiest, compared to the glitz and glitter of the others she puts up, but she swears it's her favorite."

As Ruby was a sentimental woman, Morgan imagined the tree full of precious memories really was her favorite.

"I'd like to see them someday." As soon as the comment left her mouth, she clamped her lips closed. *Seriously? What kind of com-ment was that?* She did not want to see or-naments he'd made as a little boy. Wanting that implied things that shouldn't be implied between them.

"Did you make an angel, Andrew?"

197

Greyson asked, handing the clothespin angel over to him to look at.

"Not one like this." Andrew ran his fingers over the downy white feathers glued to the back to make the wings. "Your mom was talented even back then. That must be where you get it."

Greyson turned big green eyes toward her. "Is it?"

She gave a small smile at the memories hitting her. "Maybe. Your dad didn't like to sit still long enough for most kinds of artwork."

Trey had appreciated beauty in various forms but had always joked that Greyson and any future children would be the only things of beauty he'd ever make. But there had been no future children.

"I must get that from him," Greyson said, causing everyone in the room to laugh and pulling Morgan from the past.

"You get a lot from him. Like this," she admitted, reaching out to play-pinch Greyson's nose. She didn't think he'd welcome her scooping him up for a hug with Andrew watching. He might only be five, but he was already having more and more independent moments when he didn't want to be loved on publicly. "You definitely have your daddy's nose."

Which must have been just the right thing to say and do as Greyson giggled and squirmed around next to her as if trying to get his nose back.

"Phew," Grammy said, coming back into the living room from where she'd been upstairs. "I can't believe your grandfather missed the most important box of ornaments when he was carrying things down yesterday."

"I didn't have you here to tell me what to do," Grampy teased, coming back into the room carrying a hand-painted flowerpot soldier that was almost as big as Greyson.

"Wish I'd been here to help," Andrew said. "I'd have been glad to carry all these down for you."

The sincerity in his voice had Morgan looking at him with a bit of awe. He hadn't seemed to mind one bit that her grandmother had put them to work the moment lunch was cleared. Instead, he'd jumped in and seemed to be enjoying himself.

"I'll keep that in mind next year, son," Grampy said, shooting a meaningful look toward Andrew that had another whoosh of lightheadedness hitting Morgan. Would Andrew be around next year? "Greyson," he continued, "will you get the front door so I can put this on the porch?"

First grabbing his 'nose' from where Morgan's fingers were still clinched as if she held it, Greyson went to the door to help his great-grandfather, asking questions about the painted soldier as he went. Morgan could feel Andrew's gaze on her, but she avoided looking at him. Mostly, because she knew Grammy was watching them with an eagle eye and probably had her phone recording a live feed to share with the other Butterflies. Did Andrew feel as awkward as she did over the way her grandparents were assuming that they were on their way to becoming a couple?

They weren't. They weren't anything.

Only, him being here with her and her family didn't feel as if it wasn't anything. It felt like something. Something big and important and exciting.

And scary.

"The tree looks great," Grammy said, walking over to run her finger along a branch. "I'm making note of it for future reference: you two are officially our annual tree-trimmers."

"Are you putting up another live tree today, Grammy?" Morgan asked, to emphasize that today was the only time she and Andrew would be trimming Christmas trees together.

"No, I meant—" Grammy paused, then waved her hand. "Oh, never mind. Don't you just love the smell of a live tree?"

Morgan did, but wasn't sure if she should let her grandmother off the hook that easily. Then again, she should probably be thankful her grandmother hadn't pulled out mistletoe to dangle over her and Andrew's heads. She sure wouldn't put it past her if she thought that was what was best for Morgan.

"Come look at what all I found," Grammy said.

Morgan was almost afraid to look in case her grandmother had indeed pulled out the mistletoe. "Greyson showed me the angel."

Grammy gave a sly grandmotherly look. "I have more goodies."

She did, too. Lots more goodies. Some that put a smile on Morgan's face at the same time as tears prickled her eyes. Oh, the memories!

"Andrew was telling me that Ruby puts up a tree full of handmade ornaments from her loved ones," Morgan mused, running her fingers over a plastic canvas snowflake that had her mother's name written on the tag. "I'm pretty sure you have enough here to do the same, Grammy."

Grammy smiled. "I love Christmas, but I'm not the type to have a bunch of trees. I like the one tree and want it to be super special. These ornaments will be put on it with the ones I add each year as the perfect combination of past memories and the ones we'll make this Christmas."

Morgan smiled at her grandmother. "You're right. That's the perfect combination." And this Christmas really was going to be the best Christmas ever for Greyson thanks to her grandparents. Her gaze went to where Andrew was peering in the box, smiling as he eyed different items. Yes, she was so glad she had moved to Pine Hill.

Greyson came back inside and peered in the box, too.

"That you?" Andrew asked picking up a photo ornament that had Morgan's throat constricting.

Greyson glanced at the photo ornament and wrinkled his nose. "I didn't have any hair."

Although struggling with a wash of emotions from the sight of the ornament, she smiled at Greyson.

"You were a beautiful baby," Morgan said. "Just as you're a handsome young man now."

"I'm glad I grew hair, though."

"Be careful what you say," Grampy said, laughing as he came back inside and running a hand over his partially bald head. "Some of us have lost more hair than we have left."

Her grandfather had once had a head full of light brown hair. Now, what little he had left was white. It didn't matter. Grammy still looked at him as if he hung the moon, especially now that he'd started taking her on trips. With Morgan's parents being military, Morgan had moved every few years and had seen a lot of different places. Until recently, Grammy had barely left Pine Hill's city limits. Now she and Grampy were exploring the continental US while also collecting passport stamps left and right, and they couldn't be happier.

She went over to her grandfather and kissed his cheek. "No worries, Grampy. You're a handsome young man, too."

Grampy said, "You obviously didn't pay attention in church this morning when Pastor Smith was talking about fibbing."

Morgan laughed. Busted. He was right. She'd tried to pay attention, but between making sure Greyson stayed quiet and pretending that Andrew's hand that had rested on her back when he'd draped his arm on the back of the pew wasn't burning a hole through her dress...well, she hadn't paid nearly the attention she should have. Obviously.

"This is my daddy," Morgan heard Greyson say, making her think she still wasn't paying nearly the attention she should be. Greyson had dug out another photo from the box and she knew which one it had to be.

She sucked in a breath and her gaze met her Grampy's empathetic one. Of course, Greyson would want to show Andrew that particular photo. She kept a family photo in his bedroom so he'd have it to look at and would always remember Trey. But she struggled seeing photos of him as it served as a reminder of how she'd lost him. Her heart tightening from memories, she turned to look.

Greyson held up a Santa photo frame that featured a young couple holding a one-year-old Greyson. A young couple who had been happily in love and thought they had decades of happiness ahead of them. Would she have done anything differently, had she known what fate had in store?

Greyson was looking up at Andrew to gauge his reaction as he pointed toward the photo. She was struck at the oddity of the moment, Andrew looking at a photo of her little family when it had still been intact. Andrew studying a photo of the first man who'd ever owned her heart.

First? The only man to ever hold her heart.

But it was Andrew who, for the first time since Trey, made her miss being part of a couple. When she was around Andrew, she became aware she was still young, and that maybe her heart hadn't died along with Trey after all. Was she a bad person to feel that way? It had been two years, but until recently, it always felt like every day, she awakened to remember he was gone. Every day, she had to struggle to try to make sense of life without him.

The truth was, since moving to Pine Hill, losing Trey wasn't the first thing she thought of each morning. Not even prior to meeting Andrew. And, since she had met him...Guilt hit. What was she doing? She shook her head to clear her thoughts and moved closer to where man and boy were looking at the portrait.

His face full of compassion, Andrew squatted by Greyson to get a closer look at the photo. Then, glancing at Greyson, he gave him a smile that was full of compassion and so much more. "Your mom is right. You do have your dad's nose."

Greyson's chin lifted as if to show off his nose, then maybe thinking Andrew was going to grab it, he covered it with his hand and giggled.

"But your eyes, kid," Andrew continued, "are your mom's. Most beautiful eyes I've ever seen." His gaze connected with Morgan's.

She gulped. Grammy made a happy little noise. Grampy cleared his throat.

With a nervous laugh, Morgan said, "Now, isn't it time we get started decorating the tree? Andrew, maybe you could help Grampy with the lights while Grammy and I get the ornaments sorted."

"What about me?" Greyson asked. "I want to help."

His gaze still studying her and seeing

much more than Morgan wanted him to see, Andrew put the photo down and placed his hand on Greyson's shoulder. "Come with me, kid. You're in with the men's work."

"Lights are men's work?"

"Men's work is whatever the women say is men's work," Grampy advised. "Learn it at an early age and you'll have much happier relationships."

The way Grammy was looking at Andrew made Morgan nervous. Or maybe it was what Andrew had said about her eyes that made her so nervous.

Because, heaven help her, his compliment stirred all kinds of good feelings inside her chest...and how could that be, when he held a photo of her with Trey and Baby Greyson?

Chapter Nine

ORGAN REMINDED HERSELF THAT WHAT she saw outside her Grammy's kitchen window was not what she wanted. Nope. Not at all.

Only, seeing Andrew chasing Greyson across the yard, grabbing her son around his waist and spinning him in the air as he made a 'tackle' might be exactly what she wanted. Greyson looked so happy. She didn't have to be able to hear him to know that he'd sound happy, too. She could see his giggles.

"I know you told me there was nothing between you and Andrew, but maybe you should reconsider."

Morgan's gaze shot to her grandmother's

and she sighed. "Greyson sure thinks he hung the moon."

"And you?"

"Get that look off your face, Grammy," she warned. "Regardless of what I think of Andrew, neither of us is looking for a relationship."

"Too bad because we think you make a wonderful couple."

Morgan frowned. "You've talked to Grampy about me and Andrew?"

"Not Grampy. He'd say I should mind my own business," Grammy rolled her eyes. "I meant me and the Butterflies."

Well, that was no surprise.

"Ruby wasn't that subtle this morning in church when she kept turning around and smiling at us, was she?"

Grammy Claudia laughed. "No, but Butterflies can be subtle when needed."

"They've been known to stampede when they feel it's needed, as well."

Grammy laughed. "Our reputation precedes us, I see."

"Mommy!"

Panic hit when she heard Greyson yelling for her as he rushed into the kitchen and came to a halt a few feet from her. As soon as she saw his face and uninjured body, she calmed. That was excited rushing, not the result of fear or injury. It dropped her into the same panic either way, though, until she was able to confirm that nothing was wrong.

"What are the rules about running indoors?" she asked.

His face scrunched up and he shot his great-grandmother an apologetic look. "Sorry, Grammy, but Mommy, can I sit on Andrew's motorcycle?"

Morgan's eyes widened. "Sit on it?"

"He doesn't have an extra helmet with him so he said he wouldn't take me for a ride even if you said yes."

Morgan's stomach twisted into a pretzel. She was glad Andrew had laid down the law on that point—but the fact that he'd had to still scared her, because it meant Greyson had been pushing it. "You asked Andrew to take you for a ride?"

Face glowing with excitement, Greyson nodded. "He said Big Bertha is a moody girl"—he giggled as if that was the funniest thing he'd ever heard—"but that I could sit on her if I promised to follow the rules."

"What are the rules?" she gulped.

"That I can only touch what he says I can touch."

"That's a good rule." But Morgan still wanted to say no.

Andrew walked into the kitchen. His eyes immediately sought hers.

She frowned. "Already tempting my son over to the wild side, I hear."

Janice Lynn

"I won't be wild, Mommy," Greyson promised.

Greyson's assurance plagued her conscience. She didn't want him on a motorcycle. She wanted to keep him safe and didn't that mean saying no to some things that he wanted if she felt the risks were too high? But she also didn't want to let her hang-ups hamper his life and what would it hurt to let him sit on the bike so long as it wasn't running?

"I'll stay right with him, Morgan," Andrew assured her. "What could happen?"

A few dozen possibilities raced through her mind, but she kept them to herself as she worried she was quickly becoming a fuddy-duddy in her child's eyes. How did a good parent balance keeping their child safe and allowing them to spread their wings? This parenting thing wasn't easy.

"The engine will be off the entire time?"

Andrew nodded and Greyson let out a disappointed grunt.

She knelt to her son's level. "Do everything Andrew tells you, okay?"

Greyson nodded and took off toward the door, probably for fear she'd change her mind if he stuck around. Just as he reached the door, he paused, turned to her and grinned. "Thanks, Mommy."

Her heart melted. Reality was, she had to loosen her reins. She'd boxed him in too

210

much and that had played into his isolation. She had to let him be a kid, even if it put all her Momma worries on high alert.

Rising, her gaze met Andrew's and she wondered what he was still doing there when her son had taken off.

"If you promised to follow the rules, you can have a turn on Big Bertha, too," he offered.

Morgan snorted. "As tempting as that is, I'll pass."

He chuckled. "Are you are going to come outside to watch while Greyson sits on the bike?"

She started to say no as she wasn't sure she could watch without getting worried and maybe overreacting, but the twitching of his lips had her reconsidering. She was not a fuddy-duddy. She was positive and happy. "Yes. I'll grab my jacket."

Motorcycles were dangerous. Now, being close to the bike, opposite of the side Andrew stood on, Morgan felt daunted by the motorcycle he called by name.

Greyson clearly didn't, though. He looked ecstatic as he straddled the bike and asked Andrew question after question about how it worked. Watching his delighted expressions was like a flashback to Trey.

Morgan's stomach twisted tighter.

Andrew answered each of Greyson's

question with patience and genuine enthusiasm, seeming to enjoy showing off his bike.

"When I grow up, I'm going to be a firefighter and have a Big Bertha," Greyson announced.

He's only five, Morgan reminded herself. Lots of time to reconsider major life decisions.

Andrew scratched his head. "That's all right if that's what you want, but when you get your own bike, I imagine you'll want to pick your own name."

Moving his hands in a revving the engine motion over the handlebars, Greyson made some vroom noises, then said, "I'll name mine Andrew after you."

Surprise flashed across Andrew's face, and then he grinned. "Hey, I like that. Never had anyone name their motorcycle after me."

"I might call it Andy for short."

Andrew tugged on Greyson's hat. "Just so long as you don't call me Andy for short."

"What's wrong with Andy?" Morgan asked.

"Nothing," he answered. "If you're six."

"I'll be six on my next birthday."

"When's that?" Andrew asked.

Greyson told him. "I want a firefighter-themed birthday party."

"Maybe I can bring the fire truck by for your friends to see at your party."

"Wow. That would be great."

The two chatted back and forth, talking about the birthday party, the motorcycle, and a zillion other things.

"I want to sit on Bertha," Morgan said.

Two wide sets of male eyes turned to her.

"What?"

Goodness. What had she done? She didn't want to sit on the motorcycle. Why had she said she did?

"You want to sit on my motorcycle?" Andrew asked.

"It's not scary, Mommy," Greyson said, climbing down and patting the leather seat.

It had been a long time since she'd sat on a motorcycle, but she had ridden one before. With Trey.

Memories assailing her, she straddled the motorcycle and wrapped her fingers around the handlebars. There. She'd done it. She'd conquered a fear. No, it wasn't running, but she'd gotten on the bike. That counted.

"I...can I start it?"

Greyson's eyes were huge. Andrew's, too.

"Uh, sure." Andrew glanced at Greyson. "Can I get you to watch from the porch, bud? Bertha is loud."

Greyson looked a little disappointed but didn't argue. Probably because he thought his mom had flipped her lid.

He was right. No way would she be on this motorcycle otherwise.

"Is it okay if I sit with you?" Andrew asked, eyeing her curiously.

She didn't blame him for being worried, so she nodded.

When he was behind her, he started explaining how the bike worked—lessons Trey had already given her years ago. Morgan grinned at the prospect of surprising Andrew, then stood up and kick-started the bike. It roared to life. Sitting down, she clenched the handlebars with clammy hands.

Andrew leaned in close to her ear. "You've done this before."

"Yes."

"You're full of surprises, aren't you? You want to take her for a spin?" he asked.

Greyson would never forgive her if she went for a ride when he wasn't allowed to. But she really didn't want to go for a ride. She'd just needed to sit on the bike to prove to herself that she could.

She shook her head. "I just want to sit here," she yelled back over the noise and then did just that, sitting on the bike, her eyes closed as she let memories assail her. Once upon a time, she'd loved riding behind Trey on his street bike. A single tear ran down her cheek, but she didn't swat it away, just gripped the handlebar tighter. She'd done it. She'd gotten on the motorcycle, started it, felt the motor purr beneath her.

Andrew sat behind her. His body was warm against her back as he blocked the wind. He kept his hands on his thighs, letting her grip the handlebars alone.

Taking a deep breath, she turned off the engine, then dismounted the bike.

"Thank you. I needed that."

Andrew walked into the quilt shop where a second, smaller sew-in was going on in full force. He'd heard from Cole that they hoped to finish up several more quilts, and if they managed to hit their target, they'd be able to award Quilts of Valor to every eligible resident at Pine Hill Assisted Living.

It was a lofty goal, but the Butterflies, Sophie, Sarah, and Morgan were a determined group, and they still had a few weeks prior to the scheduled presentation date. Sophie even put Cole to work maneuvering a joystick that apparently ran one of the quilting machines. His friend nodded in his direction, but kept his eyes glued on the screen that showed the pattern he was to follow. Andrew's gaze lingered on Morgan. He'd not seen her since the lunch at her grandparents nine days ago.

"I've found sleigh-pulling reindeer," Andrew announced.

Several people responded with "That's wonderful!" and "That's great!"

"There's a catch," he admitted, coming over to where his grandmother and Rosie were laying out completed quilt blocks.

"Isn't there always?" Maybelle asked, waiting expectantly for him to elaborate. "No, put that one up there," she instructed, pointing for a block to be moved to another section of the quilt.

As his grandmother moved the square, Andrew told them, "Someone will have to go pick them up."

They all stopped what they were doing to look at him.

"Pick them up?" his grandma asked.

"Where are they?" Maybelle wanted to know.

"Can't we just have them delivered?" Rosie wondered.

"East Kentucky and no, having them delivered isn't an option."

"In the mountains?" Morgan asked, keeping her gaze averted from his as she straightened a stack of material.

Andrew nodded. "Their owner used to run a Christmas village in a resort town. They took this winter off for health reasons and decided to permanently retire."

"He has reindeer?" Cole asked, having

stopped the quilting machine to come over to join the group.

"Eight of them."

"Just eight? What about Rudolph?" Rosie asked, her lower lip going out in a pout.

"No Rudolph. Sorry."

Rosie sighed. "Well, I guess the other eight will do."

"I guess they will have to do," Maybelle huffed, giving her friend a look that implied she wasn't all there.

"Mr. Harvey has said I can borrow his truck and horse trailer to go get them."

"Oh, that's wonderful, Andrew!" his grandmother said. "You've thought of everything."

Maybelle eyed him suspiciously. "Why do I feel there's another catch?"

"The owner has another offer to buy the deer. If I don't pick them up this weekend, he'll sell to them to the other buyer come Monday morning."

"Sell them?" Rosie's eyes widened. "I'm buying the reindeer rather than hiring them? What am I going to do with eight reindeer once my wedding is over?"

"You wanted reindeer, so I found reindeer." Andrew shrugged. "But Mr. Harvey has agreed to take care of them at least until after the wedding. If they're well-behaved, he's willing to add reindeer to his Christmas activities at the farm and take them off your hands permanently. Everything hinges on whether or not they're as great as the owner assures me they are."

"Looks as if you're buying eight reindeer," Maybelle told Rosie, sounding highly amused.

"Rosie's reindeers," she contemplated. "that does have a nice ring to it. "Maybe I'll keep them."

"No," the other women all said at once, then looked at each other and laughed.

"Okay, fine. I was never good with pets anyway." Rosie clasped her hands together. "Still, this is wonderful. Thank you, Andrew." She batted her heavily mascaraed lashes at him, then stretched up on her tippy toes and kissed his cheek. "This will be perfect."

"Not sure I'd say perfect," Andrew admitted, "especially when we haven't actually seen the reindeer, but they look great in the pictures."

Her eyes lit up. "You have pictures?"

"Show us," Maybelle ordered.

Andrew got out his phone and pulled up the photos the man had texted him.

"Oh, they're so cute," Rosie cooed. "Maybe I do want to keep them. Does anyone know what reindeer eat?"

"They look just like in the movies," his grandma mused.

"That one has a mischievous gleam in

his eyes," Maybelle pointed out. "You're sure they're people friendly?"

Andrew frowned at the picture, trying to see the gleam and failing to do so. "I'm not sure of anything except that if you want reindeer, then I need to head to the mountains Saturday morning."

"Saturday," Cole mused, running his hand along his clean-shaven jaw. "I won't be able to go with you." Sophie gave him an odd look and he added, "I have someone coming out to the farm to see about digging a new well."

"That's a long drive to make by yourself," Grandma Ruby pointed out.

"I'll be fine," Andrew assured her. Did they really think he couldn't drive a few hours on his own?

"Still, you'll be tired if we get many calls Friday night," Cole said. "You shouldn't make the trip alone."

Everyone looked around at each other, then all eyes landed on Morgan.

"You're off work Saturday, Morgan," Claudia pointed out. "You could go."

Morgan didn't look totally opposed, but she wasn't jumping at the chance, either. Andrew had thought they'd ended on good terms when he'd left her grandparents, but her eyes filled with hesitancy. "Oh, I...What about Greyson?"

"He could go with us," Andrew offered,

liking the idea. "He'd get a kick out of going on a Rosie Reindeer Run." He grinned at his own word play. "Plus, Greyson told me that he's never seen snow."

"I...it'll snow here before winter is over."

"Probably," he agreed. "But I think Little Man would enjoy the trip."

Morgan snorted. "You've obviously never ridden in a car several hours with a five-year-old."

Andrew shrugged. "You're right. I haven't. But I'm willing to give it a go. What do you say, Morgan? Will you go with me to pick up Rosie's reindeer, save Rosie's wedding, and show Greyson his first snow?"

"Say yes, Morgan," Rosie encouraged. "Getting these reindeer for my wedding means so much to me."

Morgan eyed Rosie suspiciously, then glanced around at everyone looking at her and apparently realized they weren't going to give her any peace if she said no. She took a deep breath, then nodded. "Sure. Greyson and I will go with Andrew to get the reindeer for your wedding."

"Yay!" Rosie cheered. "I'm going to have reindeer at my wedding."

"Only you would want them," Claudia said, shaking her head.

"That makes me think of that reindeer song," his grandma giggled.

Maybelle's lips twitched, then she started singing, "Rosie got run over by a reindeer, walking down the aisle on Christmas Eve." Several hands slapped over mouths to hide laughter, including Andrew's. "Now you can say that weddings don't have reindeer, but as for me and the Butterflies, we believe."

To Morgan's surprise, Greyson handled the trip to the mountains like a champ. Not that he was usually a bad traveler, but he was five, and being inside Mr. Harvey's truck for several hours at a time didn't exactly offer a plethora of entertainment options.

She should have known that Andrew was all the entertainment Greyson needed. Currently, the duo was belting out a country song at the top of their lungs.

"Come on, Morgan," Andrew said. "Sing with us."

"I don't sing."

"Don't or can't?"

"She can sing," Greyson piped up, sounding proud. "She sings to me when I can't sleep."

"Oh?" Andrew cut his gaze toward her for a brief second. "Tell me more. What does she sing?"

"Lately? Christmas songs," she admitted.

"Know any Elvis?" Andrew asked.

"Elvis Christmas songs? Like the ones you played at the nursing home?" He'd had a great voice and the residents had loved singing along.

Andrew nodded. "Elvis is Grandma Ruby's favorite. My whole life, she always plays a Christmas album and we sing along to it while decorating for the holiday. She still listens to that old thirty-three speed despite the fact that I set her up to just tell her virtual player to play her music for her."

"If you're wanting to sing Elvis, I could find some on my phone," Morgan offered, smiling and thinking part of her understood why Ruby played her album.

"Really?" he grinned. "That would be awesome. Elvis is my man."

"Who's Elvis?" Greyson piped up from the truck's back seat.

Morgan and Andrew exchanged a quick look.

"Hurry and find that music," Andrew ordered. "The kid doesn't know who the King of Rock and Roll is, and we're about to enlighten him."

"Snow!" Greyson exclaimed, staring out the window of the truck as they drove up the mountain. Big puffs of white danced around them.

"Should we pull over so you can touch it?"

Morgan glanced toward Andrew, amazed that he'd be willing to pull the truck and trailer over to allow Greyson to do something as simple as touch snow. The man's patience with her son was epic.

His patience with her was pretty epic, too.

Because no matter how she wanted to hold out on having feelings for him, no matter how much she knew she shouldn't... she did. Every moment spent with him saw those feelings blossoming into something that was getting more and more difficult to label as just friendship.

How could she not fall for him when he'd belted out Elvis at the top of his lungs, even after listening to the same song several times so Greyson could learn the words to sing along, too? She'd laughed until tears ran down her cheeks when Andrew had howled on "Hound Dog" and Greyson kept trying to, as well.

"I don't think we need to stop now," she told Andrew. "We're only about twenty minutes from the Christmas Village. While you check over the reindeer, Greyson and I can play in the snow." Though what he'd be checking for, she didn't know. Maybe they should have brought a veterinarian with them to be sure they weren't getting dud reindeer?

"I want to see the reindeer, too," her son said from the back seat.

"We should have plenty of time for you to do both," Andrew said. "But your mom is right. We're close enough that it doesn't make logical sense to stop prior to getting there."

Logical sense. Because she was a logical kind of girl. One who didn't do silly things like pull over on the side of the road to play in the snow. Ugh. She was back to being a fuddy-duddy.

"Do you think there will be enough snow for us to build a snowman?" Greyson asked, leaning toward the window as far as his car seat would allow.

Not taking his eyes off the road, Andrew shrugged. "There might be. When I talked to Frank, the owner, earlier, he said they had a light snow and were expecting more. Main thing is for us to be off the mountain before dark, since I'm pulling the trailer."

Morgan glanced toward him. She hadn't really thought about the difficulty of driving with the long trailer they were hauling. After all, Andrew was used to driving the fire engine, and he seemed to be a pro at handling the truck and trailer. "Would it be dangerous if we're not?"

He shook his head. "We'll be fine. They're not expecting that much snow and the owner assured me the roads are good. But I don't want to take any chances once we're off the main highway, either. I'm hauling precious cargo."

"Yeah, finding more reindeer might be impossible."

"I meant you and Greyson."

"Oh." Why did his comment fill her with warmth? "Thank you."

She'd lived on military bases all over, so snow didn't bother her. Keeping Greyson safe did, though.

"It sure is beautiful, isn't it?" she mused, looking out her window at the gorgeous snowy mountains in the distance. White clung to the trees, coating them with a wintery layer.

"I love snow," Greyson said from the back.

"Just wait until you taste it."

"What?" Morgan asked, smiling at Andrew.

"Don't tell me you've never stuck out your tongue to catch a snowflake," he said, grinning as he kept his eyes on the road.

"Never that I was old enough to remember," she admitted.

"We'll change that today."

"I want to taste a snowflake," Greyson announced.

225

"Absolutely," Andrew said. "Because it doesn't look as if this is going to let up anytime soon."

It wasn't snowing hard, just a flurry of big fat snowflakes hitting the windshield one after another to instantly melt away.

"There's the sign for the Christmas Village," Morgan said, pointing. "This must be our turn."

Within minutes they'd reached the picturesque Christmas Village's entrance.

"Frank said to pull around to the back of the main buildings rather than stopping at the parking area," Andrew told them as he drove past the parking sign.

When they'd parked, Andrew grabbed his jacket. Morgan twisted to look back at Greyson. He was already unbuckling his car seat strap.

"Put on your coat," she reminded him as she put on hers, then donned her scarf, gloves, and hat. Andrew opened her truck door, surprising her.

It had been a long time since a man had opened a door for her. Trey had loved her, was good to her, but he hadn't been the type to open doors or pull out chairs or that kind of thing. Andrew's gesture caught her completely off-guard.

"You didn't have to do that," she told him, feeling self-conscious.

226

"You trying to get me in trouble with my grandma?"

Morgan smiled. "Couldn't have that."

"Besides, my buddy needs to learn how to treat a lady."

Greyson's eyes grew big. "I do?"

"Someday you might have a girlfriend," Andrew told him as he took Greyson's hand to help him jump down from the truck.

"I already have one," Greyson announced.

"You do?" she asked, trying not to let her surprise, and horror, show.

"Way to go," Andrew said, fist-bumping with Greyson.

"Is my Mommy your girlfriend?"

Morgan's breath caught. No, she wanted to say, because she wasn't. She wasn't interested in dating at all, and he didn't date single moms. She'd never even meant for them to become friends.

Andrew's gaze cut her way, searched hers for a moment, then his expression unreadable, he answered her son, "My grandma taught me to open the door for all ladies, not just my girlfriend. It's a good habit for a man to get into. Remember that."

Although part of Morgan was disappointed at the way he'd dodged the question, her heart filled with gratitude that he was teaching her son such great habits. Just as she was about to comment on his good manners, Andrew stuck out his tongue.

He caught a drifting downward snowflake. "Mmm."

Greyson's tongue immediately went out. He bobbed his head until a snowflake fell onto his tongue.

"Mmmm," he said, mimicking Andrew. Then he started moving around, trying to catch more. Morgan and Andrew watched a few seconds, and then he turned to her.

"Come on, Morgan. It's your turn."

"You should, Mommy," Greyson encouraged. "They're good."

Stick her tongue out and dance around in the snow?

"Why not?" She stuck out her tongue and immediately a big wet snowflake touched it, instantly melting, and making her mouth water and her insides tingle with a youthful happiness.

"Attagirl."

Her gaze met Andrew's and the twinkle in his eyes caused funny feelings in her chest, much more so than tasting a snowflake. Crazy funny feelings as if her insides were floating like the snow falling around them.

"Howdy, folks." A man in his late sixties came over to the truck. "I'm Frank. Y'all here about my reindeer?"

A few minutes later, Morgan had to

admit that Andrew had done a fantastic job finding the reindeer. No surprise there. He seemed to be fantastic at a lot of things.

"This one is my favorite," Greyson said, feeding the reindeer a carrot. "He is so cute with his fuzzy white chin."

The animal in question did have a thicker tuft of white fur at his chin than the other seven deer and had taken an instant liking to Greyson. Maybe he'd known Frank would be handing over some goodies to feed them.

"Does he have a name?" Greyson asked the older man who was scratching the reindeer's neck as if he were a big pet. He sure seemed to be as he paused in eating the carrot to rub his face up against Frank.

"Ralphie."

Greyson's brows veed. "Ralphie the Reindeer? That's a funny name."

"He was brought here when he was a little thing after his mother was killed. I bottle-fed him until he was old enough to wean." Frank's face took on a sad expression. "I'm going to miss him. I'll miss them all, but especially him."

"You can come visit them," Greyson assured him. "Pine Hill isn't that far."

"Far enough," Frank said. "I might just take you up on that. Now, you folks want to come inside for a bite of lunch before we load these guys up for their trip to their new home?"

"Lunch sounds wonderful," Andrew said from where he leaned against the barn stall door, "But, what we'd really like is a chance for this little guy to build his first snowman."

Frank smiled. "I've been thinking the yard sure could use a snowman. How about I have my wife rustle up a hat and scarf?"

"Can I have an extra carrot for the nose? Snowmen need carrot noses," Greyson said just as Ralphie took the last bit of carrot from his fingers.

"There's plenty," Frank promised.

Greyson told Ralphie bye and, walking between them, clasped Morgan and Andrew's hands, swinging them happily back and forth as they followed Frank to his home.

Morgan was struck with the thought that they looked like a family.

A happy one.

Because she was happy. Happy and positive, that was her.

Scared, too, but today was too wonderful to let something like fear make her come to her senses.

Chapter Ten

"*T*HAT'S THE BEST SNOWMAN EVER," Greyson exclaimed, choosing a scarf from the box of items Frank and his wife had brought them for the finishing touches.

"I admit, he's looking pretty awesome," Andrew said.

The snow was just right, and the three of them had each crafted a snowball. Andrew's was the base, Morgan's the middle, and Greyson's was the head.

Andrew packed on more snow to round out his bottom piece while Greyson and Morgan dug through the box, looking for something to use as eyes.

At least, that's what he thought they were doing up until a thud hit his back.

Fully prepared to receive an onslaught as he turned, he said, "Seriously?"

To which Greyson and Morgan replied by both launching more snowballs at him.

"Two against one?" he asked, bending down to make a snowball.

"The snowman's on your team," Morgan pointed out. "Two against two."

Andrew laughed. "Unless I'm supposed to use him as ammunition, I'm not sure he's going to be much help."

"You wouldn't," Morgan protested.

She was right. He wouldn't. But he would use the snowman as a shield. Ducking behind him, he made another snowball and launched it toward Morgan.

As she was standing out in the open, it hit her square in the chest.

"Ooh," she said, eyes widening at the impact. "Nice shot."

Greyson ducked behind her and lobbed a couple of snowballs at Andrew that fell short. Then they both bent to gather more snow.

Andrew took aim at Greyson's boots and watched as snow splattered across them.

"He got me!" Greyson said, laughing as he threw more snow Andrew's way.

For several minutes they pummeled

snowball after snowball his way, laughing and taunting and teasing.

Apparently hitting someone with snow released happiness because with each snowball that struck him, Greyson and Morgan did a little happy dance, laughing, and Andrew found himself setting up shots for them—making himself a more vulnerable target. Hearing mother and son laugh together was addictive and he wanted more. And more.

He launched enough back as to keep them on their toes, never throwing hard as he just wanted the snow to reach them, not hurt them.

"You go that way and I'll go this way," he heard Greyson tell his mom as they flanked him.

Andrew laughed and shielded his face as they moved closer.

Greyson wrapped his arms around his waist. "Gotcha!"

Andrew's gaze cut to Morgan's smiling face. Her nose and cheeks were pink from the cold, but he'd never seen her so relaxed, so happy. "What about you? You gonna get me, too?"

"If you insist." Then she pelted him with a large snowball that caught him on the forehead. At impact, the snowball burst apart and sent snow flying. He sputtered as it got in his mouth.

"Oh, goodness. I didn't mean to hit you in the face." Morgan came rushing to him. "Are you okay?"

"I may have a concussion," he moaned, keeping his hands hidden so she hopefully wouldn't notice the snow he held.

"Oh, Andrew, I'm sorry. Let me check you," she said, kicking into nurse mode. "Let me look into your eyes."

"Ah, I knew you really liked me."

"Be serious. I could have hurt you."

"You could have," he agreed. But she hadn't. Not in the slightest. "Think you're going to have to drive the trailer home."

Her eyes widened. "Andrew, I don't think I can drive the truck with that huge trailer attached."

"We may be stuck here then."

"Yay!" Greyson cheered. "I love it here and never want to leave."

Morgan's gaze went from his to Greyson's. When it returned to his, he grinned and as he saw enlightenment dawn, he yelled, "Now!"

Giggling and immediately changing sides, Greyson threw handfuls of snow at her. But it was the handful of snow that Andrew palmed her face with that had her eyes go wide.

"Oh, that's cold!" she declared then took off to hide behind the snowman as he and Greyson teamed up, getting snowballs in where they could when she'd jump out from behind the snowman. Greyson had a blast.

Based on her laughter, so did Morgan.

"We brought out the carrot if you want it for the snowman's nose," Frank said, as he and his wife joined them, admiring the snowman.

"Can I feed Ralphie another one, too?" Greyson asked.

"Absolutely. It'll make loading the reindeer much easier if we bribe them with carrots," Frank said.

His wife added, "Why don't y'all come in and warm by the fire first? Then y'all can get Frank's babies loaded."

Andrew glanced toward Morgan to see what she wanted to do. He was in no hurry so long as they got off the mountain by dark.

"That would be great," Morgan said.

"You have such a lovely family. Before we go in, would you like a photo by your snowman?"

"I...we aren't a family," Morgan corrected the woman. "Just friends."

"Good friends, and we'd love a photo," Andrew added as the woman's face fell at her faux pas. "Like I mentioned to your husband, this guy here is Greyson's first snowman. The moment definitely needs to be captured forever."

Not that he'd need the picture to remember.

He'd never forget this day with Morgan and her son.

A soft snore from the back of the truck sounded over the music Morgan and Andrew listened to on low. Morgan twisted in her seat and smiled at where Greyson's eyes were closed. He looked so peaceful.

And happy.

Straightening, she leaned back against the headrest. "He's out like a light. I doubt he'll wake up until we get back to Pine Hill."

Andrew glanced in the rearview mirror at the sleeping boy. "I'd say not. He burned a lot of energy playing in the snow and helping me round up reindeer."

She laughed. "You make it sound as if you had to work to get them into the trailer. They were sweethearts."

Greyson had helped, but only until they got near the trailer, then Andrew and Frank had handled loading the animals themselves in case the animals got spooked. Morgan hadn't even had to remind Andrew to keep Greyson safe.

Greyson had loved petting the reindeer and feeding them. She imagined this would be one of those days that would always stand out in his memory. It wasn't every day a five-year-old got to pick up eight reindeer to pull a sleigh on Christmas Eve. Today had been a bit magical, almost as if they'd travelled to the North Pole and were picking up Santa's real steeds. The fluffs of sparkly white snow dancing in the air had just added to the magic.

And so had the man driving the truck.

Why did he have to be so wonderful?

Not that she didn't appreciate wonderful, but she didn't want wonderful for herself. She didn't want anything. Especially not with the kind of wonderful man who was into motorcycle riding, airplane jumping, and running into burning buildings. Who also had a big heart, a ton of patience, and could be a perfect gentleman when he wanted to be. John from the assisted living center would be pleased to hear that Greyson had gotten to spend the day with such a great role model.

"They do seem tame, and were quite friendly, but I worried that they might startle and stampede when we were trying to load them, that's why I wanted Greyson safely behind the gate with you," Andrew admitted. "Just in case."

Morgan had known exactly what he was doing when he'd asked Greyson to handle the important job of making sure the reindeer didn't get out the gate or near his mom. Thinking he was protecting her, Greyson had been all serious expression as he'd complied and told her to stay back.

"I appreciated that," Morgan said. "And, I'll also grant that the reindeer were great until you and Frank were loading them. Up until then, they didn't seem to understand what was happening." If reindeer could look sad, those eight had as they'd peered out through the slots in the trailer. Frank had seemed a bit heartbroken when he'd said goodbye to them, as well. "I hope they'll be happy at Harvey Farms."

"The Harveys are good people, so I suspect they will. Frank said the reindeer were all rescues. They grew up at the village so they have always been around crowds. He thinks they've been missing the attention they were used to getting when visitors were coming through his place. Once they adjust to the change of scenery, they should be fine."

"I hope so. They came across as nothing more than big pets. I do think Rosie is going to love them for her wedding."

"Maybe." Andrew sighed, then expelled a long breath. "Or she may decide to call the whole wedding off again since we weren't able to come up with a Rudolph. Or maybe she'll come up with some other reason to delay again."

Morgan cut her gaze to his profile silhouetted in the truck's cab. "I don't understand why she'd do that. It's obvious she loves Lou and I've never seen a man look at a woman with more love than when Lou's gaze is on Rosie. He adores her."

"I asked him about it once. He told me it was the blue hair that had him head over heels."

"You're joking," Morgan said, laughing.

Andrew grinned. "You're right. I am."

Morgan shook her head. "That was bad."

"Maybe," he agreed. "But it made you smile."

That it had.

"I'd imagine you'd understand Rosie's runaway bride antics more than most." His tone had grown serious and Morgan wished the glowing dashboard lights were brighter so she could better read his expression.

"Why?"

He tapped his fingers along the steering wheel. "Rosie's been married three times and lost all three husbands to various illnesses. It's only natural she's hesitant to commit again."

Morgan hadn't realized. She couldn't imagine losing another husband, much less two more, and then risk a fourth. No wonder Rosie kept finding reasons to postpone her wedding.

His gaze glued to the road and his voice as gentle and serious as she'd ever heard, Andrew said, "Risking one's heart after suffering such a great loss can't be easy. Lou knows that. It's why he continues to be patient with her no matter what outlandish reason she comes up with for putting off their big day yet again."

Tears prickled Morgan's eyes. She wasn't sure if they were for Rosie, who'd risked and lost her heart three times, or if they were for herself, who'd lost Trey when they were just beginning their life together.

She may have made a noise. She'd never be quite sure what prompted Andrew's hand to leave the steering wheel and clasp hers, but even as his gaze remained glued to the road, the fingers of his right intertwined with hers, enveloping her hand within his bigger one.

Strong, warm, firm, and yet gentle.

Heart pounding, Morgan stared at their joined hands in the dim glow of the truck's dashboard lights.

Could he feel the tremble in her fingers?

The tremble in her body?

The fear in her heart?

Yeah, risking one's heart after a great loss definitely wasn't easy even when that heart seemed—in spite of everything—so very eager to fall.

"You're humming again."

"Maybe," Morgan admitted, handing over the medicine cup to John as he scooted up a little further in his hospital bed.

Curling his nose at the cup, he took it then asked, "Saw your firefighter feller this weekend, did you?"

Morgan's breath caught at the mention of Andrew. Taking the empty cup from John, she tossed it into the trash bin. "He didn't come to church again, if that's what you're asking."

On Saturday, Andrew had carried Greyson into the house and helped her get him into bed. Her son had barely stirred so he'd not gotten a chance to ask Andrew to join them again. But as she'd been changing Greyson out of his clothes and into his pajamas, Andrew had volunteered that he had to be at the fire hall the following morning so he wouldn't be at church. Had that meant he would have come if he'd not been scheduled to work?

"Nope. That's not what I meant. I asked if you saw him."

John's hip might be broken, but his brain worked just fine.

"Greyson and I went with Andrew

241

to East Kentucky to pick up reindeer for Rosie's wedding," she admitted, wondering at the warmth that she could feel radiating from her face.

"Reindeer for her wedding?" John asked, then shook his head. "Nope. I don't want to know. That one has always been a little off her rocker."

"It's probably what I love best about her, though," Morgan admitted. "And Lou doesn't seem to mind her off-her-rocker-ness."

Andrew's comment about Rosie's blue hair driving Lou crazy played through her mind.

"I don't think thoughts of Rosie just caused that smile on your face," John accused as he lay back and eyed her.

"Actually, I really was thinking of Rosie." John wasn't buying it.

"I was remembering how happy she was about Andrew picking up the reindeer for her. She couldn't go on enough about him at church yesterday."

Of course, all the Butterflies had been spouting off wonderful things about Andrew. Did they think she didn't know how great he was? Him being wonderful wasn't the problem.

Well, it was the problem, in the sense that it made it impossible not to be attracted to him.

"A more accurate answer would've been

that you were imagining Andrew," John corrected her.

"Maybe," she admitted, surprising even herself with her honesty as she wrapped a blood pressure cuff around John's left arm.

John was quiet until she'd finished taking his reading, then he asked, "So what's the problem?"

Had the military trained him in mind reading, or what?

"I loved my husband."

"I never thought you didn't."

Morgan paused next to the valiant man's bed, taking in his Korean War Veteran's hat that he was rarely without, then heard herself say, "He died in a mountain climbing accident. Bad weather moved in much quicker than anticipated. They should have turned back, but Trey and a couple others didn't want to stop until they reached the summit." She paused, then sucked in a deep breath. "Three from their group didn't make it. They told me Trey died while trying to rescue the other two and..."

She couldn't finish. Why had she even started? This wasn't something she talked about with anyone. Not ever.

"I'm sorry for your loss, especially at such a young age, but this old mind of mine still isn't seeing why this means that you liking Andrew is a problem."

Morgan sighed. "I'm trying to learn my

lesson about being attracted to men who are so reckless with their lives."

"Reckless?" John shook his head, studying her a moment, then adding, "Not sure recklessness has much to do with it. Sounds more to me that you're attracted to men who are willing to risk their lives to save others. It's an admirable trait."

Yeah, she supposed that was one way of looking at it. But try telling that to all the fears that kept her up at night.

"Thank you for inviting me, Sarah. I was at loose ends for the evening with Greyson gone to a slumber party until Sophie reminded me about your Christmas party."

Morgan had teetered between excitement that Greyson had made friends and fear that he'd be spending the night away from her for the first time.

"Well, Harry would rather Greyson be here, I'm sure," Sarah said, taking a pan of cookies from the oven of her gorgeous kitchen. It was filled with Christmas décor, as was the rest of Hamilton House. It seemed like every nook and cranny was bright with garland, lights, and knick-knacks of all kinds that just highlighted the beauty of the grand old Victorian bed and breakfast. Morgan particularly loved the flocked garland that wrapped around the winding staircase in the entryway.

"Had Greyson known this was where I was headed, he might have chosen playing with Harry over going to the sleepover." A time or two she'd been tempted to tell him due to her teary-eyed "my baby is growing up" moments.

"He's going to have a great time," Sophie promised her, uncovering a fruit tray she'd brought. "And so are we. Sarah and Bodie throw the best parties."

Sarah smiled. "We do like to have fun, and tonight we've got something extra special planned."

"You in here giving away our secrets?" Bodie asked, coming into the kitchen and reaching for a cookie. Cole, Ben, and Andrew were right behind him, carrying in a cooler full of drinks along with bags of chips.

Morgan's face heated even before her gaze met Andrew's. She'd not seen him since they'd picked up the reindeer the week before, but they'd talked on the phone when he'd called to let her know that he'd checked on the reindeer and that they were adjusting well.

"Hey Morgan," Ben said, smiling at her. "You make some of those delish brownies for tonight?"

"Hi Ben," she said back, her gaze staying

on Andrew. "No, those require the assistance of my helper, and he had other plans tonight."

"Other plans?" Andrew's brow arched. "Hot date with the girlfriend?"

"Bite your tongue," Morgan scolded. "He's at a slumber party."

"Good for Greyson. I'm glad he's getting to know the kids here."

"Me, too," Morgan agreed, super aware that, although conversations were going on around them, they were being watched. "He's still talking about our quick trip to the mountains to get Rosie's reindeer."

"It was a good day," he agreed, his gaze locked with hers and saying so much more than mere words.

It had been a good day. A wonderful day. And she had missed him every day since.

Oh Lord. She shouldn't miss him. John's words ran through her mind. His spin made her attraction to Andrew so much more palatable.

But no less scary.

"Andrew, Morgan has never seen Hamilton House," Sarah said. "Why don't you give her a tour?"

The corner of Andrew's mouth curved upward. "I could do that."

When they were in the hallway, away from the others, he gave a low laugh. "Obvious, aren't they?"

She pinched up her fingers. "Just a smidge."

"Do you actually want to see Hamilton House, Morgan?"

"Sure. Why not?"

He held out his hands in a showy fashion. "This is the hallway."

"Really?" she asked, pretending to be shocked. "I never would have guessed."

"I could tell that by your lost expression. I'll keep the tour simple so as not to overwhelm you."

"I appreciate that," she said as they stepped into a gorgeous bedroom as fully decorated for the holidays as any other room in the house. Wow. She loved the hand-sewn red and green Christmas quilt on the bed and couldn't resist going over to touch the soft cotton material.

"You going to tell me what I really want to know?" he asked, coming to stand by the bed.

"What's that?"

"Did you miss me?" His eyes twinkled and the corner of his mouth had inched up.

"It's not been that long," she said, her heart tapping out a crazy reindeer-on-the-roof rhythm.

"Over a week."

"That long?" she asked, hoping she sounded surprised.

She must have because Andrew laughed

and asked, "Greyson get his ornament turned in for the coloring contest?"

Morgan nodded. "He did, but I'm bummed I didn't get to see it before he turned it in."

"Once Chief, Maybelle, and the other judges go through them and pull the finalists out, they'll be hung around the fire hall. I know the names are only allowed on the backs of the pages, but if I figure out which one is his, I can snap a picture and text it to you."

"That's okay. He said it was a surprise. Anyone who wants theirs back can pick them up after the fire department's Christmas open house where the winners will be announced, so you don't have to go to any trouble."

"No trouble. I can't wait to see his 'surprise' ornament design."

"Think it'll be fire trucks and ladders?" she teased as they walked back into the hallway to go into another room.

Andrew laughed. "Maybe. Whatever he chose, it'll be awesome."

"Thank you for that."

He gave her a questioning look. "What?"

"Always being so positive where Greyson is concerned."

"That's not hard to do, Morgan. He's a great kid. You should be proud."

"I am."

He gestured for her to go through an open doorway.

"This is another suite guests can book to get into the holiday spirit. It has all the quaintness of the past, and"—he pushed the bathroom door open to reveal a gorgeous bathroom with walk-in shower and a claw foot tub—"modern conveniences."

"Nice." It was, but she couldn't resist looking at him rather than the furnishings. "You sound like one of those guys from a remodel show."

"Think I have a future career in television?"

Turning toward him, Morgan smiled. "I think you have a future doing anything you want to do, Andrew. The sky's the limit."

The laughter that had been on the tip of Andrew's tongue disappeared at Morgan's comment. A future doing anything he wanted to do.

He wanted to be a smokejumper. The need burned in his blood.

"Now it's my turn to say thank you to you," he mused. More and more he'd been considering pulling the trigger on sending in that application. If he just knew for sure that his grandparents would be okay without him…

Her brow rose. "Surely, you didn't need me to tell you that?"

"It's never a bad thing to hear someone say they believe in you."

"It would be difficult for me not to," she said, not quite meeting his eyes as she moved toward the doorway.

Her comment intrigued him and he asked, "Why is that?"

Reaching the door, she turned toward him, stared up into his eyes with her gorgeous green ones, then to his surprise her gaze lowered to his mouth. Hello. Andrew's heart drummed against his ribcage.

She swallowed, then her gaze returned to his and she rocked his world by saying, "We're here, aren't we? Friends when I certainly didn't believe we would be."

"Friends," he said, letting the word roll off his tongue. It's what he'd wanted, to be her and Greyson's friend and to make their world a better place. "I'm glad."

And yet…had he been hoping for more?

"Surprisingly, me, too." With that, she ducked into the hallway and went toward the stairs.

"Hey, Morgan, wait up!" he called, going after her and just catching sight of her ducking into a room. He was about to follow when another voice called out.

"Andrew? Is that you I hear, dear boy?"

His grandma was here? Andrew sighed. So much for showing Morgan the rest of the house and continuing their conversation.

"Hey, Grandma," he said, turning with a smile on his face. He paused as he saw four women standing at the bottom of the stairs. "And Claudia, and Maybelle, and Rosie. Hello, ladies."

Looked as if the Butterflies were out in full swarm tonight.

Hamilton House was packed. Morgan had envisioned a small gathering of friends, but Sarah had apparently invited half of Pine Hill.

It didn't seem to matter how many others were there, though, as Morgan and Andrew kept ending up next to each other all evening. There had likely been some Butterfly manipulation behind them ending up at the same dining table to eat and then finding themselves sitting on the corner of the living room fireplace hearth next to each other, but Morgan didn't mind.

She wasn't even sure that the Butterflies were responsible as she and Andrew had both seemed content to fall in together.

Because she had missed Andrew in the week since she'd seen him.

Because they were friends. Had she hoped he'd correct her and tell her they were so much more? That although he didn't date single moms, she and Greyson were the exceptions because he'd grown to care so much about them?

He did care about them. She could see it in his eyes when he looked at her and her son. What she saw there made her long to let her fears go and embrace the Christmas morning bubbliness she felt inside when she was with him.

"Better watch out, Morgan," Andrew warned, leaning in close. "You're smiling again and someone is going to assume it's because you're sitting next to me."

"We'd know the truth," she said, still smiling at him.

"You're right. We would. You like me, and I am why you're smiling."

"Because you're so goofy," she said, wondering if her eyes sparkled the way his did. She was prevented from saying anything further by Sarah clearing her throat and calling the room to attention.

Sarah and Bodie stood in the midst of the living room, looking at each other with grins on their faces.

"Bodie and I have a big announcement to make tonight," Sarah said, smiling so brightly that she looked as if she were about to burst with happiness. The few people who had still been talking immediately quieted. "As many of you know, Bodie had some difficulties transitioning back to civilian life after his military career was cut short by his injuries."

Morgan's gaze went to Bodie. She could see no external evidence of injuries, but thinking back, she recalled him walking with a slight lilt to his gait after sitting for too long.

"For some time, we've been thinking of ways we could help others who, like Bodie, struggle to make that transition," Sarah continued, taking her husband's hand.

Morgan felt a pang of envy at what the couple shared, especially when Bodie lifted her fingers to his lips and pressed a kiss there. "What my wife is trying to say is that we are officially dedicating one of the guest rooms at Hamilton House into a Bed for Vets suite. It will be free to military members returning to civilian life who need somewhere to go for a few weeks or months while they figure out their next steps."

"Oh, Sarah, that's wonderful," Sophie and several others said.

"My friend Lukas is working with Walter Reed Military Hospital to help guide the right guests our way. We want our Stars & Stripes suite to be more than a place to stay, but rather a place to heal and rediscover one's self and worth."

Morgan heard the unspoken words in what Bodie was saying. He and Sarah wanted to give to others what Pine Hill had given to him.

"Beds for Vets—what a wonderful idea and outreach program. I'm so proud of you both," Sarah's father, Pastor Smith, said.

"Agreed, but I'll admit that there for a minute I thought they were going to tell us they were pregnant," Maybelle said with a laugh. Several others chuckled with her while nodding.

But rather than join the laughter, Bodie and Sarah looked at each other and Harry let out a proud yelp.

Morgan's mouth curved into a smile, happy for the couple even before Sarah said, "Well, Bodie and I do have one other announcement to make."

Rosie gasped. "You aren't."

Sarah nodded. "We're having a baby. We've known for a while but wanted to get past the first twelve weeks before announcing. Baby Lewis is going to arrive next summer, and we couldn't be happier."

A flurry of hugs, handshakes, back slaps, and congrats took place as everyone converged on the couple.

"A baby!" Maybelle exclaimed while hugging Sarah. "Oh, how I wish your aunt was here. She'd be over the moon."

Sarah kissed Maybelle's cheek. "I know she would. I'm glad she gave me such a great example of how to love and nurture a child and left me her fellow Butterflies to see me through life's good times and bad."

Sarah's watery eyes triggered something deep inside Morgan and she couldn't help but think back on when she'd discovered she was pregnant, recalling how ecstatic Trey had been. She'd been terrified at the thought of being responsible for a new little life while still trying to juggle nursing school, but he'd seen having a baby as another great life adventure. He'd been right. Greyson was her greatest adventure.

"No worries, babe," Trey had told her, pressing his cheek to her still flat belly and looking up at her with awe. "We've got this parenting thing. Together, there's nothing we can't do, even if this little guy is a mini-me."

Greyson was Trey's mini-me in so many ways.

Emotions bubbled inside her, threatening to spill forth, probably as embarrassing tears that no one in the room would understand. How could they, when she wasn't even sure she understood them, either? She was happy for the couple, and yet their happiness had thrown her into the past. How could a person be so happy and so sad at the same time?

Perhaps sensing her inner turmoil, Andrew took her hand, but Morgan just couldn't.

Pulling free from his hold, she excused herself and went to the bathroom.

Just as she got the door lock latched, the tears began to fall.

Chapter Eleven

MUCH LATER, AFTER MOST OF the older crowd had left, Andrew and several of the guys starting picked up any party mess in the living area.

Morgan helped Sarah and Sophie in the kitchen. He suspected she'd have already left if she hadn't ridden to the party with Sophie. He'd wanted to follow her when she'd left during the hullabaloo around Bodie and Sarah's announcement, but sensed she wouldn't welcome his intrusion.

She'd shown genuine happiness for the couple at their announcement, but he supposed memories had overtaken her and she'd needed a moment to herself. When she'd returned, she'd smiled and interacted with everyone as if everything was wonderful.

But it wasn't. He sensed the difference in her, in the way she looked at him and interacted with him. Whether it was a temporary glitch or permanent, the walls were back up. Maybe he hadn't helped her nearly as much as he'd thought.

Finding a saucer and spoon someone had left sitting on a hallway table, Andrew picked it up to carry it to the kitchen. Hearing his name, he paused outside the doorway.

"I, for one, couldn't be happier about you and Andrew," Sophie said.

"Me and Andrew?" he heard Morgan say. "You make it sound as if we're a couple."

"You look and act like a couple," Sarah said.

"Just because we got thrown together while playing games doesn't mean we're a couple. He's a great person, but we're just friends."

Sarah and Sophie both laughed.

"I remember you saying something similar," Sarah said, apparently talking to Sophie.

"To be fair, we weren't anything more than friends at the time," Sophie said.

"But it wasn't long before that changed," Sarah reminded her.

"It won't be for Morgan and Andrew, either. You're perfect for each other."

"No, actually, we're not," Morgan said. "We've become friends, but he's about as wrong for me romantically as any man could possibly be."

"What?" Sophie sounded shocked. "I don't believe it."

"I know you mean well, but I lost my husband because he took unnecessary risks. The absolute last thing Greyson and I need is to become involved with a man who runs into burning buildings."

"Cole is a firefighter, too, Morgan," Sophie pointed out. "He wants to save others and is willing to give his life to do so if necessary. That makes him and Andrew heroes."

"It makes them too high risk for me, Sophie. I'm happy for you and Cole, but my heart was ripped in two when Trey died. I couldn't live with the constant worrying that I might lose someone I cared about again. How can I risk getting attached to someone who constantly puts his life on the line? Especially since it's not just me. Greyson would get his heart broken too, all over again."

Her voice broke, gutting Andrew. What was he doing with Morgan? He didn't plan to settle down for the very reasons she cited. Yet, he had been trying to warm her up to him for weeks. To what end? Because he wanted to help her transition into life in Pine

Hill? Because he'd believed he could help make her and Greyson's life better? His current job was dangerous but when he applied to Hot Shot training, then on to qualify as a smokejumper, it would be even riskier. How could he do that to her, even as just friends, knowing what she'd already been through? What Greyson had been through?

He couldn't. And it was time he stopped being so selfish, monopolizing their time just because he'd been so drawn to her and Greyson. He needed to stay away from them. They'd been through enough without his exposing them to possibly going through it again.

Glancing down at the saucer and spoon, he decided now wasn't a good time to take them to the kitchen. When he turned to walk away, he locked eyes with Cole.

His friend had apparently heard everything, too.

"Want me to take that to the kitchen?"

Grateful his friend recognized his need to stay away from Morgan, Andrew handed over the dish and utensils and headed to find Bodie and Ben.

"I'm sorry," Cole said from behind him.

Yeah, Andrew was, too, because he never should have gotten involved with Morgan and staying away from her and Greyson wasn't going to be easy.

"Cole said he can't wait to see your Christmas ornament," Sophie told Greyson as they entered the fire hall for the Fire Department's Christmas Open House. The lit-up red nose on her reindeer sweater blinked. "I know it's sure to be awesome."

"Me, too," Morgan agreed. She glanced down at her own tribute to the festivities. She was getting better at this dressing for Christmas stuff. Of course, it helped that Sophie had brought her over a box of 'extras.' The red sweater with its green Christmas tree and sequined decorations wasn't nearly as blinky as her cousin's, but Morgan felt she was making progress on her overall Christmas spirit. Lots of progress.

As was Greyson. He was so excited for the holidays. She'd wanted to give him the best Christmas ever, and that was exactly what she was going to do—even if she hadn't seen or talked to Andrew in over a week.

"They have the entries hung up on the hallway walls. Chief and the other judges have already put ribbons on the winners," Sophie said. "There aren't names on the fronts of the entries so the judging would be fair."

"Mine was really good," Greyson told them. "I'll show it to you."

Morgan smiled, so glad to see her son gaining more and more confidence. "I know you worked really hard on it."

Nodding, he looked around the fire department's decorated lobby. "Do you think Andrew will be here? I want to make sure he saw my ornament, too."

Morgan and Sophie exchanged looks.

"I can't imagine him not being at the fire department's open house," Sophie answered.

Morgan hadn't seen him since Sarah and Bodie's Christmas party. He'd acted so strange when she'd gone to tell him goodbye. He'd been guarded and hadn't looked her in the eyes, leaving her wondering if he was upset with her for pulling away from him earlier. She should have taken him aside to explain her emotional reaction to Bodie and Sarah's pregnancy announcement. She felt embarrassed now that she'd been so overwhelmed. Maybe she'd get the opportunity tonight to talk to him a moment in private so she could try to explain.

"I hope so because I miss him," Greyson announced.

Morgan missed him, too. She didn't like missing him. But she did.

As Sophie had predicted, Andrew was there, talking with Ben in the long hallway that led to the deck where the fire trucks were kept and that all offices, living areas, and the dayroom branched off from. At the sight of him, Morgan's pulse skyrocketed like Santa's sleigh jetting through the sky. Everything in her yearned to go to him.

Whether because he was on duty or just to distinguish himself as a member of the fire department, he wore uniform pants and a matching button-down uniform shirt with the fire departments logo and his name over his heart. He looked handsome, professional, and so very good to her crazy, yearning heart that had missed him so much.

"He's here!" Greyson said, tugging on Morgan's hand. "Can we go see him?"

Morgan nodded.

"I'm off to find Cole," Sophie told them. "Then we'll get with you guys so Greyson can show us his ornament picture. I can't wait to see it."

Morgan let her son lead her toward his hero. As Andrew spotted them, his gaze didn't quite meet hers and his hesitancy sent shock waves through her. Had her reaction at Sarah's bothered him that much? Surely not. But there was no denying that he no longer exuded warmth toward her, and that, well, it left her bereft. Even more so when his gaze dropped to Greyson and she saw a moment's hesitancy prior to his entire face transforming with warmth. It had been as if he'd been fighting his reaction and failed.

"Hi, Firefighter Andrew and Ben," Greyson said, sounding a bit breathless with his excitement at seeing them.

"Hey, buddy," Andrew said, tousling Greyson's hair. "How have you been?"

"Good. Did you see my ornament?"

"I..." Andrew paused, took a deep breath, then shook his head. "I wasn't on duty yesterday when the coloring sheets were hung up. There are some awesome ones, though."

"We had over three hundred entries," Ben said, obviously proud of the contest's success. "Chief says we may make it an annual event."

"That's great," Morgan said, her gaze not leaving Andrew's face. Why hadn't he made eye contact with her yet? Why wasn't he teasing her or saying anything to her? Why did it bother her so much? "Hi, Andrew."

There. She'd go first and break the ice. Then, just as soon as she had an opportunity she'd explain about what had happened at Sarah and Bodie's.

"Morgan." But he still didn't look at her, just kept his gaze on Greyson, who was talking a mile a minute telling Andrew about his classroom's Christmas party and how his 'girlfriend' Brynne had gotten his name in the gift exchange.

"She knows I'm going to be a firefighter like you and gave me a fire truck. The lights work and so does the siren." Greyson talked fast, his excitement both over the gift and seeing Andrew evident. "And, it has a ladder that goes up and down, too."

"The ladder works?" Andrew looked impressed.

"You should come by and see it. I can show you how it works. Plus, Grammy and Grampy let me open a present early. It's a puzzle of a fire truck." His face scrunched. "A giant puzzle. Like a gazillion pieces, even. We've all been working on putting it together, but it's hard. I bet you could help."

Morgan watched as Andrew's throat worked, saw the emotions playing on his face. Although he was happy to see Greyson, there was still something guarded in his interactions, and that disturbed her. He'd never held back with Greyson. Even if he'd judged her harshly for her disturbing trip down memory lane, she couldn't believe he would hold that against Greyson. Something was wrong.

His brow rose. "An early present, eh?"

"I still have a bunch under the tree. I asked mom about getting a present for you, but she said we'd have to see."

Eek. Morgan's cheeks heated.

"She said she wasn't sure what you needed, but I told her we could make you brownies with lots of candies because you liked them."

Andrew nodded. "Brownies with lots of candy are my favorite."

Greyson looked up at her with an *I told you so* look.

"But I'm good, bud," Andrew continued. "You don't need to get me anything for Christmas."

"Hey, there's Lisa," Ben said, then gave them a sheepish look. "We had so much fun at Sarah and Bodie's Christmas party we decided to give it another try. So, if you guys will excuse me…"

Andrew shook his head as Ben walked over to the pretty brunette, took her hand and kissed it. He rolled his eyes. "Dude thinks he's Casanova."

"Who is Casanova?" Greyson asked.

The corner of Andrew's mouth lifted. "A ladies' man."

"Am I a Casanova since Brynne is my girlfriend?"

Morgan's jaw dropped. "Um, no. A Casanova is more a guy who leads women on but doesn't ever commit to any of them."

Andrew's gaze cut to her, but he didn't say anything. She hadn't meant him, but she suspected that's how he'd taken her comment. She wanted to reassure him that that wasn't the case. He'd certainly not led her on, or any woman, since he told them all upfront that he wasn't interested in a long-term relationship. But she couldn't think of how to say that with Greyson listening.

"Come on, buddy. Let's go find your coloring sheet," Andrew suggested. "What are we looking for?"

"A snow globe."

"You decorated your ornament like a snow globe?" Morgan asked, her attention back to her son. "That was a brilliant idea."

"Just wait until you see it," Greyson beamed. "You're going to love it."

Andrew knew immediately which coloring sheet was Greyson's even before the boy pointed out his entry. His knees felt a little wobbly at the emotions slamming through him.

"There it is!" Greyson pointed to the wall to their right.

Morgan's eyes scanned the wall, trying to find the right sheet. When her gaze hit Greyson's, it stopped. Her lips parted. Just as Andrew had, she immediately recognized what Greyson had drawn inside the blank ornament outline on the coloring sheet.

Them. There was no mistaking them playing in the snow with a reindeer and a snowman. He'd drawn white and silver snowflakes falling around them and big smiles on their faces. Andrew had never seen a more beautiful drawing than the simplistic disproportionate stick figures. Beautiful and scary.

"It's…us," Morgan said, sounding shaken. No wonder. His insides were trembling, too. The drawing appeared to be of a family. Was that how Greyson saw them? Or had the drawing just been an innocent depiction of a happy day in the kid's life?

Andrew had been so wrong to befriend them. He hadn't made their lives better. He'd set them up to get hurt and he had to figure out how to keep that from happening.

Looking proud and obviously oblivious to his mother's reaction, Greyson nodded. "It's from when we went to get Rosie's reindeers. That's us and Ralphie and our snowman."

"It's great, kid," Andrew said to give Morgan a moment to recover from her shock. He was struggling with his own shock, too.

He felt shocked. Touched. And humbled. So very humbled by this kid.

If he'd had any doubt that he needed to stay away from them, seeing the drawing sealed the deal.

Andrew's gaze went to Morgan's. So many emotions swirled in those gorgeous green depths. Mostly what he saw was questions. She didn't understand why he'd worked so hard to stay away from them.

"My picture doesn't have a ribbon, though," Greyson pointed out, sounding disappointed.

"Doesn't matter," Andrew assured him. "You're number one in my eyes always, kid."

Which wasn't exactly a distancing comment, but it had slipped out unchecked.

Greyson grinned. "I've been missing you."

Andrew wasn't sure what to say. How was he supposed to put distance between them when all he wanted to do was take them in his arms and not let go?

"I've been missing you, too, buddy." More than Andrew cared to acknowledge. Greyson wasn't the only one too attached.

Smiling, the boy wrapped his arms around Andrew's waist. "I love you."

Stunned and moved to the core, all thoughts of distancing himself gone, Andrew gave in to the emotions within him, hugged Greyson back, and heard himself say, "I love you, too, kid."

"You okay? 'Cause you don't look so good."

Taking a sip of her Christmas punch, Morgan blinked at her cousin, Isabelle. "Um, yeah. I'm fine."

Isabelle glanced around where Morgan

stood by the snack table the fire department had set up and asked, "Where's Greyson?"

"With Sophie and Cole. He wanted to show them his ornament." Under normal circumstances, Morgan would have gone with them. This didn't feel as if it were normal circumstances. Seeing that ornament with its obvious depiction of the day they'd spent with Andrew shredded her raw insides. And then the emotional intensity ratcheted up even further when she watched her son throw his arms around Andrew and declare his love for him.

Greyson had meant what he'd said. He did love the firefighter.

Which had Morgan asking herself how she felt about him and why it bothered her so much that he'd been standoffish, why he hadn't met her eyes earlier, why she could feel the difference in his interactions even with Greyson?

"Aunt Claudia and Uncle George are on their way. They were a bit nervous as Annabelle got her license and is driving them," Isabelle continued, then frowning at Morgan, her blue eyes narrowed. "Are you sure you're feeling okay?"

"I...yeah, just a little shaken up." She took a deep breath, then needing to give voice to the sentiments overwhelming her, she gave a tight smile. "At Sarah and Bodie's, I got emotional during their pregnancy announcement and pulled away from Andrew. He's not acted the same towards me since then."

Isabelle touched Morgan's arm. "I'm sorry. I can't imagine your pain at Trey's death."

Morgan closed her eyes, nodded, then took a deep breath. "Greyson's ornament has me, him, and Andrew drawn on it. I should have known something was up when he wouldn't let me see it, saying it was a surprise, but it still caught me off guard."

Isabelle's lips formed an O. "I take it that you aren't happy about it?"

Taking a deep breath, Morgan shrugged. "I...I'm not sure. I mean, it's not what I expected." Not that she knew what she'd expected. Maybe something more along the lines of what the other kids had drawn with more traditional Christmas colors and ornament patterns. "We had a great time that day, so I shouldn't be surprised that it stood out in Greyson's mind."

"And yours?" Isabelle guessed.

Meeting her cousin's blue eyes, Morgan nodded. "Am I crazy?"

Isabelle snorted. "Remember who you're talking to. I think anyone who falls in love is crazy. I'm never doing anything that insane, and I'm stunned you'd even consider it again. But ask my sister"—Isabelle gestured to Sophie, Cole, and Greyson, who were heading back toward them—"and she'll

271

tell you falling in love is the most wonderful thing in the world. For her, maybe she's right. I won't deny that it's made her happy. In fact, she continuously bubbles with happiness. But it isn't for me."

Morgan eyed her cousin curiously, wondering what had Isabelle so anti-romance. "You don't want to bubble over with happiness?"

"Falling in love isn't all happy bubbles. Not for my mom and not for you. I do just fine on my own, with my family and my quilt shop, and I don't need a man messing with my life," Isabelle pointed out, then smiled at Greyson as the trio stepped up next to them. "Please don't tell me I missed the viewing by the artist, because I'm super excited to see your coloring sheet."

Greyson grinned at her, then glanced up at Sophie and Cole. "We need to show Isabelle my ornament, too. Mommy, are you coming this time?"

Morgan swallowed. "I—"

"Actually, Greyson," Isabelle said, "I think Rosie was looking for your mother to ask her something about the wedding. Are you okay with giving me a private viewing?"

Morgan gave her cousin an appreciative look as Greyson said, "I can do that."

"Hey, Grandma," Andrew said later that night, surprised to see his grandmother at his front door. Usually, it was him showing up at her place, not the other way around. "What's up and what's in the box?"

"The box is what's up. I need a taste-tester for this recipe for Rosie's wedding rehearsal dinner. The girls and I are hostessing the rehearsal for her and Lou. You available?"

"To try something you've cooked? Absolutely." Smiling at her referring to the Butterflies as 'the girls,' he stepped aside to let her into the house. "Having you show up with food is sort of like Santa Claus showing up with presents when it's not even Christmas."

Grandma Ruby laughed. "I knew coming to see you was the right choice."

"Everything okay?"

Placing the box on his kitchen counter, she nodded. "Everything's fine. I'm just worried about Rosie. Her wedding is getting so close and she keeps changing her mind about every little detail."

"Don't tell me she doesn't want the reindeer now?" Andrew asked, eyeing the containers his grandmother was unpacking. Amazing smells were already filling his small kitchen and his mouth watered in anticipation.

"Oh, no, that's not it. At least, not yet.

273

But she completely changed her rehearsal dinner menu and the catering company had a fit, so she let them go."

"Two weeks before the wedding?"

"Exactly. Lou offered to have the diner cater it, but she wasn't having that, either." His grandmother sighed. "So, now we Butterflies are trying to save the day. Although, it would serve her right if there wasn't any food to be served."

Poor Lou. And, Rosie, too, for that matter. With as emotionally wrenched as Greyson's ornament had left Andrew, he totally got Rosie's hesitation. The fears that had Rosie stalling were the same fears that had Morgan refusing to date at all. Which was just as well where he was concerned, because he wasn't the right guy for her.

"Well," he told his grandmother, opening a drawer and pulling out some silverware, "you've come to the right place to have someone sample your goodies. Let the taste-testing begin."

His grandma started opening small plastic containers that were stuffed with various homemade entrees.

"This one is my favorite," Andrew said a few minutes later, taking another bite of the succulent lemon chicken as they sat at his kitchen bar. "Man, that's good, Grandma. You outdid yourself."

She beamed at him as if he'd done her

a grand favor in stuffing his face. "Great. It's settled then."

Taking another bite, then slowly pulling the fork from his mouth so as not to miss a single morsel, he eyed his grandmother. "Not that I'm complaining, but I do have to wonder why you're here rather than having Rosie and Lou do the taste-testing for their wedding."

She waved off his concerns. "Rosie has enough to figure out without me piling on. Besides, after sixty years of friendship, I know her food likes and dislikes and Lou said he didn't care so long as Rosie was happy."

It was hard to fathom friendships that had lasted so long. Then again, he imagined that no matter what, he, Ben and Cole would always be close. In fifty years, they'd be the new Butterflies. Only they'd call themselves something hypermasculine like Flaming Hornets or the Fiery Spiders.

"Now," his grandmother shifted on her barstool, eyeing him in a way that had him thinking there was a price to be paid for the treat he'd just consumed. "Tell me about you and Morgan. I noticed you barely talked to her at the fire hall this afternoon and you didn't stick around long, which was surprising."

Bingo. He'd suspected all along that her

being there had something to do with Morgan.

"Nothing to tell."

"Nothing to tell, or nothing you're willing to tell?" she asked, giving him that grandma look that had him resisting the urge to squirm on his barstool. He hated when she gave him that look. Usually because it meant she already knew the answers and was going to keep him on the hot spot until he fessed up.

"Greyson's ornament was just the sweetest. I think he should have gotten first place," she continued, not waiting for his response before launching her next attack. "That was the three of you on his ornament, wasn't it?"

Taking another bite, a big one so his mouth would be full, eliminating the possibility of a verbal answer, Andrew nodded.

"Greyson obviously adores you," she pointed out.

The food he'd just swallowed formed a lump in Andrew's throat. Greyson's sweet words as he'd hugged him played through Andrew's head. Greyson loved him. Pain stabbed him and Andrew beat his fist against his chest, trying to help the food that had obviously gotten stuck to move on down.

"I've noticed you've not been to church the past few Sundays."

"I only went the once because Greyson invited me," he reminded her. He shouldn't have gone then. To have done so had set the poor kid up to think there was something more between him and his mom. Something that could never be.

Greyson loved him.

"Not sure that liquid soap stuff would work nearly so well as a good old-fashioned bar of soap, but I'm not beyond giving it the old college try," his grandmother said.

Knowing she was threatening to punish him for lying, Andrew sighed and gave in. "I like Morgan, Grandma. A lot. Greyson, too. I wanted us to be friends. But you saw his entry in the coloring contest. He wants a father. Any involvement I have with them will just get in the way of him ever having that."

Grandma Ruby frowned. "Why would you think that?"

Because even though she'd recognized from the beginning that he wasn't right for her, Morgan had feelings for him. And they'd just deepen if he let things continue on. So the more he stayed away from her, the better for everyone involved.

"I'm not what they need. They deserve someone who can give them what they deserve long term."

His grandmother placed her hand over his and gave it a squeeze. "You're positive that's not you?"

"One hundred percent. I fight fires, Grandma. They've already lost love once." The pain in Morgan's voice when she'd been talking to Sophie and Sarah at the Christmas party pierced him anew. "The last thing they need is to get more attached to me when I..."

"When you what?" Her gaze bore into him and a new quivery wave of emotions hit him.

Here it was. His moment to tell his grandmother about what his future held.

"When I want to fight wildland fires."

His grandmother's eyes widened with surprise. "As in, forest fires?"

"Yes. That's the job I want," he admitted. A heavy weight lifted off his shoulders at giving his dream voice to his grandmother. "Ever since I volunteered during the big fire in East Tennessee a few years ago, wildland firefighting has called to me. I want to smokejump."

It was rare that Andrew surprised his grandmother, but her expression now was one of complete shock.

"Goodness, child, why haven't you said anything before now?" Her hazel eyes bore into him. "Better yet, if that's what you want to be doing, why aren't you?"

Wasn't that essentially what Greyson had once asked him? His answer was the same.

"Life isn't that simple, Grandma."

"Life is as simple or complicated as you make it," she countered as she gave his hand another squeeze. "Your future is your responsibility, Andrew. Whether or not you pursue it is up to you. If being a smokejumper is what you want, you're the only person standing in the way of you doing that." She gave him a sharp look as she added, "Your grandfather and I would certainly never stand in your way."

Not intentionally.

"I promised you I'd always be here for you and Grandpa," he reminded her, surprised at his admission. Maybe there had been some truth serum laced into the goodies she'd brought over for him to sample. If Rosie's grandmother's cinnamon bread made men fall in love, then it sure wouldn't surprise him for his grandma to be able to whip up a confess-all confection.

Grandma Ruby gasped. "Please don't tell me you've been holding back from following your heart because of your grandfather and me?"

"That's not what I said," Andrew hedged, choosing his words carefully. He hadn't meant to put guilt on her face and wanted it gone. She had nothing to feel guilty for. She was amazing, and so was Grandpa. He was the one who kept messing everything up, including this conversation. "You and Grandpa are my heart. I love you and will keep my promise because I want to. There's no choice to be made as long as you need me."

His grandma stared at him, love shining in her eyes as she slowly shook her head. "I'm not sure whether to hug you or box your ears."

"If it's up for debate, I pick the hug."

"Silly boy." Leaning over to him, she wrapped him in a hug, kissed his cheek, and thankfully left his ears alone. "Your grandfather and I love having you around, but we never want to hold you back from living your dream."

"You're not," he countered. "I choose to stay here because its where I need to be."

"Oh, Andrew." Love shined in her eyes. "You're such a joy and I'd miss you terribly, but I want you to follow your dream. Always." She paused, gave him a questioning look. "Unless perhaps, there's another reason you want to stay in Pine Hill."

"You mean Morgan," he guessed. "She and Greyson are wonderful, but I stand by what I've said all along. I'm not interested in a serious relationship." Even if he reconsidered, how could he ever risk putting her and Greyson through such loss again? He couldn't. "Nor is she interested in dating me, casually or otherwise. And don't go saying I'm assuming that. I overheard her telling Sarah and Sophie that she'd never date me."

She shook her head again. "How any sane woman could not want to date you is beyond me."

Andrew snorted. "Spoken as a completely unbiased grandmother, of course."

"Of course." She smiled at him. "But biased or not, you're a jewel and don't you ever forget it. I'm sure that deep down, Morgan recognizes that."

Deep down, Morgan might recognize that, but that didn't mean she would risk a long-term relationship with him. Why would he even want her to?

"Grandma, I love you, but let's talk about something besides Morgan and Greyson, okay?"

Because his grandma knew him too well and he didn't want her seeing just how much he struggled with the decision he'd made to stay away from Morgan and Greyson.

"Okay, for now." She sighed. Then she smiled and patted his hand. "Tell me more about this smokejumper dream. I recall you talking about how much you enjoyed volunteering during the Gatlinburg fire and knew you took that wildland firefighting course afterwards, but I never guessed that you'd felt a life calling. I want to know more, my gem of a grandson."

Andrew was quite positive that it was his grandmother who was the true gem, but she wouldn't listen to him even if he argued that point. So, he grabbed his laptop and pulled up a website and began showing her the program he was considering. He'd work as a Hotshot for six months or so, then get qualified as a smokejumper. Just thinking about living that life had his blood pumping.

"You should apply."

Part of him wasn't surprised by her comment. She was such a selfless person. But another part of him was stunned that she seemed so genuinely enthused for him to apply. "Seriously? You're okay with me going?"

"Will I spend a lot more time on my knees praying for your safety? Absolutely. But I couldn't be more proud of you for your commitment to saving others, Andrew," she paused and gave him a tight smile. "I just wish it wasn't at such a high cost to yourself."

"I'm hoping it's never that high of a cost," he pointed out, thinking she meant the ultimate cost too many of his fellow firefighters paid.

A horrified look wrinkled her face. "Oh, goodness, not that. I meant the sacrifice of a personal relationship and family of your own."

Morgan and Greyson popped into his mind, then he reminded himself that he wasn't sacrificing anything that could ever be his, anyway. The greatest thing he could ever do for them was to stay away.

Which, with a few clicks of the laptop's keyboard, shouldn't be a problem.

"I have a family of my own," he said, typing in his name on the application. "A great family with you and Grandpa at the helm."

It was enough. It would have to be.

Chapter Twelve

"ACCORDING TO THEIR WEBSITE, THE mission of the Quilts of Valor Foundation is to cover service members and veterans touched by war with comforting and healing Quilts of Valor," Sophie said from the front of the cafeteria room at the Pine Hill Assisted Living Center. The space, converted into an award room for the afternoon, was full of those gathered for the awarding of the patriotic quilts that had been made at the recent sew-ins. "To carry out that mission is why we are gathered here today."

Morgan's heart swelled with pride that she'd been able to participate in a small way in something so meaningful. She glanced over at where Greyson stood with her grand-parents and hoped he felt joy in having helped, too.

Rather than watching the presentation, her son's gaze was focused on a certain fire-fighter, though. Morgan sighed. She under-stood the temptation. Keeping her own eyes away from Andrew wasn't easy.

"The Quilts of Valor Foundation started in 2003 when Blue Star mom Catherine Roberts had a dream where a dejected sol-dier was wrapped in a quilt meant to com-fort, offer hope, and to welcome him home." Sophie paused, looking around at the group. "As many of you know, my father served in the military. He wasn't able to deal with his return home and left when I was a child."

Morgan wished she could hug her cousin as Sophie's voice broke with emotion.

"Every quilt I make, present, or have anything to do with makes me feel as if I am somehow helping to heal him, wherever he is." With watery eyes, Sophie gave the crowd a wobbly smile and continued, "Just as we wrap up in a quilt when we're ill or we swaddle a baby in one when they're up-set, quilts comfort and make us feel better. That's what each and every one of the quilts being presented today are meant to do—to comfort, heal, and welcome home the fine men and women being honored today. We thank them for their dedicated service to our country and the role they played in protecting our freedom."

Morgan glanced over at where John sat in his wheelchair. Such a good man, and so deserving of every recognition. Scanning over the row of recipients, Morgan couldn't help but think how each and every one was owed so much for the sacrifices they'd made.

"Our first quilt being awarded today is being presented to Major Glenda Jackson who served in the Korean and the Vietnam Wars as a nurse. Her quilt is being awarded by Sarah Smith Lewis."

Sophie turned the microphone over and Sarah ran through a quick introduction about the woman, how she'd been touched by war, then asked permission to wrap the woman in a beautiful red, white, and blue quilt.

"Welcome home, and thank you for your service," Sarah told the woman, giving her a big hug, then handing the microphone back to Sophie.

Sophie ran through several other awards, each being presented with an emotional introduction and concluding by wrapping of a veteran in a patriotic quilt.

"Last, but certainly not least, we have a very special gentleman with us today. John Harper served in the Air Force as a gunner on a Douglas B-26 Invader and flew in seventeen missions during the Korean War. Our local Quilts of Valor group has a new member and she's going to award John his quilt."

Morgan took a deep breath, then walked to the front of the room, smiling as she took the microphone from her cousin. Public speaking wasn't her thing, but she hadn't been able to say no when Sophie had asked her if she wanted to award John his quilt.

"Hi," Morgan said to the group, thinking back to every public speaking piece of advice she'd ever heard to get her through the next few minutes. "Since I'm off duty and out of my uniform, many of you may not realize that I work here as a nurse. Not long after I started I had the privilege of meeting John. For those of you who know him, then you already knew all the things that I quickly learned—that he is an honorable man and a humble one. If you ask him, he will say he's no hero, that he just did his job. He went to war, did his duty to protect our country and his fellow countrymen, and then he came home and picked up the pieces of his life."

The group listened attentively as she continued. "But there's so much more to his story than that. Prior to his admission here, he was an active volunteer with the local American Legion. Based upon how they've come to visit him and how many times they have called checking on him, I know how much they love him."

She smiled at him. "John, you inspire

me to be a better person and to do more for my country and those who have so valiantly served. That's why, even though I can't sew, I joined the Quilts of Valor Foundation, and why I'll continue to volunteer and work with them to wrap as many of our military as we can in quilts of comfort. Because of you and the impact meeting you has had on me. You are a true American hero, John, and I'm so proud and honored to award you this Quilt of Valor that's even more special to me because my son helped sew some of the blocks. May I wrap you in your quilt?"

John, looking a little weepy himself, nodded. "I'm sure there's someone who deserves this more than me, but I'm not going to say no to being wrapped in a quilt of healing by a pretty lady. My Carla was a quilter. I know how much time and love goes into making a quilt. I'm the one who is honored."

Morgan shook her head. "I'm not going to let you downplay your greatness. Not today." She unfolded the quilt, then draped it across his shoulders. "John, welcome home and thank you for your service."

Then, fighting to keep from choking up, she hugged him.

"Now you've gone and done it, girl. You've embarrassed me in front of Maybelle," he whispered, sounding a little choked up himself.

Morgan pulled back to look at him. "I didn't mean to embarrass you, but you deserve this recognition."

"I'm not embarrassed by the quilt. I'm embarrassed by the way you're making me cry like a big baby."

Sure enough pink rimmed his old blue eyes and tears flowed down his cheeks.

Morgan lost it and started crying, too, pulling him into a hug.

"Now, look who's crying like a baby," she whispered.

"Yeah, but whereas I'm just embarrassed by my tears, yours are making your firefighter look as if he's going to come teach me a lesson for making you cry," John whispered back.

Straightening, Morgan swiped at her eyes, then glanced toward where she'd seen Andrew with his grandparents. Sure enough, he was watching her and his eyes were filled with...compassion? Empathy? Or was that something more in how he was looking at her?

And oh heavens, what was that moving through her? Surely it was just because she was so emotional over presenting John's quilt to him. As the crowd was clapping in honor of John, Morgan handed the microphone back over to Sophie, who immediately began putting out a call for more volunteers.

"As Morgan mentioned, she doesn't sew,

but she was still able to participate. There are so many ways a person can help beyond quilting. If you're looking for a way to serve and honor our precious military service-men and women past and present, please consider joining Quilts of Valor Foundation or making a donation. Anything you can do will help us meet our goal to wrap all nomi-nated service members with a Quilt of Valor. All service members are heroes and can be nominated. Thank you for joining us today and help yourselves to some of the yummy snacks provided for us by the Pine Hill Church's ladies class."

Morgan made her way over to her grandparents. They were close to Charlie and Ruby, and thus Andrew, and she hoped she got the opportunity to talk to him. She needed to explain what had happened at Sarah and Bodie's.

"You did a fantastic job," her Grammy said, hugging her. "I'm so proud."

Morgan smiled, hugged both her grandparents, then got similar praise from Andrew's grandparents, who were just the cutest couple ever.

"Oh, there's Pastor Smith. We must go say hello. Greyson, you, too," Grammy grabbed Ruby's elbow and the two women along with a reluctant Greyson headed over to the preacher. "Come on, guys," they called to their husbands. Grampy and Charlie looked at each other, shrugged, then followed the women, leaving Morgan and Andrew semi-alone.

"Subtle," Andrew harrumphed, rocking back on his heels.

"Weren't they just?" Morgan smiled nervously at him.

"You did a great job awarding the quilt."

"Thank you. John is a wonderful person."

"Sounds it. I remember when he was Grand Marshall of the Christmas parade a few years ago. Maybelle nominated him, I believe."

"Interesting. She nominated him for his Quilt of Valor, also." Morgan studied him, trying to see through the small talk to what was really going on inside his head. "How have you been?"

"Fine," he answered. "But probably still on Santa's naughty list."

"I didn't realize you were ever on Santa's naughty list," she mused. "To tell you the truth, I thought I was on it."

His gaze met hers "You?"

Morgan's breath hung in her throat. "I'm sorry I rushed off at Sarah and Bodie's when you tried to hold my hand. I…" she searched for the right words, "Please don't think badly of me. I was thrilled for them, but memories hit and I felt all panicky, and I just needed a moment."

"I didn't think badly of you, Morgan. I figured it was something along those lines when you rushed off," he told her, sounding sincere.

She couldn't stand not knowing a moment longer. "If you're not upset about that, then why have you been avoiding me since that night?"

"Who says I've been avoiding you?"

"You think I haven't picked up on the change in the way you act around me and Greyson? I've noticed and I don't like it." She closed her eyes. "Actually, I hate it."

His eyes darkened as he studied her. "What are you saying, Morgan?"

"That you were right." Lord, was she really doing this? Really admitting to him that she didn't like how long it had been since they'd seen each other, that she didn't like the distance she'd felt between them at the fire hall's open house? "Going too long in between seeing you is bad for me. I've missed you."

His jaw tightened and he swallowed. "I should go."

Morgan's heart squeezed. "Because you don't want a serious relationship?"

"Is that what you want, Morgan?"

She knew she should tell him no. He was backing away from her, so why expose herself to rejection?

Everyone's always told you that he runs

when a woman gets too attached, and you're acting like you're covered in Velcro.

"Yes," she admitted, unable to lie about how she was feeling. "Is there somewhere we can go to talk?"

He closed his eyes for a second, then shrugged. "I planned to head by the station after I left here. You can walk with me to my truck."

"No motorcycle today?" she asked, following him out of the cafeteria.

"Nah. Too cold. Fortunately, my truck has been running like a charm since I replaced the alternator a few weeks ago."

"That's good." Ugh. They were back to small talk. Was that his way of telling her not to press her luck?

They paused in the lobby. A large Christmas tree was to the inside of the doorway and an empty reception desk was opposite it. No doubt the receptionist was still at the presentation.

As uncomfortable as the thought made her, Morgan took a deep breath and lifted her gaze to his. "You once told me going too long in between seeing you was hazardous to my health. Based on the way my pulse went crazy when I saw you today, I think you were right. So when can I see you again?"

Andrew's insides shook. He'd always known Morgan wasn't immune to him. That truth had been in her eyes from the moment they'd met at the school. There had been some innate recognition between them that transcended logic. He'd felt it, had wanted to ask her out right away, but then believed he couldn't be more than friends with her once he'd realized Greyson was her son. If he'd been thinking straight then he never would have pursued a friendship with her, but he hadn't seemed able to stay away.

"You know I'm not a serious relationship kind of guy," he reminded her.

Morgan paled a little, then she nodded. "That is one of the first things I was told about you."

"It's true," he confirmed. He'd never wanted a serious relationship and now, more than ever, that was out of the question.

"I didn't think I'd ever want to date again, and especially not someone with a dangerous occupation and pastimes." Looking nervous, she inhaled sharply. "So, the fact that I can't stop thinking about you makes me think you're the exception."

Andrew gulped.

Her eyes were big and full of hope as she said, "Maybe Greyson and I are worth you making an exception, too."

Oh, Morgan. Her words had him twisted into knots, making him want to leap for joy all the while knowing what she was saying would only further torment him. Because he was about to hurt her even though he'd never wanted to do that.

"If ever I was going to make an exception, it would be for you and Greyson."

But he couldn't do that to them. He wouldn't.

"There's something I should tell you," he began, knowing that when he told her of what his future held, it would all be over. "I'm leaving Pine Hill."

"What?" Confusion furrowed her brows. "Why would you do that?"

"I'm heading to California to train at a wildland fire fighting base. I leave the second week of January. My plan is to stay out west permanently, working full time at one of the base camps."

"Wildland fire fighting?" she asked, not sounding as if she fully understood what that meant.

"I'm going to be a Hotshot, and eventually a smokejumper, Morgan. It's what I've dreamed of doing for a long time, what I've been preparing myself for over the past few years, getting my wildland qualifications."

"This is why you skydive? Because you want to jump out of planes where forests are on fire?" she asked, her pitch heightening as understanding dawned. "What if your parachute catches fire?"

"I'll have a back-up parachute on me. All smokejumpers do."

"It's still dangerous."

He nodded. "It is, but wildland fires cause so much damage, Morgan. They have the potential to consume entire towns if they're not gotten under control. Do you realize how many lives I can possibly save by doing this?"

"Andrew, please no. I…" her voice trailed off and she flinched. "I don't think I can handle you doing this."

"I'm not asking you to." The urge to take her into his arms hit so strong it was all he could do to hold himself back. Instead, he did his best to mask how much it ripped into him that he was causing her pain.

"I know you're not, I just…I don't want you to go."

"I know—I always knew. This is why I had my rules: no serious relationships, no single moms. Because I knew this was where I was headed, and I never wanted to hurt anyone with it. I couldn't seem to stay away from you—but that's because I'm a heel. I knew you were a forever kind of girl and that I wasn't a forever kind of guy."

"So you're really going," she said, her tone too flat to be a question.

He couldn't stop himself from trying to explain, wanting her to understand. "Being a smokejumper is something I need to do, not just for me but for those I might save by doing so. I want to make a difference, to save lives, because this is who I am. But knowing that, I should have stayed away from you and Greyson. I realize that now. Forgive me that I didn't."

And with that, he left because he couldn't bear the anguish shining in her tear-filled green eyes a moment longer.

Especially when he knew he was the cause.

"Sophie keeps asking me about you."

Gripping his game controller tighter, Andrew glanced over at where Cole was stretched out working on a crossword puzzle. The fire hall had been slow that night. They'd worked a motor vehicle accident earlier in the day, but otherwise they hadn't had any calls come in. "She finally looking to upgrade?"

The look Cole gave him was meant to slay.

"As if you'd be considered an upgrade," Ben pointed out from where he sat next to Andrew. "You can't even be relied upon to help me save the world from these aliens."

There was that.

"She is worried about Morgan," Cole

added, messing further with Andrew's concentration.

"Is something wrong with her?" he couldn't help asking. He'd thought of her and Greyson so much since the Quilts of Valor presentation. How shattered she'd looked when she'd finally understood that he was leaving would haunt him all his days.

"According to Sophie, you're what's wrong. Sophie wants to know what happened. I keep telling her it's not our place to ask, that if you and Morgan wanted us to know, you'd tell us."

"True that," Andrew agreed. He didn't want to be what was wrong with Morgan, but he was certain that it was much better for him to back away now than to risk growing even closer between now and the time he left for training camp.

"But," Cole continued, "she wouldn't let up until I promised I'd ask. You know how Sophie is when she gets something on her mind. The woman is persistent."

Andrew returned his gaze to his game. "I'm leaving in January. That's all that needs to be said."

His buddies had been happy for him when he'd told them his plans. He'd miss them and suspected the same was true for them, but they could tell he had a real passion for what he was going to do.

"You'll be back to visit after your training is complete," Ben pointed out.

"Eventually, since my family lives here."

"Family?" Ben asked. "Who do you think you're fooling? You'd miss me too much to stay gone too long."

"Sign up and go with me."

"Me?" Ben shook his head. "I love what I'm doing right here. Smokejumper is your dream, Wilderness Boy, not mine. I'd say ask your buddy there, but there isn't any way you'd talk him into leaving Sophie to go save Bambi and some trees."

"It's about a lot more than just the trees and wildlife and you know it. Wildland fires left unchecked can reach towns with thousands of homes and tens of thousands of lives. I want to help prevent that from happening."

"You know Ben's just giving you a hard time," Cole said, eyeing him over the crossword puzzle book. "Mostly because we aren't too sure about you breaking up a good thing."

"I've already told you that Morgan and I were never a thing. Not really."

"I was talking about us," Cole pointed out. "Not Morgan. No worries, though, I'll do my part by taking over as Greyson's hero while you're gone."

Andrew's heart squeezed.

"You do that." It would be best if Cole

really did. "I expect you both to watch out for Morgan and Greyson, make sure they're okay."

"You're not sounding too uninterested there, bud."

"Lack of interest was never the problem," he admitted. "I'm the wrong guy for them. I thought Morgan and I could be friends, but that was a mistake. She needs someone who is safe and secure and who doesn't take risks. Maybe a dentist or something. Y'all find her one."

"And what about you?"

"I don't need a dentist. My teeth are good." He bared them to prove it.

Cole rolled his eyes. "I meant what about you if Morgan finds someone else?"

"I'll be happy for her." He'd also tar and feather the guy if he hurt Morgan and Greyson, but other than that...yeah, he'd be happy for her. He wanted her to have all the things she deserved in life. Things like a husband who came home every night to her and Greyson.

"And too stubborn to admit you care about her," Cole added.

"Stubbornness has nothing to do with this." Andrew shook his head. "It's because I care about her that I'll be happy she's with someone else. So long as the dude is good to her and Greyson. If not..." his voice trailed off.

"If not, that 'dude' will be answering to all three of us," Ben finished. "We got your back, bro."

Andrew started to reply but the alarm sounded, signaling a call had come in.

Looked as if it wasn't going to be a slow night, after all.

Smoke billowed all around him and Andrew didn't think he, Ben, and Cole were ever going to reach the section of the automobile parts factory where Bob, Jules, and a female factory employee were trapped. He wasn't even sure what he was going to do to get them all out of here.

Going back in was crazy. Leaving part of their crew trapped inside was crazier and had never been an option. Chief hadn't even had to ask. He, Cole, and Ben had already grabbed their Rapid Intervention Team packs, gleaned where in the building to look, and busted into the building from an outside door closest to where they expected to find the others.

Thick smoke limited visibility. The stench of burning plastic and Lord only knew what cut through his respirator and made his eyes water. The fire roared around them, almost deafening him to the cracking of beams and wood as the building around them threatened to collapse.

Finally, through the smoke-filled passageway, they reached the area where Bob and Jules had been searching for the missing plant employee. Through the dusky haze, a movement caught his eye.

"There," Cole said.

Jules was bent over a pile of rubble, trying to clear it. When Andrew rushed over, he saw that beneath the rubble was Bob and the missing employee. Good grief. Of course Jules wouldn't have left Bob behind—but she must have known there was no way she could have cleared that mess before the fire reached them. Andrew worried that the four of them might not be able to.

"I almost had them out, but another section fell," Jules said, continuing to pull rubble away.

They immediately jumped in and began helping to clear the rubble on top of the two. Around them, the smoke grew thicker. Finally, they uncovered a small opening where Bob was sharing his respirator with the employee, letting the woman take big, clean breaths of oxygen. Andrew and the others continued to lift wood and tiles. Although it had probably been two or three minutes, it felt as if hours had passed since they'd found them. They had to hurry. At any moment another part of the ceiling could cave in.

Or the fire could reach them.

As soon as they had them uncovered enough to reach, Ben handed over the spare respirator from the RIT pack for the woman to put on.

"Missy's leg is broken," Bob told Andrew as the man helped to push a beam off his lower body. "Jules and I were dragging her out when the roof caved in and trapped us. Jules got free. We couldn't. And then another load crashed onto us. Now, I'm useless and going to make this even harder on y'all."

He gestured to his own legs. Andrew winced. His buddy's legs were crushed. There was another loud pop then the sound of falling debris came from nearby.

"We've got to get out of here fast. Where's the closest outside wall?" he asked Missy. He had a good idea, but since she'd worked there, wanted to verify.

She pointed to his left, which was the same direction he'd thought.

"Is there a door we can go out?" he asked.

She nodded. "Yes. A metal one that leads out to a picnic table." Andrew knew roughly where she meant.

"How far are we?"

She gave him a blank look. "I don't know. A hundred yards? Maybe more."

A hundred yards? Safety was a football field's length away. Andrew winced again. He'd been hoping she'd say just around that smoky turn.

He glanced toward Ben, Cole, and Jules. "Can you manage Bob?"

"Piece of cake," Cole assured him, already wrapping a special webbing around Bob that they'd use to drag him.

"This is embarrassing," Bob muttered. "I should have started that diet last year. Y'all are going to break your backs pulling me."

"Save your breath," Jules warned.

After warning her about what he was going to do, Andrew hoisted Missy over his shoulders. She cried out in pain. "Sorry, ma'am."

As long as the fire allowed, he'd carry her. If the smoke and heat got to be too much, he'd drag her, but he hoped he wouldn't have to and that the exit was closer than it seemed right now.

As he said a prayer that their exit plan wasn't blocked off by flames or debris, he also prayed that Morgan and Greyson wouldn't hear about this until he and crew were safely outside the building.

He hadn't wanted to worry her.

At the moment, he was pretty worried himself.

And, yet, he'd never felt more alive than

as he made his way through the treacherous dark building.

Fighting fires really was who he was.

Chapter Thirteen

WORN OUT FROM A TWELVE-HOUR shift that had run over when her replacement was late, Morgan let herself into her grandparents' home.

"Hey, Sophie, Isabelle, and Aunt Darlene," she said, surprised to see all three there. She'd recognized Isabelle's car in the driveway but hadn't been expecting to see them all in the living room with her grandparents. Nor had she expected to see Sophie pacing across the living room floor. "Where's Greyson?"

"Already down for the night, dear," Grammy said. "Sorry. I know you prefer to be the one to put him to bed, but when you called and said you were running late, I went ahead and bathed him and put him to bed. He might still be awake, if you want to pop your head in."

"I'll go say goodnight." But she paused, Sophie's agitation too much to ignore. Anxiety hit as she realized something was wrong. "What's going on?"

"Sit down, dear," her Grammy said.

Fear filled Morgan. People only told you to sit down when something bad had happened. If Greyson was in bed asleep, then...

"Tell me what's happened."

"There's been a fire at a local factory."

A fire...that meant Andrew.

Oh God, please let him be okay.

"A malfunctioning boiler blew," Isabelle said, her concerned gaze jumping back and forth between her pacing sister and Morgan. "The explosion triggered an electrical fire in another part of the building and then that spread before anyone realized because everyone was distracted with the explosion. Crews from all over the county are trying to get the fire under control, but apparently it's a doozy and people were trapped inside."

Morgan's legs buckled and she collapsed onto the sofa. No wonder Sophie was in such a tizzy. Cole and Andrew were there, fighting the fire and no doubt doing everything they could to get to whomever was still inside the burning building.

"We've been listening to your grandfather's scanner. We turned it off when we heard your car in the driveway so we could tell you rather than risk you hearing something over the radio."

Morgan's chest constricted and it took everything within her to ask, "Hear what?"

Because she knew there was more news. More bad news.

"Two firefighters were trapped in the building when a roof collapsed, along with a woman they were trying to get out."

No. Just no.

Tears slid down her cheeks and she swatted them away. "Andrew?"

"No. Andrew and Cole aren't the two trapped firefighters," Sophie assured her.

Morgan was instantly filled with guilt that she hadn't thought to ask about Cole. But, oh God, she'd thought Andrew...

"But they are on the Rapid Intervention Team, along with Ben."

Morgan's stomach clenched, knowing she wasn't going to like what her cousin was about to tell her next.

"They went back to extricate them."

Of course, Andrew had gone back in. If there were people inside, he'd rather die trying to save them than to watch the building burn around them while doing nothing.

"Not long after they went back in, another large section of the roof caved," Isabelle picked back up when Sophie's voice broke off. "Even if more fire crews arrive, they can't get to them. Not now. So, we wait to see if they find their own way out."

Oh God.

Andrew. Cole. Ben.

Andrew!

Oh God. No. Please, no. Nausea hit Morgan and she thought she might throw up. Throwing up might make her feel better.

She might never feel better again.

She slumped over, putting her head between her knees, partially to hide the heavy flow of tears cutting across her cheeks.

Grammy moved next to her and wrapped her arms around Morgan. "There, there, sweet girl. They're going to be okay."

Morgan didn't bother lying or pretending that Andrew wasn't why she was upset. They all knew anyway. They'd known long before she'd admitted as much to herself. She hadn't wanted to care for Andrew. But she did.

"You don't know that, Grammy." She covered her face with her hands. "Sometimes things aren't okay. Sometimes the people you love die and they leave this huge hole in your heart that seems ever expanding."

"And sometimes they live to fight the good fight another day," her grandmother said.

Please let that be the case. Please. Please. Please.

"They know what they're doing, Morgan," Sophie said, coming to sit on the other side of her. Her cousin placed her hand on Morgan's shoulder. "This is what they've trained for. I'm nervous, too, but we have to trust in them, in their skills, and in God to watch over them. I pray He does."

At that moment, Sophie's phone began playing, "Here comes Santa Claus," which was Cole's special ring tone.

Morgan sat up, her gaze meeting her cousin's, then Sophie scrambled to answer the call. "Hello? Cole? Everyone's out safe? Jules, Bob, and the lady who was still inside, too? Thank God."

Andrew was out. Relief washed over Morgan, as did exhaustion and she fought breaking down into sobs.

"I love you, too, Cole. I'm so glad everyone is going to be okay," Sophie continued.

Morgan's body began to tremble. She loved her family, but she needed a moment alone to process how utterly wound up she was over the thought of something happening to Andrew. Ever.

She'd looked up Hotshots and Smokejumpers online. Statistics of injuries—some serious, some fatal—were much higher than with other firefighters. She'd been right to tell him she couldn't do this. She couldn't.

"I...I'm going to tell Greyson goodnight."

Her grandmother gave her an odd look, but Morgan shook her head.

"I'm fine." Not really. Inside she was falling apart for so many reasons. "I just want to tell my son goodnight. My son who says he wants to do this for a living when he grows up." Her voice broke but prior to rushing from the room, she managed to say, "I'll be praying extra hard that he changes his mind."

"You're not your usual bundle of sunshine today. You that upset they're letting me out of this joint?"

"Devastated," Morgan assured John, smiling as he swung his legs over the side of the bed without assistance. "I think they're making a huge mistake and that I need to talk with the medical director to get things cleared up."

He used his hands to push up against the bed to help himself stand. "Bite your tongue, girl. I've took all those pills you keep throwing at me. I deserve to be set free."

"Set free?" She arched a brow at him. "You make it sound as if we've held you hostage."

"Guess that would be my own body doing that," he admitted, taking a step, then another. His gait was cautious and he had to use his quad-cane, but he was getting stronger each day. "Either way, doc says I'm well enough that I can go home. I'm out of this place just as soon as doc gives the final okay."

She didn't blame him for being excited about being back in his space, with his things. As much as she loved Grampy and Grammy, she planned to find a place of her own after the holidays. She'd forever be thankful to her grandparents, but it was time she and Greyson had their own home, again.

"Don't think that you no longer being here means I'll stop worrying about you," she admitted, walking beside him as he made his way toward the doorway.

"That's something you do too much," John accused.

"Worry?" she asked, glancing toward him.

He nodded. "You need to stop."

Morgan stared at him, then sighed. "You're right. I worry too much, but I don't know how to stop. It seems to have become ingrained."

"It's useless, you know. Worrying doesn't change anything and it robs you of your happiness."

"I'd say easy for you to say, but I know you've dealt with your own tragedies."

"And survived them. You will, too." Leaning out to steady himself against the doorjamb, he paused, "What's triggered this relapse? I can tell something's changed since I saw you yesterday."

Everything changed the night of Sarah and Bodie's party. From that point onward, she'd felt the loss of Andrew's absence from her and Greyson's lives. Last night had just served to remind her that she'd been foolish to ever think she wanted him with them in the first place.

"There was a fire at a factory in the industrial park last night."

John's face grew concerned. "Was anyone hurt?"

"An employee and two firefighters. Jules just had scrapes and bruises, but the other two people are in the hospital still with serious injuries."

John's blue gaze studied her. "Not Andrew?"

Just the memory of not knowing if he was okay had Morgan feeling jittery, but she reminded herself he was fine and shook her head. "No, I'm told he's well."

John frowned. "You're told? Why don't you know firsthand?"

"I've not seen him. We're not a couple. We never were."

"Pfft. So you say."

"It's just as well that we weren't. He's

313

leaving for wildland firefighter training in California in a few weeks. He plans to be a smokejumper."

John shrugged. "So?"

"So, even if he was interested in a committed relationship, I couldn't deal with how I'd worry about him and he'd be far away for who knows how long? It's best that we were never a couple."

John straightened and began walking again as he said, "I'm just a practically senile old man, but seems to me that whether you're involved or not, you worry about him anyway."

John might be in his eighties, but he wasn't in the slightest bit senile.

Lost in her thoughts, Morgan stayed beside him as they made their way to the dining area.

"Tell me, Morgan," he said, slowly walking down the hallway, "because I'm curious. If you and Andrew were a couple, would you have been any more worried about him last night?"

"I..." She considered what he was asking, then shook her head. "No, I don't think it's possible to have been more worried than I already was."

John gave her a smug look. "Because love doesn't work that way, does it?"

A noise sounded deep in Morgan's throat

and she shook her head forcefully. "Love has nothing to do with this."

John had the audacity to laugh. "Love has everything to do with this. It doesn't make any difference if that young man is halfway around the world or standing right beside you, you're going to worry about him. It's on you to figure out how to deal with that."

"I...when I said I don't know how to stop worrying, I was telling the truth," she admitted. "I used to not worry, but then when Trey started pulling riskier and riskier stunts, anxiety set in and now I can't seem to stop worrying."

"What are you so worried about?"

"Everything," she admitted.

"Too vague." His blue gaze put her on the spot. "What are you so worried about, Morgan?"

Heart pounding, she said, "Losing Andrew."

"No reason to worry about losing him when it seems you've already pushed him away," he said so matter-of-factly Morgan could only stare at him. "So, what else are you worried about?"

But Morgan had stopped walking, eyeing him as they stood just outside the dining area. "I never had Andrew to lose him. I told him I wanted a relationship, John, and he pushed me away. He said that wasn't what he wanted."

John's bushy white brow rose. "You sure about that?"

"It's snowing!" Greyson said, running to the window for a better look, smushing his nose against the windowpane that overlooked Grammy's front lawn.

Morgan followed him to the window and placed her hand on his shoulder. It was Christmas Eve, and she was blessed to have the next two days off work. Greyson had crawled into bed with her that morning with a stack of Christmas books and they'd lain there reading, talking about Rosie's wedding, and about Santa coming that night.

"Wow," she said, staring at the heavy layer of white covering everything. "It must have snowed all night."

"Almost four inches and it's still coming down," Grammy Claudia said. "Looks as if we're going to have a white Christmas."

"It's been a long time since I've had a white Christmas," Morgan said.

"I've never had a white Christmas," Greyson added, then glanced up at Morgan. "Have I?"

"No, honey. We never had snow where we lived in Georgia."

"Then, I'm extra glad you're getting a white Christmas this year and that Rosie has snow for her wedding later today," Grammy said. "Goodness knows she probably threatened to cancel the wedding again if she didn't have real snow. God must have decided it was time to intervene since half the town has already bought ugly Christmas sweaters for this thing." She shook her just-coiffed-that-morning head.

Thinking how lovely her grandmother looked, Morgan smiled. "Hopefully, today will be everything she's ever dreamed of."

"Ha." Grammy snorted. "It already is literally everything she's ever dreamed of. She's come up with every outlandish idea imaginable—I don't think even her dreams could come up with something new. It's going to be a winter wonderland zoo. This morning, while we were getting our hair and make-up done, she informed us that she added a live nativity."

"That's very Christmas-y."

"Yes, I suppose so. I don't even know where that woman gets these ideas," Grammy continued, shaking her head. "But she sure keeps our lives exciting."

"Well, I guess there's been stranger things to happen at a wedding than a live nativity."

"Oh, I'm sure she'll manage to top those stranger things, too, before the day is over. It wouldn't surprise me one bit if she finagled a polar bear to walk her down the aisle or if she's planned some great runaway bride getaway."

Morgan smiled. No doubt, Rosie might have a few surprises in store, but hopefully not of the runaway bride variety.

"Is there anything I can help with, Grammy?"

Her grandmother shook her head. "Not that I can think of. I'm going to get changed into that ugly Christmas sweater dress that bridezilla insisted we wear—talk about your ugly, never-wear-again bridesmaid dress!—and say another prayer that I make it through this day without snapping her precious butterfly wings."

Morgan placed her hands over Greyson's ears. "Grammy!"

"No worries." Her grandmother smiled sweetly. "I wouldn't really, dear. Not that I'd have to." She giggled and covered her painted red lips. "Maybelle is going to beat me to it if Rosie doesn't cooperate today."

"You don't really think she'll back out again?"

Sighing, Grammy shrugged. "I hope not, but with that one you never know."

"Oh, Grammy, Lou would be heartbroken."

"That he would." Her grandmother nodded, then headed toward her bedroom to get ready.

"Do we have time to play in the snow before Rosie's wedding?" Greyson asked, giving her a hopeful, puppy-dog look.

Glancing at her watch, she calculated how long it would take them to get ready, then nodded. "We can play for a few minutes."

She bundled Greyson up, then put on her coat, gloves, and hat. Once outside and off the front porch, Greyson ran around the front yard. With his tongue stuck out.

Memories hitting her, Morgan swallowed hard. John's accusations still played through her head. She tried to push them away. She cared for Andrew, but she wasn't in love with him. And he wasn't in love with her.

"Mmmm, these snowflakes taste yummy, Mommy. You want one?"

Pasting a smile on her face, she decided that she was not going to think about Andrew, what John had said, or anything else other than this precious time with her son. She was done with worrying—for the moment at least.

"Absolutely," she told Greyson. "You didn't think I was going to let you gobble them all up by yourself, did you?"

Greyson giggled and made a chomping sound. "Better hurry. I might eat them all."

Together, they ran around the yard, tongues out, catching snowflakes, and making silly chomping noises. After a few minutes, Morgan wrapped her arms around him and swung him around, laughing, and laughing even harder when they fell back into the snow.

"Again!" Greyson cheered.

The cold biting through her pants, Morgan spread her arms and made a snow angel. Smiling, she stood and dusted snow off her clothes, then took a photo of her snow angel and several of Greyson. They played for a few more minutes, then she went to the front porch and sat down on the middle step to watch him.

"Mommy?" he asked coming over to stand in front of her.

They'd been having so much fun that the solemn expression on his little face startled her. "What, baby?"

"Do you think Andrew is tasting the snowflakes, too?"

She swallowed, then put on a smile for Greyson's benefit. "How could he resist?"

Greyson nodded, then put his mittens on her cheeks, looked in her eyes, and said, "I miss him."

Morgan's smile slipped. "Me too, baby." So much her insides ached.

Greyson's brows drew together. "Do you think he will be at Rosie's wedding?"

"You think he'd drive all that way to get reindeer for Rosie's wedding and then not be there?" She shook her head. "I imagine his grandmother has him helping do all kinds of last-minute things to make sure the wedding goes smoothly."

He sighed, his breath making a white puff of air. "It feels like it's been forever since we've seen him."

Morgan couldn't argue. It felt like forever to her, too—and she'd seen him more recently than Greyson had. John's words ran through her mind again. Whether they were a couple or not, whether she wanted him there or not, Andrew had made his way through her defenses.

She might not have wanted to risk her heart again, but from the moment she'd met him and he'd flashed that smoldering grin and winked at her, her heart had been on the line.

"If we see him today, I'm going to tell him I've missed him," Greyson announced. "And that we caught snowflakes today and I wished he'd been here to build a snowman with us."

"Good idea," Morgan told him, thinking back on the last time she'd told Andrew she missed him. It had been the last time she'd seen him.

He'd told her he was leaving.

She didn't want him to go. And not just because he was heading into a dangerous job.

But because she wanted him to stay with her and Greyson. Forever.

Later that day, Morgan drove her car up the winding drive that led to the main buildings at Harvey Farms where Rosie's wedding was taking place. Snow capped the black picket fence that lined either side of the road and the large evergreen trees at regular intervals were decorated with giant red balls and gold ribbon. Twinkling lights peeked out from snowy branches. Long before they reached the farm, Morgan had decided they'd left Pine Hill and been transported to some magical place. Greyson obviously agreed.

"Wow," he breathed as Morgan drove through two giant candy canes. Once through them, a 'toy soldier' directed her on where to park her car. An elf waited in a utility vehicle to haul them to the picturesque barn with its giant wreath centered in the gable just beneath the roof. "Are we at the North Pole?"

"It does look that way, doesn't it?" Morgan had only been to Harvey Farms a couple of times. It had always been charming, but nothing like the snow-capped scene visible beyond the parking area. Rosie had said she wanted a winter wonderland wedding, and that was certainly what she'd gotten. The snow had stopped an hour or so ago, leaving a fluffy white layer over everything. The sun had come out, warming the nip in the air and making the world around them glisten.

"It's magical," she said out loud as she and Greyson climbed up on the utility vehicle and pulled up the provided thick wooly blanket over them for the short trip to the barn.

"I want a Christmas wedding when Brynne and I get married," Greyson announced.

Morgan's eyes widened. "Um, yeah, that's great, but let's wait a few years before we start planning your wedding, okay?"

Greyson giggled. "I know, Mommy. I have to go to firefighter school and get a job first. Then Brynne and I can get married the next Christmas."

Seeing the excitement in his eyes, the love of firefighting that he'd had for months, she smiled at him. "I'm proud of you, Greyson, that when you grow up you want to do something that makes the world a better place."

She'd worry about him, but ultimately, didn't she want him to be happy? If firefighting made him happy, then she couldn't stand in his way. She still hoped he changed his mind between now and then, though.

He grinned at her. "Like Andrew?"

Morgan's heart squeezed. "Yes, honey, like Andrew. He is a hero."

Greyson patted her thigh. "You are, too, Mommy. I'm glad you take care of sick people."

"Thank you, honey." Morgan's chest swelled with pride and love and gratitude to the Lord for blessing her with such a precious child. She hugged him a little closer to her. "Brrrrr."

"I'm not cold," Greyson said. Most likely he really wasn't, as he was bundled up from head to toe with only his round little face peeking out, and the blanket covered them as well.

Morgan wasn't really, either, not with her layering beneath her fuzzy 'ugly' Christmas sweater, but she snuggled up to him anyway just because she wanted to be close. "Good, then you can keep me warm."

Greyson hugged up with her, trying to warm her, until something to their left caught his eye. "Is that a ballerina skating with that soldier?"

Morgan's mouth dropped. "It's a ballerina ice skating with a nutcracker! Oh, wow."

Morgan had heard Rosie was having a small skating rink set up, but she hadn't known the bride had arranged for professional skaters to be there to entertain. Wow. Wow. Wow.

"Is that the book we read with the rat?"

Morgan nodded.

Greyson's nose crinkled. "I hope there aren't any rats here."

"I don't think Rosie would want rats to come to her wedding," she said.

A choir group dressed like characters from a Dickens novel sang Christmas carols just outside the gorgeously decorated barn and Morgan couldn't resist humming along.

The elf drove past the barn, where Morgan had assumed they'd be going, and instead delivered them to a spot surrounded by so many Christmas trees, it was like walking into an enchanted Christmas forest. Once inside, as a focal point, an altar decorated with snowflakes and butterflies had been set up with the pines behind it, providing a perfect Christmas backdrop. Hay bales with red coverings were set up in long rows creating an aisle leading to the altar. Splashes of color came from decorated Christmas trees that included stacks of presents of various sizes, some as tall as Greyson.

"Y'all have a great time," the elf said as he assisted them out of the vehicle. "Bring the blanket with you to use during the ceremony."

"Oh, okay." Morgan grabbed the blanket

and together she and Greyson made their way to a log near the back of the ceremony area. She smiled and waved at several familiar faces.

Spotting her Grampy, she went over to join him. Greyson sat beside her, and they wrapped the warm blanket around them.

"Let the circus show begin," Grampy said, making Morgan laugh.

"Let's just hope it doesn't involve a runaway bride."

Chapter Fourteen

"**L**ET'S MAKE SURE I HAVE every-thing," Rosie said, glancing around at her friends in the bridal 'suite' of the Harvey Farms event barn. "Let's see, something blue—"

"I think your hair has that one covered," Ruby giggled as she checked over Rosie's wedding dress, smoothing out the train. It was a lovely gown, trimmed with sequins, pearl, and lace snowflakes and butterflies covering the long silky train.

"Something old—"

"No worries. She's definitely got that one covered," Maybelle muttered under her breath.

Rosie gave her friend a squinty-eyed,

sugary-sweet smile. "So nice of you to have volunteered for that position for me, Maybelle."

Ruby and Claudia giggled.

"For your 'something new,' too bad you didn't 'borrow' some new best friends to wear these ugly bridesmaids' dresses," Maybelle said dryly.

"They're supposed to be ugly," Rosie said, taking another look in the mirror to check her makeup. "It's an ugly Christmas sweater-themed wedding. All the guests will be wearing them."

"You could have at least spared the bridesmaids."

"Now, now, Maybelle, this is my day so just smile and pretend you love your dress."

"Don't think I don't know that you purposely put me in this...this..." Maybelle glanced down at the gaudy sweater clinging to her body. "This monstrosity of a Christmas sweater to ensure I didn't outshine you on your big day."

"Now, Maybelle, would I do that?" Rosie smiled sweetly again. "But I tell you what, if you ever find someone crazy enough to marry you again, I'll wear whatever you pick without making the slightest whimper of complaint."

Maybelle eyed her, then slyly smiled. "I'll keep that in mind."

Rosie snorted. "After five decades of you being single, I'm not worried."

Maybelle just kept smiling.

"Oh! It's time," Ruby said, fluffing Rosie's dress once more, then sighing. "Our dresses may be lacking in beauty, but this really is one of the most beautiful wedding dresses I've ever seen. I love the pearls and iridescent sequins and, oh, it's just gorgeous. Not sure you qualify to wear white, though."

Claudia slapped her hand over her mouth.

"I'd have gone with something bold, maybe in blue to match my hair, but Lou wanted me in white. I wasn't so sure that wouldn't be boring, but I do make it look good, don't I?" Rosie asked with a waggle of her drawn-on brows. "Now, y'all come give me a hug, but don't mess up my makeup, and definitely don't say anything too sweet or I'll cry."

"No worries there. Just you make sure you make it down the aisle or we'll never forgive you for making us go out in public in these hideous things."

The gleam in Rosie's eyes had the other three Butterflies exchanging looks even before she said, "Now, Maybelle, do you think I'd do something so diabolical as to set you up that way?"

"I can't wait to see Ralphie," Greyson said, wiggling around to take in all the festive activities around them. "He's so cute. Maybe I can feed him a carrot again."

"Maybe. If not, we'll definitely come to visit another time," Morgan promised, thinking it would be a fun mother-son trip.

The music changed and Morgan turned back to see the Butterflies lined up in comical Christmas sweater dresses. Her mouth fell open. *Oh my.* Rosie had outdone herself with those numbers.

Her Grammy was first. She carried a bouquet of neon pink and green poinsettias and wore a green sweater bedecked with tinsel garland and a tribute to the twelve days of Christmas, complete with a partridge in a pear tree. Ruby was next and carried bright blue and green poinsettias. Her sweater dress was a different shade of green and had similar tinsel garland zig-zagging across it. It was dotted with colorful gumdrops, and oversized plastic candy canes and peppermints dangled all over it. As the matron of honor, Maybelle was last and carried silver and gold poinsettias. Her red and green dress was decorated with stuffed abominable snow monster faces—along with every other grumpy Christmas character to ever exist.

Morgan covered her mouth to keep from giggling, but not everyone was able to suppress their humor and a wave of laughter sounded.

Soon all three Butterflies were at the altar next to Lou, who looked a little nervous. A group of little girls dressed as elves made their way down the aisles, stopping along the way to hand out candy canes to guests. A pretty little dark-haired elf, spotted Greyson, waved, then came over and gave him a candy cane.

"Hey Brynne," Greyson whispered.

Rather than answer, the little elf smiled, waved, then took off to hand out more candy canes. Morgan wasn't quite sure what she thought of the way her son's pink cheeks were glowing, but she had to admit that Brynne was adorable. When all the elves were at the front near the altar, they sat down with their legs crossed and the music changed again to cue the bride.

As several seconds passed and there was still no Rosie, Lou's nervousness grew, as did that of the guests.

Come on, Rosie, Morgan silently urged. *Don't let Lou down.*

Just as Morgan was deciding that maybe someone needed to go look for the bride, six toy soldiers stepped up and blew trumpets.

"All may rise," one announced in a stern voice after the fanfare.

Everyone stood and turned toward where the soldiers stood at attention. The sound of bells could be heard from outside the tree perimeter. Faintly at first, but the sound gradually grew louder and louder.

"On Dasher. On Dancer. On Comet and Cupid," a very jolly Santa called. "Donner and Blitzen," he said as he drove the reindeer-led sleigh up toward the aisle.

Greyson's eyes were huge as the sleigh came to a stop. "Look, Mommy. There's Ralphie and our other reindeer Santa borrowed for Rosie's wedding!"

"And Rosie," Morgan added. "She didn't run away, after all. And look how beautiful she is."

Two of the toy soldiers went to the sleigh, lifted Rosie out, and spread out her glistening train. Morgan glanced toward the altar, then smiled at Lou's awed expression.

"She looks like a magic snow queen from a movie or something," Greyson whispered. "Do you think we can ride in Santa's sleigh and say hi to Ralphie?"

"Maybe after the wedding," she whispered back. "Shhh, watch Rosie."

Because as Rosie took a step toward the altar, toy soldiers on both sides of the aisle opened the lids to the giant presents, releasing what looked like hundreds of white and silver butterflies.

Lots of ooohs and aaahs sounded.

"Wow," Greyson and Morgan said at the same time.

As they weren't real, Morgan wasn't sure what caused them to rise from the box and flutter around, but watching Rosie walk down the aisle amidst the dancing butterflies, with the sun reflecting off the snow, giving the world a diamond shimmer, was absolutely breathtaking.

As Rosie passed where she was sitting, Morgan caught sight of Andrew sitting on the opposite side of the aisle. She'd looked for him earlier and not seen him, so he must have slipped in just prior to the ceremony starting. He apparently noticed her at the same time as their gazes met and held.

He didn't smile, just stared back at her, his hazel eyes filled with emotions she couldn't quite understand.

Oh Andrew, she thought. She'd not seen him since prior to the fire. Seeing him living and uninjured had her wanting to leap across the aisle, wrap her arms around him, and to hold on tight for however long he'd let her. Had he missed her as much as she'd missed him?

"I see Andrew," Greyson said.

"Shhh." Morgan returned her gaze to the wedding. Rosie reached the altar, and the guests were asked to sit down.

It was so hard to keep her gaze from shifting back to Andrew as Rosie and Lou exchanged the vows they'd written for each other. Their words caused a few shed tears and some laughter, too, when Lou promised to spoil her rotten and Rosie said, "But of course."

"By the powers vested in me, I now pronounce you man and wife," Pastor Smith said, then smiling at the crowd added, "I present to you, Mr. and Mrs. Lou Hudson."

Hand in hand, Lou and Rosie walked back down the aisle, all smiles as the soldiers assisted them back up into Santa's sleigh and tossed a furry white blanket over them to snuggle underneath.

Next the Butterflies came back down the aisle, all smiles—no doubt because Rosie had finally said I do.

"If everyone will make your way over to the main barn, the bride and groom have lunch available for you while they have their wedding photos made," Pastor Smith told them. "It's buffet style, so help yourselves. There's plenty."

Rather than walk, Mr. Harvey pulled up with his wagon that had been decorated to look like a sleigh. Fuzzy white blankets covered hay bales. Three soldiers pushed three sturdy presents of varied sizes over to the end of the wagon to make a tiered staircase and stood beside each one to assist each person up them.

"I'm definitely having a Christmas wedding. One with reindeers and soldiers," Greyson said from beside her. "This is so cool."

Deciding she should probably start saving her money now, Morgan smiled.

"Let's go find your grandmother," Grampy said. "I need to tell her that even with eleven pipers piping and ten lords a-leaping on her dress, she looks beautiful, and makes three hundred and sixty-five days a year feel like Christmas, not just twelve."

"Ah, that's sweet, Grampy," Morgan said, kissing her grandfather's cheek. "She'll love you saying so."

So rather than head directly to the make-shift sleigh wagon, Morgan and Greyson went with Grampy to find the Butterflies to tell them all how beautiful they looked. From the neck up, at any rate.

"George, do you mind staying here for a few minutes?" Grammy asked. "I'm going to ask the photographer if he'll shoot a few shots of you and me together."

Morgan looked around for Andrew but didn't spot him anywhere at the ceremony area. Had he already headed to the reception? She and Greyson headed that way, too. It was a quick five-minute wagon ride.

Inside the barn, more elves waited to dry their footwear and take their outerwear and the backpack of extra clothes they'd been advised to bring for playing in the snow after the nuptials. A girl elf with a black marker wrote their names on a large white plastic bag, then took it to hang it by its tie straps alphabetically with the other bags.

Holding Greyson's hand, Morgan walked into the barn, her breath catching at the magic of the large open room. The scent of pine and Christmas filled the air. There must've been some type of fragrance being pumped in, since Morgan couldn't imagine the live pine trees at the front of the barn generating that much of a scent. Whatever was causing it, it smelled heavenly.

"Can we stay and have Santa visit us here tonight? I don't ever want to leave," Greyson exclaimed, looking around the room that had been set up with gorgeous Christmas table settings, including a centerpiece consisting of a wrapped present with huge ribbons alternating in colors of red and gold. On each place setting was a name card.

"Morgan?" Sophie called from a nearby table. "You're over here with Cole and me. Hi, Greyson!"

"Wow, Sophie. You guys look amazing," Morgan told her cousin and Cole. She'd seen them outdoors, but they'd all had their coats and blankets covering their 'ugly sweaters.' Sophie had taken plain red sweaters and embellished them with tinsel on the shoulders. Cole's had a large Santa on the front, and Sophie's had Mrs. Claus. Both wore Santa hats. "You, too, Isabelle," she told her cousin who sat next to Sophie.

Isabelle glanced down and shook her head, the movement causing the tiny bells on her sweater to jingle. "Who ever heard of an ugly Christmas sweater wedding theme? Leave it to Rosie."

"I think it's fun," Sarah said from where she sat on the opposite side of the table. "Bodie and I sure had a great time coming up with what we were going to wear. He's the cutest reindeer ever."

His arm protectively draped across the back of her chair with his hand on her shoulder, Bodie just smiled indulgently at his wife, whose pregnancy was just starting to show.

"I like your antlers, Mrs. Sarah," Greyson piped up, pointing to her headband. "You're a cute reindeer, too. Did you see Ralphie?"

"Thank you, Greyson. I did get to see Ralphie. It's so great you helped get those reindeer for Santa to borrow for Rosie's wedding today. Today has been magical," Sarah said echoing Morgan's thoughts. "A perfect wedding day, Christmas eve, and anniversary eve."

"Happy one year anniversary eve," Sophie said, smiling at the blissfully happy couple.

Morgan felt a pang of envy. Once upon a time, she'd been that happy.

A realization hit her. She was that happy.

Perhaps not the "I'm so in love and loved back" relationship kind of happy, but she was happy. Really, truly happy. Glancing down at Greyson, at where he was checking out the present that had been in her chair, she acknowledged that he was happy, too, and not just because Brynne had given him a candy cane, although that had been the topic of conversation the entire ride over to the barn.

This was what she had wanted. To give Greyson his best Christmas ever. To make Christmas magical for him. Now her biggest worry was how to ever have another Christmas to compare to the magic of this one.

"Andrew!" Greyson dropped the present onto the table, rushed over to where Andrew was returning to the table with a drink in his hand. Greyson wrapped his arms around Andrew's waist and squeezed him in the biggest hug.

"Hey, bud." Sitting his drink on the table, Andrew knelt and hugged him back.

Morgan's breath caught. She'd been fighting to keep her gaze from searching out Andrew because she knew once she let her eyes feast on him, they weren't going to want to go elsewhere. She'd been right. But why would she want to look anywhere else when she could be watching that hug? That was a real hug. An *I've missed you* hug. An *I care about you* hug. An *I don't want to let go* hug. A hug like she wanted to give him. She wanted to wrap her arms around him and feel life surging through him with his strong heartbeat against her cheek.

"Nice snowman sweater," Andrew said, avoiding looking in her direction as he pulled back to take in Greyson's outfit.

Greyson proudly glanced down at his snowman sweater and grinned. "It's like the one we made on the mountain. Your sweater has Dalmatians. I like that, but not the pink." Which caused Andrew to laugh. "Someday I'm going to have a dog. Maybe a Dalmatian, but Brynne has Lab puppies and says I need one 'cause they need a good home and I have a good home."

Morgan's heart swelled. He did have a good home. A home filled with love. And as long as they had each other, that would always be the case.

"Lab puppies, huh?" Andrew said. "Maybe Chief can be talked into a Lab, but since they chew on things a lot when they're little, I'm not sure he'd let one be around the fire hall until it was older and trained not to chew."

While Andrew and Greyson talked, she took in how handsome he was in his jeans and ridiculous pink sweater with Dalmatians in Santa hats, fire hydrants with wreaths on them, and fire trucks decorated with Christmas lights.

When Andrew stood, their gazes collided. His eyes not leaving hers, he picked up his cup and took a drink. After a moment, he asked, "What about you? Do you think I'll win the ugly sweater contest?"

"Just the ugly contest," Cole piped up, causing Ben to laugh and Andrew to roll his eyes.

Morgan swallowed, taking in that he was talking to her. She knew it was probably just to break the ice to keep everyone at the table from feeling awkward, but it still thrilled her that he was looking at her, talking to her.

"Maybe. That sweater is definitely…" Keeping it light despite the heavy fireworks going off inside her, Morgan gave a dramatic pause. "Something."

He was something. Something wonderful. Being so near, hearing his voice, made her head a bit woozy. Did he have any idea how worried she'd been about him? How much she wanted to hold him as tightly as she could and never let go? But even if he let her hold him here and now, she'd have to let go before long. Because soon, he'd be leaving Pine Hill.

"Grandma got it for me," he said. That Ruby had found the sweater for him wasn't surprising. Nor was the fact that Andrew was proudly wearing it. "Yours is great, too."

Morgan's blue sweater was covered with gingerbread men and a big *Oh, Snap* written on it with a fabric paint pen she'd bought at The Threaded Needle.

"Greyson, Rosie has a special place set up for young guests," Sophie said, standing. "A lot of fun things will be happening. Would you like Cole and me to take you over to where the others are?"

Greyson gave Andrew a pleading look, then turned big eyes on Morgan. "Can Andrew take me, please? I need to tell him about Brynne."

"I...I don't mind, so long as he doesn't," she said.

Was Andrew imagining the way Morgan was looking at him? She looked...no, he wasn't going to think on that. He'd be leaving in a couple of weeks, following his plan to be a smokejumper. His dreams were coming true. He was happy. Ecstatic. Only...

Only her words to him plagued that happiness. If he'd not been leaving, Morgan would've been willing to open her heart to him. He'd have her and Greyson in his life. But the smokejumper drive within him was real. He'd put it off for so long. When he'd look back at the end of his life, if he didn't train as a smokejumper, didn't fight wildland fires, he'd feel as if he'd been a failure. He had to go. It was now or never.

"No problem," he said, focusing on Greyson. He'd missed the kid, wanted to hear about Brynne, and he needed to tell him goodbye. That wasn't going to be easy. He wasn't even sure if Greyson was aware that he'd be leaving. It was possible Morgan had already told him, but Greyson didn't act as if he knew. "It'll give us a chance to talk."

Greyson beamed up at him. As Andrew tried to find the right words, he listened to Greyson excitedly tell him one thing after another while they walked to the back of the large open room.

"And Mom and I ran around the yard tasting snowflakes and laughing. We had so much fun, but we wished you were there," Greyson talked a mile a minute. Off to the side of the room was a hallway that led to an area set up with 'reindeer games' for the kids. "I've been missing you bunches. Where have you been?"

"I've been missing you, too," Andrew admitted, knowing he'd be missing this kid a long time. "Bud, do you remember when we first met? You told me you wanted to be a firefighter and I told you that I wanted to be a firefighter who is part of a special group who battles wildfires?"

"A smokejumper." Greyson nodded. "I didn't tell anyone your secret. Not even Mom."

"That's right. You pinky-promised. Like I mentioned then, I really want to be a smoke-jumper."

Understanding began to light in Greyson's green eyes. "You're going to do that now?"

Andrew nodded. "I'm going to train as a Hotshot and, Lord willing, earn my qualifications to then train as a smokejumper. I'm excited to finally be making my dream come true."

"That's cool," Greyson said, obviously not understanding the full ramifications of what this meant.

"It is cool," Andrew agreed, wishing he could leave it at that but knowing he had to make the boy understand. It wouldn't be fair to leave that to Morgan to deal with. He wanted to make sure Greyson knew how special he was and how much he'd miss him. What he didn't want was to hurt him. Ever. "But I admit to being sad about a few things, too. Things such as not getting to see you and your mom." He took a deep breath. "I leave in two weeks, Greyson."

"How long will you be gone?"

"A long time," he admitted, thinking his

sweater must have spontaneously shrunk a few sizes, as it seemed to be cutting off his breathing.

Greyson went watery-eyed, and he sighed. "I'm gonna miss you lots."

Something deep in Andrew's chest jerked. "I'm going to miss you lots, too, kid."

More than he would have dreamed possible. This boy was in his heart and he knew he'd think of Greyson, wondering what he was doing, how he was doing, for years to come.

"Is that why my mommy cried the other night? Because you're leaving us?"

Andrew's heart did its jerky thing again. "Your mom cried?"

Greyson nodded solemnly. "She used to cry at night a lot before we moved here. But not now. Except she cried after the big fire where people got hurt." His lower lip trembled a little. "I think she thought you got hurt, too."

Andrew's throat constricted. This was why he had to leave, had to let Greyson and Morgan move on without him standing in their way. If he'd needed a reminder, there it was.

"There were some people hurt, but they're going to be just fine," he said, not wanting Greyson to worry. "No matter what happens, I never want you or your mom sad, bud."

"Mommy says it's okay to be sad when something bad happens." Greyson's face scrunched up, but he took a deep breath, then bravely said, "I'm glad you get to be a smokejumper, but it does make me sad."

"I understand," he admitted. He felt the same. Overjoyed to be starting wildland fire fighting training. Sad at the thought of leaving Pine Hill, his grandparents, his friends, Greyson, and Morgan.

He hugged the boy to him, held him close, smelling his kiddie shampoo, and searing the moment to his memory. Yeah, he was going to miss Greyson a lot.

"I need you to promise me something else, bud."

Greyson nodded.

"I need you to take care of your mom." Andrew swallowed and pressed forward. "I won't be here, so I need you to always make sure she's loved and taken care of. She's special, so it's important that I'm able to count on you. Can you do that for me?"

Nodding, Greyson held up his pinky. "I pinky promise."

"I knew I could count on you." Andrew locked his pinky with Greyson's much smaller one and fought the emotion clogging his throat. He'd known this wasn't going to be easy, but he hadn't realized how gutted telling Greyson was going to leave him.

"Okay, enough of this mushy stuff," he

---

said, straightening, and reminding himself this was the right thing to do. For him. For Greyson. For Morgan. "Let's get you to Rosie's Reindeer Games. I saw a pretty little elf named Brynne head that way a while ago."

Chapter Fifteen

"*D*O YOU SEE WHAT I see?"

Morgan nodded at her cousin's question. She saw and was filled with so many different emotions as she watched Andrew kneel down to talk with Greyson. She was sure Andrew was telling him of his decision to leave Pine Hill.

And no doubt her son was telling him that he didn't want him to go.

I don't want him to go, either, she thought again.

"He's so good with Greyson," Sophie continued, her words coming out as a sigh.

"Sophie, leave Morgan alone," Cole said, coming to her defense. "She knows Andrew is great with Greyson. She also knows he is leaving in two weeks."

Two weeks, and then he'd be gone for Lord only knew how long. Even when he came back, it would likely only be for short visits with his family.

Sophie frowned at Cole. "A lot can happen in two weeks. There's always hope."

Hope. Morgan swallowed. Andrew hoped she'd be happy, that she'd live the life she wanted to live, that she and Greyson would get all the good things they deserved. She hoped he'd be happy fighting fires in wide open spaces. And safe. Lord, she hoped he'd always be safe.

Staring at where he hugged her son, she bit her lower lip. John was right. It didn't matter where Andrew was or whether they were a couple, she'd always be praying for his safety.

"She just needs to tell him how she feels," Sophie insisted to Cole as if Morgan wasn't sitting within hearing distance.

"Not everyone responds to your 'bulldoze them with love' technique, Sophie," Isabelle spoke up, casting a worried look Morgan's way.

"I think it was those cookies Sophie made him that had Cole falling head over heels," Ben said from the opposite side of the table. "Those were great."

"You like cookies? My mom's recipe for

chocolate oatmeal cookies are a-mazing," Lisa said, launching the couple into a discussion about different types of cookies.

"Was that it?" Isabelle asked Cole. "Was it my sister's cookies that won you over?"

His eyes sparkling with humor, Cole's gaze skimmed over Sophie as if trying to recall what it had been, then he grinned. "Nah, she knows what it was that sealed the deal."

Sophie's smile was bright enough to light up the room. "It was my joy."

Morgan was pretty sure she was missing an inside joke as Isabelle rolled her eyes and Sophie kissed Cole's cheek. She'd also missed when Andrew and her son had headed to the Rosie's Reindeer Games area and was startled when Andrew returned to their table. Without a word, he sat down and took a long sip from the cup he'd left earlier.

"You look as if you just lost your best friend, and I know that isn't true because we're sitting right here," Ben said, gesturing back and forth between him and Cole.

Andrew sighed. "I sort of feel as if I did." He glanced toward Morgan. "I told Greyson that I'm leaving. I know you know this, but just to reiterate, he really is a great kid."

Crazily feeling as if she were losing her best friend as well, she nodded. "Thank you."

Morgan was saved from saying anything else by the toy soldiers making an appearance and blowing their trumpets.

"Ladies and Gentlemen, let me introduce your wedding party. Claudia Bradley, Ruby Jenkins, and Matron of Honor Maybelle Kirby." A round of applause went up. The soldier announced Lou's groomsmen, then paused dramatically before saying, "And now for your groom and his lovely bride, Mr. and Mrs. Lou Hudson."

Lou and Rosie came into the room. Everyone stood and clapped. A bunch of *woot-woots* that sounded loudly from Morgan's table.

Rosie and Lou had their first dance, and then Bodie took Sarah's hand to lead her onto the dance floor. Several other couples joined them, including Ben and Lisa.

Morgan smiled when she saw John ask Maybelle to dance and the older woman wisely said yes. He wasn't doing any crazy moves, just slowly shuffling his feet back and forth, but he seemed steady and the look on his face at having Maybelle in his arms was priceless. How sweet.

Sophie gave Cole a look and cleared her throat. He grimaced. "I don't dance."

"Neither does Bodie, but look at him now," Sophie pointed out with an expectant look on her face. Sighing, Cole got up and went out on the dance floor with her. His smile suggested that he might not enjoy dancing, but he liked the excuse to have Sophie in his arms.

Which left Andrew, Morgan, and Isabelle at the table.

"Hey, I want to talk to Carrie about how Sophie's pet bandanas are selling at her shop," Isabelle said, standing up, then pausing before she walked off. "Andrew, you should ask Morgan to dance."

Then she left. Morgan sat there surprised by the suggestion from anti-romance Isabelle.

After a moment Andrew said, "Telling Greyson goodbye wasn't easy."

"I imagine not," she admitted, staring at the dance floor to keep him from seeing the tears forming in her eyes. "He adores you. He was disappointed you weren't there when we picked up his entry from the fire hall."

"I still think his colored ornament was the best," Andrew said, his gaze searching hers. What was he thinking? Was he wishing they could go somewhere and talk in private—or was she alone in longing for that? But even if they did go talk, what would they say? She wanted to beg him to stay, but she couldn't do that, could she?

"You two coming out here or what?" Sophie called from the dance floor where she was lovingly wrapped in Cole's arms.

Embarrassed at Sophie's question, Morgan gave Andrew an apologetic look.

"Hey, Andrew, you going to show us some of your smooth dance moves?" Ben teased as he and Lisa sashayed in front of them.

"Maybe we should dance to appease them," Andrew suggested. "Otherwise, they'll just keep on."

Dance with Andrew? Morgan swallowed. "I..." she paused. What was she doing? Andrew was leaving. This might be her last opportunity to touch him. "I'd like that."

Her agreement seemed to surprise him, but he quickly stood and held his hand out to take hers. Her belly flip-flopped as his warm fingers clasped hers, feeling strong and capable and yet gentle as he led her out. They didn't go far, stopping just at the edge of the dance floor.

He let go of her hand and wrapped his arms around her waist. "This okay?"

She nodded. It was. Beautifully, perfectly, okay as they moved slowly back and forth in rhythm with each other. His arms around her felt...right. Unable to resist, Morgan laid her head against his chest to listen to his heartbeat. It pounded loud, strong, steady against her cheek.

"Greyson told me you cried the night of the fire."

"I didn't know he saw that," she admitted, not looking up because she was afraid she might cry right here and now if she did.

"I'm sorry if I'm why you cried. I never want to hurt you, Morgan."

"I...I cried for a lot of reasons that night, Andrew," she admitted. "You were one of them."

"I'm sorry," he repeated.

"Don't be," she said and meant it. Emotions overwhelmed her and she lifted her head to stare up at him. "I don't want you to go, Andrew. You have to know that. But I'd never want to hold you back from going after your dreams."

His expression tightened. "Not even when you hate what I'm going to be doing?"

"I don't hate it," she countered. "Far from it. I admire what you're doing, Andrew. What every firefighter does whether they are fighting structure fires or forest fires. You're heroes. I...I've been doing a lot of thinking." She really had, thanks to her conversation with John. "I regret that I've been giving Greyson such a hard time about wanting to be a firefighter. I tried to hide how I felt some, but he knew. I shouldn't have let my biases come through so strongly."

"That kid is going to do great things no matter what he does."

Morgan nodded. "He has a good heart."

"Like his mom."

"And his father."

"...Tell me about him?"

Andrew's request surprised her. But talking about Trey felt much easier than addressing the ache inside her at the thought the song would soon end and Andrew's arms would no longer be around her.

"Trey was fun, full of life, not afraid of anything." She half-smiled. "A lot like you."

"He died while mountain climbing?"

She nodded. "The weather changed unexpectedly. Apparently, the blizzard was blinding and a few of their group stumbled off the trail. Trey attempted to rescue them and lost his life in the process."

"I'm sorry, Morgan. For you and for Greyson."

"Me, too." She bit into her lower lip. "He died a hero, laying his life down to try to save others. That's something I didn't ac-knowledge until recently."

"He sounds like a good man."

Trey had had a love of adrenaline, but he truly had been a good man. A very good man, and she'd loved him so much. As the thought hit her, she realized that although the deep sadness was there, it was different. She was no longer filled with anger that he'd taken such risks with his life or that he'd left her much too soon. Instead, the gratitude she felt for the time they'd shared soothed the hole in her heart that losing him had caused.

"There's something else you have in common with him." Morgan stared up at Andrew. "For a long time, I was so buried in my grief and anger that he'd taken such risks that I couldn't see beyond the walls I'd built around myself. Thank you for helping to improve my life's view by tearing down those walls."

Swallowing, he stood still. "I'm leaving in two weeks, Morgan."

"You think you need to remind me of that?" she asked, determined to say what was in her heart once and for all. "That I don't keep thinking of how soon you're going to disappear from my life? I finally find someone who fills me with such hope, and now I have to let him go."

"I'm sorry," he said again, his body stiff against hers. "I never want to be the reason you cry."

Morgan's eyes prickled, but her tears stayed checked as she admitted, "I didn't think I wanted you to be the reason I cried, either, but I was wrong."

His brows veed as he stared down at her. "I don't understand."

Finally, she did. Fully and completely.

"Crying meant I cared and once upon a time I didn't think it possible for me to care about another man. But then you came along and I…"

"And you what?" he prompted, his gaze searching hers.

"Oh, look at you two!" Sophie exclaimed, popping the bubble they'd been inside and pulling them back to the reality. As she and Andrew turned to glance Sophie's way, Morgan noticed one of the soldiers standing nearby, holding a giant candy cane with a sprig of mistletoe tied to the top. A sprig of mistletoe that was dangling above her and Andrew's heads.

"You have to kiss. It's tradition."

Mortified, Morgan's gaze met Andrew's. He didn't look any happier about the situation than she did.

"No, sorry, but we can't," she said. "I mean…"

"Morgan, you have to kiss," Sophie insisted. "It's bad luck if you break the mistletoe tradition. You can't send Andrew off to training with bad luck."

No, she couldn't do that. It wasn't as if she didn't want to kiss him. She did want to. Only, she wanted him to kiss her back because he wanted to and not because mistletoe hung above their heads.

"Fine," she murmured, placing her hands on his shoulders and standing on her tiptoes. She'd just press a quick kiss to his lips to appease her cousin and to satisfy her own curiosity.

But when her lips touched Andrew's, pulling back was the last thought on her mind. Instead, she looked into his beautiful hazel eyes. They locked with hers as he kissed her back with the gentle pressure of his lips against hers. Morgan forgot there was anyone else in the room and that the kiss was only happening because of a Christmas tradition. She forgot Andrew was leaving. She forgot everything except that she was in his arms and he was kissing her, and nothing had ever felt more right.

His kiss was a sweet tasting of her lips that filled her with hope. Andrew kissed her as if her kiss was precious to him.

When he pulled back, his gaze didn't waver and what she saw there confirmed everything she'd just felt.

"Wow," she whispered, her hands clinging to his shoulders to keep herself steady on her feet. "Who needs a flashy red truck and sirens when he has that in his arsenal?"

Although he looked torn over how to feel, his eyes lit with recall. Smile playing on his lips, he asked, "Are you saying you were finally impressed?"

Morgan nodded.

He gave a slight shake of his head. "This is complicated."

Her heart pounded. "So you keep reminding me."

Clapping sounded around them, pulling Morgan from the fantasy she'd been in where she and Andrew were alone and that he was going to tell her he'd changed his mind, that he wasn't going to leave her and Greyson. Ugh. How could she keep forgetting they were surrounded by their meddling friends and family?

"Way to go," Ben congratulated Andrew, slapping him on the back. "You impressed me, too."

They'd been able to hear their conversation? Morgan's cheeks flushed so hot that she felt like she'd gone up in flames. How embarrassing!

"Ahem!" Maybelle said into a microphone, calling everyone's attention to her and rescuing Morgan from further mortification. "If I could have Andrew, Ruby, and Claudia to join me at the front of the room. We've prepared a special wedding treat for the newlyweds."

Morgan's gaze cut to Andrew in question.

"I've got to go, but we'll talk later," he said, then surprised her by bending down to press his lips to hers for one last, quick taste before joining Maybelle on the stage.

"What was that?" Sophie asked, immediately coming over to her.

Morgan shrugged. "I'm not sure."

Because Andrew was leaving, and what could a Christmas kiss change about that?

What had Andrew been thinking? He

shouldn't have kissed Morgan, no matter if a canopy of mistletoe was hung over them.

But what a kiss. Morgan had kissed him with her heart in her eyes.

She didn't want him to go.

His insides wrenched. Part of him longed to tell her that he'd changed his mind, that he'd stay in Pine Hill for her and Greyson. That if it would make her happy, he'd give up firefighting and find a much safer desk job.

But if he did that, how long would they be happy before he grew restless? How long before his love of firefighting beckoned him back? Firefighting was a part of who he was, ingrained in his very being. He'd never wanted anything else.

Until Greyson and Morgan.

But he couldn't think about that now.

Not with Maybelle, his grandma, and Morgan's grandma expecting him to help them pull off their surprise for Rosie. He walked over to where he'd stashed his guitar and their song props earlier.

"Rosie," Maybelle continued, somehow managing to still look regal in her ridiculous 'ugly' sweater bridesmaid dress. "For as long as I've known you, you've added color to my and the other Butterflies' lives. Today, we're adding some color to your wedding."

Andrew got his guitar and the props. He handed the cardboard posters over to the

Butterflies, then put the main microphone in its stand and adjusted the height. Then, he waited for the three Butterflies to get together at their back-up singer microphones. They held the props so that only the plain white backs showed to the crowd.

When they appeared ready, he grinned at the newlyweds. "When my grandma asked me about doing this, I wasn't so sure, but Rosie and Lou, this one's for you." He strummed his pick across his guitar strings, then let loose with Elvis's "Hound Dog."

Lots of eyes widened and a few jaws dropped, including those of his back-up singer Butterflies who hadn't been expecting that particular song. Then chuckles rippled over the crowd.

"Oops. Wrong song." Laughing, Andrew started over with the correct Elvis number the Butterflies had requested. "Blue Christmas." The Butterflies sang backup in unison, flipping their props to reveal large poster cutouts of Rosie's face with her blue hair.

As Andrew sang, he couldn't keep his gaze away from Morgan. He'd kissed her. It had been such a perfect kiss. Well, it would have been perfect had they not been surrounded by people.

But he supposed it was just as well that they had been, because he never should have kissed her. Now, that kiss was just one more thing to miss about her. As he sang the melancholy lyrics, he knew he told the truth. No matter where he was, no matter what he was doing, Morgan would be on his mind and his heart would be blue without her. That was a given.

The Butterflies swayed, getting into their backup singer roles as they danced the blue-haired Rosie faces back and forth. Grinning, Andrew tapped his guitar in rhythm as the Butterflies took over completely, singing the chorus with as much gusto as any dynamic women's trio in history.

Looking as if she was having the time of her life, his grandma bopped back and forth with her friends as they danced in their ugly Christmas sweater dresses. Then they flung their arms out, laughing, and took a bow.

Yeah, Andrew was going to miss this, but how could he ignore the incessant call of his dreams when it was finally within his grasp?

Chapter Sixteen

ALTHOUGH SHE WASN'T THAT COLD, Morgan wrapped her arms around herself as she watched her son play in the snow with Brynne. The little girl's mother had asked if Greyson could build a snowman with them. He'd been looking at her with those big pleading eyes, so Morgan had quickly agreed and followed them outdoors.

Seeing him laughing as he and Brynne rolled up snow, Morgan couldn't help but smile. No matter what, she would cling to her happiness and remain positive. No matter what, she was back on her feet and could withstand whatever life threw at her. No matter what, she'd do what was right for her son. No matter if her heart broke because of Andrew, she'd keep a smile on her face and focus on all of life's blessings.

"He looks happy."

Wondering if fate was immediately testing her resolution, Morgan turned toward Andrew. "He is happy. I loved your song with the Butterflies. That was so great. I thought Rosie was going to die laughing at their antics."

"They do think they're pretty funny, pulling one over on Rosie. And when they asked me about doing the song, I couldn't resist singing Elvis with my grandma." Smiling, he gave Morgan a look that let her know that he'd not sought her out to talk about the Butterflies. "Walk with me? We won't go far—I know you don't want to be away from Greyson."

"I'd like that," she said. "As for Greyson, I doubt he'll notice I'm gone. Brynne's mother is planning to take them for hot cocoa when they're finished with their snowman. He's quite in heaven getting to see and spend time with Brynne today. I think he's missed her since school let out for Christmas break."

"She was happy to see him when I brought him to the reindeer games, too."

"He's started talking about marrying her and having a Christmas wedding. Five years old, and he already has his whole life mapped out," she mused, but with a smile. "Moving here is the best thing I ever did. Pine Hill has been a place of healing for both of us." She glanced Andrew's way. "Meeting you and getting to know you helped us, too, Andrew."

Without looking at her, he kept walking, then finally said, "If I've played any role in giving you and Greyson happiness, then I'll count that as a blessing."

He sounded so sincere, so overflowing with emotions, that she stopped walking and turned to him, letting her own emotions take over. "I can't believe you're really leaving."

"There's part of me that wants to stay, Morgan, but I can't."

She bit into her lower lip. "Can't or won't?"

"I know you don't understand, but this is something I have to do."

She took a deep breath. "For how long?"

"I'm not sure. Maybe just a few years. Maybe longer. I just know it's what I'm meant to do."

She nodded as if she understood, but she didn't.

"For what it's worth, you and Greyson make me wish things were different, that I was different and didn't feel this drive..." His voice trailed off and he sighed. "You make me wish I could be everything you ever wanted in a man and in a father for Greyson. That I could somehow have it all—you and being a smokejumper."

There was such anguish in his words that Morgan's breath caught.

"But you need someone who will be there for you. Someone who will come home every night and help Greyson with his homework and cook dinner when you're too tired to. That's not me. There will be weeks, sometimes months, when I'll be out in the wilderness fighting fires and even phone calls will be impossible."

Morgan swallowed at the grim picture he was painting.

"When you're out there, fighting those fires, know that you'll be in my prayers and in my heart," she told him, staring up at him with so much emotion bubbling inside her she thought she might burst. "And that I'll be so proud of the man you are, that you're willing to give so much of yourself to help others."

"Morgan, I," he began, then paused before he took her gloved hand into his and lifted it to his lips. "Thank you for everything."

Knowing he was telling her goodbye, she fought tears and nodded. "You're welcome, Andrew. Take care of yourself, and if you do make it back to Pine Hill, please let Greyson and me know." Then she remembered something. "Greyson wanted to get you a gift. Is it okay if we drop it off tomorrow?"

"I'll be at the fire hall all day. Got to be there at eight in the morning to relieve the crew working tonight." She should have known that he'd have volunteered to work the holiday so others could be off. "But we're working partial shifts tomorrow and I should be off around four. I could swing by on my way home to save you from having to take Greyson out."

"Sounds good." She smiled at him, then decided it was time to take an interest in this new path that was so important to him. After all, she'd need to know what to be praying for. "Now, tell me exactly what you'll be doing at your training and how long that lasts, and where you'll be going to fight fires. I want to know everything."

"Really? You want me to tell you about becoming a smokejumper?"

"Shocking, I know, but I really do." Too bad every excited word from his lips was a reminder that he'd soon be gone.

"Your firefighter does a decent Elvis imper-sonation."

"He's not my firefighter, John." Morgan patted the bench beside her where she was

taking a break from her ice-skating at-
tempts. Greyson was still on the ice, holding
hands with a nutcracker-costumed skater
on one side and Brynne on the other as they
got a personalized ice-skating lesson. "I've
told you that before."

"It was my hip that was broken, not
my eyeballs," he reminded her. "I saw that
mistletoe kiss and was a bit jealous that elf
never made his way over to where Maybelle
and I were. Had you ever offered me that
kind of cane, I wouldn't have complained so
much about using one."

Morgan laughed. "You think so? I can
put it in the suggestions box at work."

"Good idea."

"I was tickled when I saw you and Maybelle dancing," she told him, smiling.

"Not much of a dance with this still-
healing hip, but at least I didn't fall on my
face. Then again, if I had, someone might
have brought that cane over to me."

"Can you imagine the comments Rosie
would have made about you throwing yourself at Maybelle's feet?" Morgan smiled. "She
seemed to be enjoying herself. And as far as
my and Andrew's kiss, it was just the mistletoe."

"You don't expect me to believe that, do
you?"

"I told him that I didn't want him to go,
John, but when I listened to him talk about

being a smokejumper…well, I've realized that I was wrong to ask him to stay."

"You're going with him?" John asked, sounding shocked.

Stunned, she shook her head. "No, of course, not."

"Why 'of course not'?"

"I can't go with him."

John stared at her blankly. "Why not?"

"Because Pine Hill is my home and is where my grandparents and family are. I don't want to leave."

"Then you'll let him go and forget about him."

"I won't forget," she admitted.

"Yes, I agree. Because love doesn't work that way."

"Would you quit saying that?"

"You saying you don't love him?"

No, Morgan admitted to herself, she couldn't say that.

Christmas Day proved to be boring at the fire department, which was a good thing for the fine folks of Pine Hill. It meant all was well.

It was less good for Andrew, who was plagued with a restlessness that he couldn't shake. He had a week left to work out his notice, and then he'd be unemployed until he started his new position in California. He'd miss his Pine Hill crew, especially Cole with his crossword puzzles and Ben with his grand visions of beating Andrew at the latest video game sensation. Change, even good change, was never easy.

"I'm headed to Sophie's for Christmas dinner. You want to tag along?" Cole offered.

Andrew shook his head at his best friend. "Thanks, but I have plans."

"Your Grandma Ruby cooking?"

"Yes." She was, but Andrew had a stop to make first that he decided not to mention.

"I'm going to ask Sophie to marry me."

Cole's announcement had Andrew pausing, then slapping his friend on the back. "Congratulations, man. I'm happy for you."

Cole nodded. "Save your congratulations. She hasn't said yes yet."

Andrew snorted. "Is there any doubt that she's going to? She's crazy about you."

"I guess we'll know for sure soon enough." Cole dug in his pocket, pulled out a velvet box, opened it to show Andrew an impressive diamond. "I've been looking at rings for months. When I saw this one, it seemed right."

"It's impressive," Andrew said. "Seriously, I'm happy for you."

"What about you?"

"What about me?"

"Are you happy?"

Andrew raised his eyebrows, taken aback. "I'm about to do what I've dreamed of doing for years. Of course, I'm happy."

Cole seemed unconvinced. "What about Morgan and Greyson?"

Frowning, Andrew shook his head. "They're better off without me."

Cole closed the lid and slid the velvet box back into his pocket. "You know, I thought that about Sophie once, that she was better off without me. Then I realized no one could ever love her as much as I do. There's nothing I wouldn't do for Sophie. If she says yes tonight, I'll spend the rest of my life knowing I'm a lucky man."

"She'll say yes. Not hard to see she loves you."

"If she does, you'll come back and be my best man?"

"Finally, after all this time, you're admitting I'm the best man."

He and Cole exchanged grins, more back slaps, then clocked out from their shift.

Later, as he waited on Morgan's grandparents' front porch, gifts in his hands, Andrew's stomach was an anxious mess. Which didn't make sense. He was just there to drop off presents and to pick up whatever Greyson had gotten him.

Morgan opened the door, laughter shining in her eyes. "Andrew, come in."

Woof. Woof. A chocolate lab raced over to Andrew, jumped up to put his paws on Andrew's shin, woofed some more, then raced back over to where Greyson sat in the living room floor.

"You got a dog?"

"That Santa," Morgan complained with a wink. "Can you believe he left Greyson a puppy?"

"Mommy, you got me my puppy," Greyson reminded her, laughing and rolling on the floor with the dog climbing all over him. "Mommy had him in a box and brought him in to my room this morning to wake me up. I could hear him whimpering and knew what was inside. I love him."

"I can see why," Andrew said, smiling as the puppy licked Greyson's face and sent the boy into giggles. "Where are your grandparents?"

"They're at Sophie and Isabelle's for Christmas dinner. The whole family is gathered there. Greyson and I are going later."

Realization hit.

"You waited here on me, didn't you?" he guessed. "I could have come by at a different time, Morgan. We didn't have to do this tonight."

"Today is Christmas. Giving you your present today is important and waiting wasn't a big deal. We've had fun playing with the puppy, haven't we, Greyson?"

Still laying on the floor playing with the puppy, Greyson nodded. "Andy's the cutest puppy ever, aren't you, boy?"

"Andy?" Andrew asked, shocked. "You named your dog Andy?"

Greyson nodded.

Andrew knelt down to scratch the dog's head. Andy wouldn't hold still long enough for much of a petting, though, jumping around and licking Andrew's hand, before going back to pounce on Greyson and eliciting more happy little boy giggles.

Andrew glanced up at Morgan and, eyes looking a bit watery, she shrugged. "I tried to talk him into Rover, but he insisted upon Andy."

"If I'd known, I'd have gotten him puppy supplies."

"I'm sure he'll love whatever you got him," Morgan said, sitting down on the sofa to smile at where Greyson played.

"Do you want to open your present?" Greyson asked, going over to the tree and pulling out a large, rectangular gift.

"Sure. I have one for you, too. But my gift is going to seem underwhelming next to a puppy."

Morgan laughed. "Topping this Christmas in years to come won't be easy, that's for sure."

Andrew glanced at where she sat on the sofa, smiling, and was struck once again with how pretty she was. "It has been a good Christmas, hasn't it?"

She gave him an odd look. "You've been at work all day."

"I'm here now."

"Here's your present." Greyson handed the gift to Andrew.

Andrew took the present, then while Morgan and Greyson watched, opened what felt like a frame. What it was took his breath away.

On one side was Greyson's colored snow globe ornament. On the other side was the photo that Frank's wife had taken of them standing next to their snowman.

Teeth clenched from the emotion hitting him, Andrew swallowed. "Bud, this is great."

"I knew you would love it."

"But I feel guilty taking your snow globe ornament rather than your mom having it."

"I drew her one, too," Greyson said. "Grammy helped me frame it for Mommy's Christmas present."

"I'll treasure this always," Andrew said, thinking he'd snap a picture of the gift so he could keep it on his phone with him wherever he went. How many times in the future would he look at this photo and wonder what life would have been like if things had been different?

"Is that for me?" Greyson asked, pointing to the presents Andrew had set down prior to petting the puppy.

"Greyson, that isn't polite," Morgan said, causing Greyson to make an apologetic face.

"Sorry," the kid said.

"My fault. What was I thinking, not giving this to you first thing?" He handed over the larger box to Greyson, then picked up the smaller one and handed it to Morgan. "This one is for you."

Morgan stared at Andrew. "You got me a present?"

She'd gotten him one, but had never dreamed he'd reciprocate. Not that she was positive she was going to give him his gift. She'd not even put it out under the tree because she hadn't wanted anyone to know what she'd done in case she opted not to give it to him.

"I think you'll like it, and it's certainly a trendy gift this Christmas."

"Wow, I love this!" Greyson exclaimed, having ripped into the package to unveil an extensive fire department block set. "This has a lot more stuff in it than my other set."

Andrew and Greyson talked firefighting block sets a moment, then he said, "Open yours, Morgan."

Hands trembling, Morgan tore the paper from the box, unveiling a solid dark green box. She opened the lid, pulled out a Styrofoam casing, and when she pried it apart, she sucked in a breath. "Andrew, it's beautiful."

"Shake it and make the snow go everywhere," Greyson requested.

Morgan complied, loving the building a snowman scene inside the globe.

"It plays music, too," Andrew told her, causing her to glance at him.

"Elvis?" she asked, smiling.

He shook his head. "No, but that would be great if it did."

"I'll never hear him without thinking of you," she admitted.

"Lucky you that he doesn't get much airtime these days."

She ran her fingers over the smooth glass. "I don't mind thinking of you, Andrew."

"You'll forget me soon enough."

Was that what he thought? Out of sight out of mind? If only she believed that would be the case. But she knew better.

"Love doesn't work that way," she quoted John.

Andrew's eyes darkened and he started to say something, but Greyson tugged on his sleeve. "Do you want to go with me to my room to open this? Mommy says I can't open presents with small pieces around Andy because he might chew something that could be bad for him, or choke on something that's not supposed to be chewed at all."

"I...I probably should head out, bud. You and your mom are supposed to be heading to Sophie and Isabelle's and I'm going to my grandparents."

"Oh," Greyson's disappointment was palpable.

"Greyson, why don't you put your present up in your room and gather Andy's bag so we can take him with us to meet the rest of the family?" Morgan told her son who nodded. After Greyson had left the room, she reached into her purse and pulled out his present.

"I wasn't sure I'd have the nerve to give you this," she admitted, her stomach feeling as topsy-turvy as the snow globe when she'd shaken it.

"Now you have me curious," he admitted, his gaze going to the small box. "About what's in that and your comment a minute ago."

"Here." She handed him the present and watched as he opened it, pulling out the small velvet bag. Opening the draw strings, he turned the bag up to drop its contents into his hand.

A shiny stone dropped into his palm. Engraved on it was Be Safe. You're Loved.

"You're supposed to keep it in your pocket as a reminder," she explained when he just kept staring at it.

"To be safe?"

She nodded, noting that he hadn't commented on the other part. Was he just going to ignore that she was opening up her heart to him? Silly woman, she berated herself. He probably didn't know what to say when he'd already repeatedly told her that he wasn't into commitments.

He stared at the stone for long moments, then said, "I should go."

Morgan's heart cracked, but she managed to keep her disappointment from showing. "Ruby is expecting you."

He nodded, picked up his photo frame, then stood and walked to the front door. Legs feeling weak, Morgan followed him.

"You'll tell Greyson goodbye for me?"

"If that's what you want."

"It's what's best." He stared down at her and she knew he was thinking about kissing her goodbye and weighing the pros and cons.

Taking a deep breath, she solved his dilemma for him by stretching up on her tiptoes and pressing her lips to his.

"What was that?" he asked.

"Tradition," she answered, pointing to above the doorway where Grammy had hung mistletoe.

Janice Lynn

He nodded. "Thanks. I wouldn't want seven years of bad Christmases or whatever it was that Sophie said would happen."

"Andrew," she ventured, feeling that she had to know and fearing that if she didn't ask it would always haunt her. "If you weren't leaving, what would happen? With us, I mean?"

His gaze locked with hers, he took a deep breath, then said, "I'd ask you to spend all your Christmases with me."

Morgan's heart raced. "Why?"

He opened his palm and glanced down at the engraved stone he still held there. "Because you are loved, too."

Eyes watering and heart burgeoning with hope, Morgan swallowed. "Ask me to go with you."

He flinched as if her words had struck him. "I can't do that. You and Greyson are happy in Pine Hill. Your family lives here. I could never ask you to go with me and give that up."

"Because you love me?" she pushed.

His gaze held hers. "With all my heart."

Joy filled her.

"You and Greyson have already suffered tragedy once," he said. "I'd never risk putting you through that again. It's better this way. Being a smokejumper is one of the most dangerous jobs in the world. Forget me, Morgan."

She wasn't letting him go so easily. Not when so much hope had sprung to life. "Will you forget me?"

"Never."

"Then you'll understand when I say that I won't be able to forget you, either. You're in my heart." She paused, then corrected herself. "You are my heart, Andrew. You and Greyson. I love you both so much."

"Morgan, you're not making this easy. I'm trying to do the right thing."

"Then take us with you."

He studied her. "You'd do that? Move Greyson to California to live near a wildland firefighting base just to be with me?"

She nodded.

"I love you," he said. "You know I do. I think I have from the moment I spotted you in Greyson's classroom that day. But, Morgan, I can't wrap my head around putting you through the pain of being with me, of never knowing where I'll be sent next or when I'll be home." He paused, closed his eyes and added, "Or even if I'll be home. It would be in yours and Greyson's best interest if you forget about me. Forget and fall in love with someone else."

"Love doesn't work that way," she repeated. "Besides, do you really believe things will be any easier for me if I'm here? I can assure you that they won't. Something I've learned is that life is short, Andrew, and

Janice Lynn

none of us are promised tomorrow. I loved Trey and I lost him. But I loved, Andrew. I wouldn't change that even if it meant taking away the pain of losing him. I wouldn't change loving you, either."

His throat working, he studied her. "You're sure? Sure that you understand what you're saying? Sure what you would be getting yourself into? Sure you want that life? Because it's not an easy one."

"Will accepting that life mean that in exchange for all the worries, I get your heart?"

"You already have my heart, Morgan."

"Then I'm sure."

Andrew searched her gaze for the longest time, not looking quite as if he believed she'd really go with him. "I'll be back after I finish my training. If you still feel the same, if you're sure you want the life of being hitched to a smokejumper, I'll bring you and Greyson to California with me. If not, I'll understand."

Morgan blinked up at him. "Are you asking me to marry you?"

"You think either of our grandmas would be okay with our moving in with each other without my putting a ring on your finger?"

"I don't want you to marry me because of our grandmas."

"I'd marry you because I love you and want to be with you. I'd do it sooner rather than later so I can move you to California with me, with our families' blessings. We can spend off season here in Pine Hill." He bent, kissed her long and hard. "That one wasn't because of tradition."

"No?" Morgan smiled up at him.

"That one was for me." He cupped her face.

"Are you kissing my Mommy?"

Morgan's eyes widened as she stared up at Andrew, then watched as he knelt to talk to Greyson.

"Yeah, I am. You know I'm leaving for California soon, right, bud?"

Greyson nodded.

"How would you feel if, when I finish my training, I moved you and your mom to California with me?"

"Would we get to live with you?"

Andrew nodded.

Greyson looked up at Morgan. "Would Andy get to come?"

She knelt down next to Andrew so she would be eye level with her son, too. "Absolutely. We adopted Andy into our family, remember?"

"And we'd come back to Pine Hill to visit Grammy and Grampy and Brynne?"

"Every chance we got," Morgan promised.

Greyson's gaze turned to Andrew. "Would you be my daddy?"

Andrew ducked his head, and when he

raised it again, he was smiling. "If it's okay with you, I'd like that very much, bud."

Greyson nodded. "Okay. Now, can we go to Sophie and Isabelle's so I can show everyone my puppy and tell them you're going to be my daddy?"

Morgan and Andrew exchanged a look, then Andrew winked at her and the world felt brighter. Part of her couldn't believe this was happening...but then again, it was the most magical day of the year, one when hope could blossom into reality.

As if he'd read her mind, Andrew said, "Merry Christmas, Morgan."

"It's the best Christmas ever!" Greyson called from the floor where he was playing with Andy again.

"He's right," Andrew said. "It is the best Christmas ever, but I suspect I'm going to feel that way every Christmas spent with you and Greyson."

Morgan wrapped her arms around his waist and smiled up at him. "One can hope. Merry Christmas, Andrew."

The End

Lemon Chicken Scaloppini

A Hallmark Original Recipe

In *Wrapped Up In Christmas Hope*, Andrew's grandmother and her friends take over catering a wedding rehearsal dinner. They bring various delicious entrees to Andrew's house for a taste-testing...and they grill him about his attraction to Morgan, the single mom who's new in town! Avoiding their questions, Andrew chooses this succulent chicken dish as the winner...and anyone you serve it to will be just as impressed.

Prep Time: 10 minutes
Cook Time: 10 minutes
Serves: 6

INGREDIENTS

- 4 boneless, skinless chicken breasts
- 1 cup flour
- 1 tablespoon salt
- 1/2 cup butter
- 1/4 cup olive oil
- 1/4 cup white wine
- 1 cup chicken broth
- 2 tablespoons capers, drained
- 1 lemon, sliced very thin
- Salt and pepper to taste
- 1/2 cup parsley, finely chopped

DIRECTIONS

1. Place chicken breasts on cutting board and slice in half horizontally, forming 8 thin filets.
2. Place each chicken filet between two pieces of plastic wrap and pound until 1/4inch thin.
3. Combine flour and salt in shallow container. Dredge pounded chicken in seasoned flour; shake off excess flour.
4. Heat butter and oil in large skillet.

Working in several small batches, sauté chicken for 5 minutes mover medium heat, turning once.

5. Add white wine and chicken broth. Simmer until the liquid is reduced by half.

6. Add lemon pieces and capers.

7. Season to taste; garnish with parsley.

Thanks so much for reading
Wrapped Up in Christmas Hope.
We hope you enjoyed it!

You might also like these other
books from Hallmark Publishing:

Christmas Charms
Wrapped Up in Christmas
Wrapped Up in Christmas Joy
Christmas in Bayberry
At the Heart of Christmas

For information about our new releases
and exclusive offers, sign up
for our free newsletter at
hallmarkchannel.com/hallmark-
publishing-newsletter

You can also connect with us here:

Facebook.com/HallmarkPublishing

Twitter.com/HallmarkPublish

About the Author

USA Today bestselling author Janice Lynn loves to spin a tale that puts a smile on her reader's lips and a tear in their eye as they travel along her characters' journey to happy ever after. Her favorite read is one with a strong heroine who is able to laugh at herself and a hero who appreciates the heroine's strengths and imperfections.

Janice's books have won numerous awards including the National Readers' Choice Award and the American Title, but she is most proud of her seven children. From actor, engineer, nurse, student, to Army National Guard, they are her greatest accomplishments.

Janice lives in Tennessee with her family, her vivid imagination, lots of crafting and quilting supplies, and numerous unnamed dust bunnies.

Turn the page for a sneak peek of

ON
CHRISTMAS
AVENUE

A feel-good small-town romance

NEW YORK TIMES BESTSELLING AUTHOR
GINNY BAIRD

Chapter One

MARY WARD STARED AT HER boss and blinked.

"Where did you say I'm going again?"

Judy cocked her chin and her asymmetrical bob swung sideways. She had a slender section of her black hair pinned back on top, offsetting her dark brown eyes. "To Clark Creek," she repeated matter-of-factly, like she'd just said Atlanta or some other highly recognizable place. In addition to being Mary's boss, Judy Ramos was also her bestie, and had been for a decade—ever since they'd been roommates in college.

They stood in Judy's tenth-story office in a corporate building on the outskirts of Richmond, Virginia. Snow fell beyond the floor-to-ceiling windows, coating the pines abutting the parking area. Davenport Development Associates specialized in fund-raising initiatives for nonprofit entities, but generally not towns, so this wasn't a typical assignment.

"Well, I've never heard of it."

"Neither had I," Judy said, "before I got their mayor's cry for help." She stepped toward Mary, extending her cell phone, and Mary had to crouch down to see. She towered over her shorter and more athletically built friend.

Judy pulled up a map of Virginia and tapped at a spot in the state's western portion.

Mary's brown curls spilled forward and she held them back with one hand, attempting to get a better view of the screen. Nothing obvious jumped out at her, besides mounds of mountainous terrain. "I'm not sure I—"

"Hang on." Judy enlarged the map on her navigational app and a tiny dot appeared. The name *Clark Creek* sat adjacent to a curvy blue line, indicating a narrow body of water connected to a larger tributary.

"That looks like it's in the middle of nowhere."

"Not completely nowhere," July replied. "The Blue Ridge Parkway's nearby."

Judy was big into hiking, kayaking, and skiing...all sorts of things that meant spending time outdoors. She'd been president of the sporty Outdoors Club at their university.

Conversely, fair-skinned, easily-sunburned Mary was more of an *indoor* yoga person. The only club she'd belonged to in college was the Christmas Club she'd started.

While other charities donated seasonal gifts and meals to those less fortunate, few delivered uplifting decorations, like live Christmas trees and festive garlands, to folks who wouldn't otherwise have them. Mary had been pleased to learn her club had continued operating even after she'd graduated from college.

For her part, she'd never really gotten out of the habit of buying Christmas decorations whenever she found them on sale. She loved saving them up to drop off at nursing homes or other places where they were appreciated. Her apartment closets were so jam-packed they couldn't absorb any more holiday cheer, and the cargo area of her SUV was loaded.

Judy motioned for Mary to have a seat in the chair facing her desk, and Judy sat behind it. A small plastic Christmas tree stood on its corner wrapped in colorful lights, and the wreath above Judy's bookshelf behind her showcased a red-and-green-checkered holiday bow.

"What's going on in Clark Creek?" Mary asked her.

"Not nearly enough." Judy sighed. "The email from the mayor was honestly a little sad, and a lot frantic. Clark Creek barely has enough reserves to fund its daily operations."

"Oh no. You're talking local government?"

"I'm talking all of it. Government operations, the sheriff's office...and the shops and restaurants are hurting, too. The town council learned about our company's reputation for raising capital quickly and reached out to us for help. If they don't get relief soon, the whole town will go under."

"Bankrupt?"

Judy nodded. "Everything will take a hit in that case, including funding for parks and schools."

That sounded perfectly awful for the poor people of Clark Creek.

Mary shifted in her chair, growing uncomfortable. She normally helped smaller organizations like charities run their fundraisers, functioning as part of a team. Lately, she'd been spearheading those teams. But none of them had tackled anything this big.

"How many of us will be on this?"

"I tried to suggest sending you, Natalie, and Paul—at a minimum." Judy grimaced. "But the mayor said they can only afford one consultant."

"One?" Mary swallowed hard. "I don't know, Judy. This sounds like a challenge."

Judy scanned something on the laptop

in front of her, then shut it. "Since when have you backed down from a challenge?"

Mary chuckled, feeling called out. "Never."

"See? You're perfect for the job. Smart. Determined. Innovative! Plus, you can think on your feet."

"Let's hope I land on them, too."

"You will." Judy took on a serious tone. "I'm not supposed to tell you this," she said in a whisper. "But if you pull this off in Clark Creek?"

"Yeah?"

"It could mean Seattle."

Mary's heart thumped. "What?"

"Headquarters," Judy confirmed. "And a promotion to program manager, like me. You won't even have to apply. Upper management already has their eye on you. All you need is this major victory to seal the deal, and my recommendation, of course. Which you know you have."

Anticipation coursed through Mary. This was just what she wanted—what she *had* wanted for the past year, ever since Judy had been promoted ahead of her. They'd started at the firm at roughly the same time as implementation specialists, after both having earned their MBAs and working for different universities' development offices.

Mary had been glad to move to Virginia, and extra happy about working with Judy, who'd already accepted a position at Davenport. Things became privately awkward for Mary when Judy got named her boss. Even though Judy was always kind and fair about it, being her subordinate felt weird after being equals and friends.

Then again, Judy was more assertive than Mary, and not afraid to advocate for herself. Like she had when she'd applied for the supervisory position she currently held.

Mary frowned. "But that would mean leaving Virginia. And you."

"Don't be silly, Mary! We'll keep up like we did before. Besides..." Judy playfully rolled her eyes. "You've got to know, if the shoe was on the other foot—"

"You'd jump at the chance in a heartbeat."

"Yeah."

Mary knew this was an opportunity she couldn't refuse. She really did love rising to a challenge, and moving to the West Coast sounded exciting. Virginia was great, but she'd already lived here for nearly two years, and grass was growing under her feet. While Mary wasn't stellar at maintaining long-distance connections, she'd always managed to stay friends with Judy—in part, due to Judy's bullheaded persistence. Mary loved her to death for her loyalty. Judy was the closest thing to a sister she had.

"So all I've got to do," she said, "is pres-

ent this little town with some new strategies?"

"For fiscal viability, yes. That's what
they're counting on. An economic reboot."

Mary inhaled deeply, thinking things
through. She could do this; of course she
could. Given enough time to strategize.
"Okay. Why don't you send me the particu-
lars: demographics, chamber of commerce
information, that kind of thing. Oh! And forward that email from the mayor. I'll do some
research on Clark Creek and come up with
a proposal to run by you before presenting it
to the mayor and the town council."

"Super. As soon as it gets their approval,
you can go on site to implement your plan."

"How long have I got?"

"They're wanting results by Christmas."

"Christmas?" Mary's stomach clenched.
That sounded impossible, even to her. She
was accomplished at her job, but she wasn't
a miracle worker. "That's only two weeks
away."

Judy shot her an encouraging grin.
"Sounds like you'd better get busy."

Read the rest!
On Christmas Avenue is available now.